STIXX

Remy Porter

A Wild Wolf Publication

Published by *Wild Wolf Publishing* in *2013*

Copyright © *2013* Matthew Bridgeman

ISBN: 978-1-907954-32-0
Also available as an e-book

www.wildwolfpublishing.com

Other titles by this author

Dead Beat

The Monster of Coniston Water

For Hannah, who has always been a beautiful, loving sister

Chapter 1 – First Blood

The garden was a neat, cared for square of trimmed greenery and lawn around which a dense border of shrubs and bushes grew tall enough to protrude over the top of the head-height wall. Leaves were sparse and blood red in colour. The drizzle funnelled like a tap all the way down into the saturated, black cloying peat.

An earthworm writhed and twitched in the wet soil beneath the bare foot. The naked figure stood in the garden, oblivious to the rainwater running in rivulets down his porcelain, hairless body. There was a splatter of dirt reaching up his legs, intruding on perfection. He snorted at the air, a crack of sharp discoloured teeth visible beneath his lips.

Creepers stretched out black tendrils, veins etching onto the uneven surface of the house. He could sense the people inside like a beacon calling to him. His hand wiped the water droplets off a window, one long dirty nail making a faint scratching sound. His face pressed distorted against the glass.

The room was small. On one side cardboard boxes were piled on top of each other beside a big bookcase housing a jumbled array of books. A children's art easel was on the opposite side, with loose papers and paints scattered across the floor. A faint glow from a nightlight highlighted the bed in the centre of the room. It was that which held his attention, the patterned covers moving fractionally. A little girl sat up in bed watching him, no more than five years old.

Hands no bigger than a doll's.

He pushed his palms against the glass, feeling the single pane flex, his breath steaming and condensing angrily on the glass. Reaching down he teased at the window frame, feeling it start to rise without any great resistance. The child opened her mouth and screamed; a thin high-pitched noise.

He reached in a hand and then a foot, the soil marking the carpet. A noise from behind stopped him as headlights from a car arched over the garden as it passed to climb the single lane track next to the house. A light came on in the hallway, the slow footfalls of approaching family. Nimbly the naked figure stepped back out into the garden and moved quickly back to perch on the wall he had come over. Hidden and out of sight, he watched the twin headlights twist up O'Halloran Hill, illuminating at times the open fields and woods that lay either side.

Dropping down to the track he chose to follow, falling into a loping stride unbothered by the harsh gradient. He watched the car slip from view, over the rumbling cattle grid and into a gateway of trees. There was only one way up and down The Hill. He passed the gated entrance of Ridgeway Convalescent Home, a derelict hulk of a building. Behind him the village lights sparkled, dotted around the horseshoe of the estuary bay. A few thousand sleeping souls; he wanted to see them all.

He crossed the cattle grid to where the track became more broken and rutted, all rocks and potholes. Taking small, agile leaps, he moved past the tourist map and the charity well, close to where the car was parked under the canopy of conifer trees. He moved using the tree line, not one foot in the open now, being no more than a shadow. There was heat from the engine and he let his nail peel away a sliver of metallic paint.

'Should we even be here, Patrick?' The voice drifted out of the half open driver's window.

'Nobody drives up here this late. And nobody in their right mind walks their dog this late either,' another man's voice said. 'Saying that, I wouldn't put it past your mad bitch of a wife to break out a search party if she wakes up and finds you absent from the matrimonial bed.'

'No danger of that, the strength of those sleeping pills she's on these days. Basically, if anyone ever tried to date rape her, those roofies would just bounce right off.'

'Let me have some of that dope, Mr Meek and Mild. Heart of a lion when everyone is asleep, aren't you Patrick? I'd love to hear you talk like that in actual daylight.'

The men smelled the herbal smoke. The naked man wrapped his hand around the car door handle.

'Yeah well, whatever, Devlin. Real life isn't that simple, is it? There are things called careers and kids, and all those other things that are part of life's mystery to you.'

'You should leave her you know. I can make room in my man-cave, no problem.'

'Can you imagine what the village would make of that? My kid's friends would find out at school, can you imagine that happening as well, Devlin? And her indoors? If she didn't kill me for real, she would gut my finances. I wouldn't have a pot to piss in for like forever!'

'She must suspect. Come on, she must do!'

The naked man could see them in the side mirror. Patrick was older and heavier. The other one, Devlin, looked skinny and fidgeted in his seat, his nervous hands flicking around like a trapped wasp. Patrick was smoking the herb, the burning end showing up in the darkness like a red bead.

'I would love to see her face though. We could sit down in your kitchen with a glass of Shiraz and just lay it all out to her. You could sell tickets to that one!' Devlin said.

'In another life, maybe.'

'Hell, you know me. I like all this sneaking about like James Bond shit. Now you sharing that pot, or what?'

'You still buying it from that lanky kid Stixx? Funding his love of expensive comic books or whatever? What is he, like eighteen or something? Probably thinks he's some kind of gangster.'

'You know how hard it is to get weed in a village like this? Guy's a godsend!' Devlin said. 'Now are we going to get busy or what?'

The stranger watched them start to kiss, the bigger man rolling over, on top of Devlin, taking control. The seats started to go down, juddering and awkward jumps with all that weight on them, followed by the sound of slurping, hungry kisses. The naked man stood up, no chance of being seen now. Both of the men in the car faced downwards. The heavy one had his hairy backside in the air, the pair of them starting to grunt like animals.

The naked man reached through the driver's window, and just for a fraction of a second felt the throb of Patrick's jugular vein, before letting his nails tear through the hot, sweaty flesh. There was a jet of blood, and the man flailed around the inside of the car like a punctured balloon.

'What the hell, Patrick? Get the fuck off me! Is that blood, Patrick?'

Patrick was a dead-weight.

The naked man opened the car door and climbed inside. He bit Devlin on the neck before he even knew he was there.

Chapter 2 – Stixx

'Hey, my buddy! Didn't know you were on the choo-choo.'

Stixx looked at his ghostly thin reflection in the train carriage window and wished that he was a ghost. *Or perhaps the invisible man.* People were definitely right though, he did look a little like a young Thom Yorke with his sallow cheeks and pale skin. However, it was his eyes that stood out the most – an icy cold blue. 'What do you want Marco?'

'I just really wanted to ask you something.'

Stixx looked across at Marco Marx, standing in the train aisle with that familiar, expectant over-inflated face; a giant among oompa-loompas. Marco was wearing the same light blue fleece he always wore, full of the multiple burn holes all degenerate pot monkeys had from dropping hot embers. Stixx had spent five years sharing a playground with Marco at junior school, before he finally disappeared off to a special school for kids with Down's Syndrome. He had saved Marco from the odd playground beat-down back in the day, and ever since, Marco seemed convinced they were like *forever friends.* They were both nineteen years old now, and junior school was a long time ago.

'Marco, if I said fuck off, would you get the subtle hint?' Stixx rubbed his face again. Looking down he realised he still had his ASDA name badge pinned to his chest. He plucked it off in disgust. 'Pot will rot your brain you know.'

'Ah come on, Stixx, don't be mean.' Marco had sat down next to him, blocky pink thighs spreading over the seat like melted butter. Only Marco would wear shorts at Christmas. 'You got any of that stuff for me?'

'What would your mother be saying now, short round?'

Stixx thought of himself as a morally righteous drug dealer. He was the only drug dealer he knew of in the village where he lived; a small fish in a very small pond. It was just a little extra pocket money. He only sold the soft stuff though, grown from scratch at a secret location.

'Don't be a jerk all the time, Stixx!'

'I am a jerk. Beef jerky! Anyway, Marco, I can't be seen to be dealing to undersized people. You know the rules.'

'You're making me sad. There is no one here to tell on you. Look!' He flapped his sausage around the carriage. The last train to Greystones was definitely empty apart from the two of them. 'Come on, we're nearly there. And you don't walk my way.'

'Okay, but we need to take some precautions. Feds or anyone might be watching with their satellites.'

Two minutes before the train got to the village, Stixx slid past Marco and went up to the train toilet door. 'I'll make the drop in there,' he said, pointing theatrically.

Stixx waited ten seconds in the toilet and came back to Marco. 'I stashed it in the paper bin. You better hurry yourself!'

'Is it good stuff?'

'It will blow your tiny mind.'

Marco practically ran to the toilet. Stixx stood up as soon as the toilet door shut. His Swiss army knife was out, and he selected the flathead screwdriver. He twisted around the bolts and slider in the train lock. The train was slowing down.

Easy does it.

'Is that you, Stixx? Hey, Stixx what did you do? This door won't open' The door rattled, then started to get a pounding. 'My stop, Stixx. It's my stop, Stixx!'

'Hang tight, Marco, let me just get the guard.' Stixx pressed the door release and stepped out onto the platform. He watched the train pull away, the toilet door flexing crazily, but it didn't give. Those Downs kids were strong with all their extra shoulder muscles. Stixx shook his head and started the walk home. In the distance he saw the two carriages crossing the estuary on the viaduct; a glow worm disappearing into the dark.

He had a choice, either to take a short cut path up the steep hill, or to circle the village along the promenade. It was longer that way but took less effort. Stixx went long.

Greystones was a big village. He remembered the figure of three thousand people being mentioned from when he went to the local junior school and guessed there must be at least another five hundred residents since those days. Certainly there had been

10

plenty of new houses built in the last ten years, fresh cul-de-sacs where there were once just farmers fields.

More often than not it was failed businesses like a garage or a sprawling garden centre that would disappear to be replaced by easy living, retirement homes, or assisted living apartments. Greystones was an elephant graveyard of a place, where the affluent middle classes came when they got old, to watch the tidal flows over the estuary sands, and walk the myriad trails through the National Trust woods that covered O'Halloran Hill. When finally they became too old to move, they could just sit and stare at the world going by through their Victorian bay windows.

Stixx passed a few of the shops that remained; a chip shop, a newsagent, *The Mariners* public house. All were closed up and dark, but every one was significant to Stixx. The newspaper round he once did before school, that first time he could drink a pint of beer legally, the jumbo sausage and chips on a Friday night with his mum. Little memories which were all part of him like some ornate jigsaw puzzle.

He made the turn and walked up the private road to his house. Why it was private he didn't know. Certainly it was one of the most ill-maintained roads in the whole village. His road contained a mish-mash of houses, hundred year old terraces, semi-detached cottages, leading to more modern houses further up the road.

The Blackfriars Guest House was where he lived, a large, bleak Victorian house, laid against a factory-sized diesel lorry garage which generally was very noisy and probably equally carcinogenic. The garage and the lorry car park halfway along the road were owned by the Colonel and seemed to be winding slowly down towards inevitable oblivion. The 1960's diesel trucks inside the vast garage appeared mainly on blocks or broken up for spares as haulage contracts were thin on the ground due to the recession. No one really saw the Colonel around the village anymore either. Rumour had it some hereditary genetic disease was slowly turning his brain into soup.

Stixx went up the concrete steps to the guest house and turned a key in the heavy lock. Inside it smelt of home, as well as old carpets and even older furniture. It was pitch black in the hallway, but after ten years living there he could find his way. He passed the guests' dining room, the too-small kitchen and the frosted glass of the guests' lounge door.

Stixx opened the door to the cellar rooms and flicked the light switch. There was a steep set of concrete steps down to the two dungeon rooms. Once upon a time he had fallen down here, and had the dent in his head to prove it.

The sound of David Essex singing about aliens wafted up. There were two rooms down here, one a standard cellar room and pantry, full of junk, washing machines, ironing boards and a homemade table tennis table. The other had been converted into a private lounge, a retreat away from the unwanted intrusions of annoying paying guests.

'Hi, Mum,' Stixx said loud enough to catch her attention.

'I didn't hear you come in,' Margie Stixx said, waving a tube of glue in his direction. She was in her preferred evening wear, which was paint splattered dungarees. There was an air of youthfulness about her, despite just turning forty-five. Her light blonde hair was pulled back into a neat ponytail, was perhaps five foot two, and slightly chubby. Stixx's best friend Red thought she was gorgeous and never failed to tell him that. Margie appeared to have made a statue out of gold painted acorns. 'What do you think?' she asked.

'Nice err... thing. Not a present for anyone I know I hope?'

'I thought ebay! Would you help me with the advert? You know how I am with computers.' She was like kryptonite.

Margie liked to make tie-dye tee-shirts, garish splotches of greens, oranges, reds and purples she brewed herself in an old cauldron in the other basement room. His best friend Red also liked to describe her as a new-age witch, a hot new aged witch. Margie Stixx was his only parent. His dad was a will o' the wisp, a grey clouded memory of whom he couldn't recall a single solitary image, like a black spot somewhere in his past. The topic was thoroughly off-limits with Margie.

'So what did we learn today?'

'We... I... did learn that Sebastian my supervisor is a fat twat. Yesterday he was a fat wanker, so things have developed.

Tomorrow is Friday, and I think he's aiming to be a fat cunt for the weekend.'

'Swear box,' Margie said, pointing to a shiny red and black handcrafted box resting on the fireplace with assorted other knickknacks. Above it, the entire wall was filled with Margie's other passion – photography.

Stixx cracked a smile, and wandered over to the open fire and prodded it with the poker. His gaze drifted up and briefly he scanned over the familiar photographs his mum had taken around the village. She made the estuary look beautiful in black and white, not at all the festering mud puddle he knew it to be, full of the backwash of bacteria and crap from effluent pipes.

'I'm going to hit the hay.'

'Do you want breakfast tomorrow?'

'Sounds like a plan.' He kissed her goodnight and left her to gluing acorns, like some crazy nocturnal squirrel.

Stixx walked up the creaking wooden stairs to the first floor, the guest floor comprising four bed-and-breakfast bedrooms of varying size and quality. None were en-suite and the only bathroom in the house was on this floor. This was a bitch when your own bedroom was another floor up. He could hear the not-so-gentle snores of some foreign guy who came without fail every Christmas. German or Austrian, he could never remember the guy's name.

Stixx climbed the next set of near vertical stairs up to his attic bedroom. On this floor there was a walk-in attic and his mum's own bedroom. His was the smallest of the six bedrooms, bitter cold in winter and sweltering in the summer. He had gotten used to it over the ten years they'd lived there.

He jumped on his three quarter sized bed and flicked on the portable TV. Channel 4 had some 1970's horror movie on with Edward Woodward from *The Equaliser*. Such films usually had a scene worth waiting for. Stixx wasn't that interested in the gore and the horror, but he did like the scenes halfway through when the resident bimbo starts to get frisky and loses some clothing. Edward's film wasn't looking too promising on that front, but then the tidy barmaid stripped off unexpectedly and started banging on the wall. *Good enough!* Stixx pushed down his work trousers and released the wee man from captivity.

When Stixx woke up he thought he was still dreaming about being in the Vietnam War with Willem Defoe. There was a deafening noise over the house followed by a blazing white light briefly illuminating his room. He rubbed his eyes and looked at the red digits on his alarm clock – 4.07am. Standing on the radiator he poked his face up to the attic bedroom window. A helicopter with a search light was strafing its way up O'Halloran Hill, circling above a mass of flashing blue and red lights from emergency vehicles.

'What's going on?' Stixx heard Margie come in behind him, switching on the light. She didn't look like she'd been to bed yet.

'I'm going to find out.'

'Don't be doing anything stupid.'

'Sure.'

Stixx jumped the stairs two or three at a time, not really caring if he did wake up some nameless foreigner. He pushed his mountain bike out through the cobwebbed passageway that ran off the cellar rooms. Old paint tins clanked and got unhelpfully underfoot in the darkness.

Finding a gear, Stixx peddled hard. He clearly wasn't the only one puzzled and intrigued by all the noise and lights. People were coming outside their homes. Living next to an estuary filled with quicksand meant he'd seen a few bodies both living and dead plucked from the waters, but this was something else. This was inland and bigger.

He passed another row of shops, the post office, the supermarket, the bakery, the chemist, and all the tourist shops. All shut up and in darkness, as was the second village pub, *The Noble Man*. The one he liked best.

Breathing hard up The Hill, he saw other people wrapped in warm coats walking in the same direction like sheep. *Like zombies.*

'What's going on?' he heard one man call out to him.

'Don't know!' Stixx panted back, trying to keep his skinny legs cranking the pedals.

He turned onto the flat of Hill Road, and went down a gear. He was in the expensive heart of the village now where nearly every house was large and detached, each one unique and with a fancy high-walled garden. The chopper passed close overhead again, before veering off towards the coast with its laser beam search light.

What was this?

After a dramatic dip in the road and passing another one of Greystones ten hundred old folks homes, he saw he was finally as close as he was going to get to O'Halloran Hill. Multiple blue lights strobed in his face and he saw more police vehicles parked than he'd ever seen in the village before. Stixx figured he really must have been deeply asleep to miss their entrance, and guessed they must have come in without their sirens screaming. There were at least twenty police officers behind the police tape cutting across the road ahead of him. The house at the base of The Hill had its lights on and he could see police with notebooks out talking to a man holding a small girl in pyjamas. In the distance there were men in white 'scenes of crime' suits walking up the O'Halloran Hill lane.

Stixx pushed past the other confused locals to get a better view. There was more than one curious old lady there in dressing gown and slippers. *'What's going on?'* seemed to be the words on everyone's lips. Stixx caught the eye of the only policeman he knew, Sergeant Flint. The guy hated him with a passion. 'What's going on, Flint?' he asked.

The sergeant squinted at Stixx, a slightly constipated look, perhaps now remembering all the cautions he'd handed him in his youth to save on paperwork. They hadn't physically spoken for years, probably since Stixx outgrew his passion for pyromania. Flint had maybe twenty-five years in the force, and had been the village beat cop for most of that time. His skin looked grey and lined in the flashing blue light, half-dead no doubt from a lifetime of shift work. He was retiring soon, or was being retired, depending on which village rumour you chose to believe. His one man village police station was being closed down and sold off by his constabulary. Everything was going to be centralised and modernised, and Flint wasn't necessarily going to be invited to the party.

'What do you want, Stixx?' His voice was gruff.

Like rubble.

'What do you reckon? Your whirly bird woke me up.'

'People are dead up there, Stixx. Sorry if it disturbed your little beauty sleep.'

Gasps erupted around the crowd. Flint was about as subtle as a brick.

'Can everyone please move away, we will be extending this cordon now. There will be official announcements in due course. Please let us do our jobs,' barked a plain clothes officer. He looked a little like a hunchback, with a severe nose and badly receding hairline. Stixx caught him scowling at Flint; it was the modern against the old. Stixx turned and started to cycle away, narrowly avoiding being run down by a Border Television van.

Had life finally become a little more interesting around here?

Chapter 3 - The Day Job

'It's gone national. It's all over the news!' Margie wouldn't shut up.

Stixx stared at his eggs and bacon through gritty eyes, his brain trying to navigate the worse than usual early morning fog. It was as if it had been injected by candyfloss. *How was it his mother could get by on less sleep than Margaret Thatcher and not feel the same way?* He squinted at the minute portable TV they had in the kitchen, watching morning television news. *'A ritual double murder,'* the newscaster finished saying.

'I just can't believe it!' Mrs Phillips was joining in now. She was a little wizened Irish lady in her sixties Margie paid to come in and help around the guesthouse twice a week. It was mainly ironing and cleaning she was paid pennies for. Stixx's mum had always hated both. 'This puts Greystones on the map, but not in any good way. No. It's just going to be lots of them gothic kids coming to the village because they think it's cool. Know what I'm saying?'

'So are you not a little worried there's a murderer out there, Mrs Phillips?' Margie was stacking plates.

'Well I'll be double locking the doors and taking a kitchen knife to my bed, I'll tell you that!' she said, and went back to scrubbing the enamel off a frying pan in the sink.

'Good for you, Mrs Phillips. In fact you know we can always make up a guest bedroom here if you like... until this thing blows over.'

'Until they catch the deranged serial killer you mean, Mum? And what does it mean about all this ritual killing stuff? Red texted me and said it was two blokes from the village we didn't know,' Stixx said, but as usual nobody was really listening to him.

'That's okay,' Mrs Phillips said to Margie. 'I think you'll be needing the extra space anyway.'

Stixx stood up. 'Going to catch my train. Hopefully they've turned it into a crime scene so I don't have to go into work.' On the TV a row of uniformed and plain clothes police officers were giving a press conference.

17

'*The investigation is ongoing, along several avenues. We do strongly emphasise the need to be vigilant and careful, especially at night. Do not go out if you don't need to. Always travel in pairs or groups, and stick to main roads and street lit areas...*' The caption underneath said Detective Inspector Neil Hastie. Stixx recognised him as the balding hunchback-like officer from the night before, the one who didn't like Flint's big mouth.

'Got to go. See you all later.'

Outside the front door he nearly bumped into a tall woman with a lot of makeup. Behind her was a short hairy-looking guy, struggling with a lot of cases in his hands. Parked below was the heavily logoed Border Television van that had nearly run him over.

'We heard this place had vacancies,' she said a little breathlessly. 'I'm Veronica Myers and, lucky us, it looks like we'll be here for the duration.' Veronica offered her hand like she was royalty. Blood red nail varnish.

'There are three spare rooms. I'll shout Mum for you. Say, do you know what they meant by ritual murder?'

'It means gory, lots of blood and guts, you know like those *Saw* films,' the hairy guy said grimacing with all the cases of equipment. The name on his lanyard said Diego and he looked like he had some hygiene issues.

'Yeah, that's what I thought.'

Disappointingly the train station wasn't cordoned off for any further ritual murder, and standing in the cold drizzling rain Stixx watched the 8.13 am train rumble over the viaduct like clockwork. When it arrived, he half expected Marco Marx to come flying out looking for some payback, but the carriage was nearly empty. Thirty minutes later he was in the shiny metropolis that was Furness, a place so grim that the only colour allowed was grey, and if it wasn't raining people thought something was wrong.

Stixx trudged the three quarters of a mile to his lousy job. It was just his bad luck that when he sent out fifteen job applications to all the local supermarkets the only one interested in employing him was the one furthest away. Eighteen months ago it was supposed to be a temporary job, a springboard to something better after leaving school at sixteen. Now it was like a spider's web – a sticky permanent ASDA coloured fly trap.

'Hello, James,' said Sebastian. He was one of the very keen trainee managers: a dweeb with round spectacles and a near fetishism for cycling everywhere. His ASDA uniform was a different colour to Stixx's because he was special.

'Hello, Seb,' he mumbled back, and loudly closed his locker. He didn't like being called James.

'You look a little creased today.' Sebastian was actually inspecting him.

Stixx looked down at the uniform he'd slept in, and then made a show of looking Seb up and down. If that guy spent less than an hour ironing himself into the perfect Nazi, he would be surprised. 'Whatever!'

He walked out onto the show floor already buzzing with early morning shoppers, their trolleys filled to bursting with Christmas goodies. Passing the checkouts he nodded over to Crazy Claire Bibby, who had dyed blonde hair and a scary, near-black fake tan. If they ever found themselves on a break together she would always talk incessantly about her two boys, the divorce and the mother-in-law who once went out with one of the Great Train Robbers. *'She's still got connections. Worries me, James!'* she would say a lot. Stixx didn't mind all that. He figured that she would pass for MILF, so what the heck!

Stixx wasn't a lowly till monkey though. He wasn't even a double lowly shelf stacker. No, he was a backrooms and warehouse amoeba, a shifter of cardboard mainly, shuffling boxes on jack trolleys for eight hours a day. It didn't so much addle your brain, as suck it forcefully out of your ears and make you shamble about in a daze wanting to bite people. Stixx grabbed a trolley and started breaking down a pallet of frozen goods that had just been fork-lifted off a lorry.

'Say, Stixx, what the hell is going on down in your manor?' boomed a voice behind him. It was Fat Les, the warehouse foreman of sorts. He was twenty stones easy, with a gigantic hairy belly that usually peeped through the gap left between his XXL work shirt and his enormous pants: a walking coronary waiting to happen.

'I don't know. Something about a ritual sacrifice. Looks like two blokes have been killed on O'Halloran Hill, and not in a nice way.'

'Sounds like Satanism to me. You better watch yourself, Stixx, them occultists might decide to go all *Blair Witch* on your ass when you're not looking.' Fat Les actually crossed himself and was looking serious, but probably he was just fooling around.

'You're not religious. What was that?'

'Saw it in the films man. People reckon those crazy killers might strike anywhere. Next stop Furness. I'll be locking my fucking door up tight, hombre.'

'I suppose you'd like a little weed... for the stress and all?'

'Well, since you mention it...'

The day went like it always did – slow, bordering on reverse time travel. Stixx found that if he didn't look at his watch it helped. What didn't help was that ear phones and iPods were banned in the warehouse since some guy had managed to side-swipe a pallet of garden furniture through the side wall of the warehouse while listening to Lady Gaga. That dead beat had spoilt it for everyone. Now they had to make do with Radio One being played through tinny wall speakers, and a wicked cold draft from the botched repair job on the wall.

At around 3 p.m, with an hour and a half left on his shift, Stixx treated himself to a dump in the ground floor staff toilets. He preferred these ones to those upstairs, due to the better standard of graffiti, half of which was his. Using a fine black permanent marker he began to sketch a caricature of a man on a bicycle. There was a new type of attachment on the back wheel; a piston with a large dildo. The caption read *SEB LOVED THAT BIKE!* Stixx wondered if that was too much. He tilted his head.

Nah!

He rode out the last hour and a half on a small triumphant high.

Chapter 4 – The Noble Man

By 7 p.m that Friday evening, Stixx was burrowing into the piled layers of clothing at the bottom of his bedroom wardrobe. Coat hangers not hung in guest rooms were thin on the ground to non-existent. Finally he found a vaguely clean looking jumper, to go with his vaguely clean jeans and his one pair of halfway smart shoes.

Red was sitting eating chips on his bed. 'Always were a tart, Stixx!'

Red was unfortunately not a buxom red fire-breathing Amazon warrior, he was Stuart Richardson, Stixx's oldest and best friend. Stixx pondered, not for the first time, how it was exactly his borderline mental school mate should deserve a cool nickname. The moniker had arisen sometime in that first week at secondary school, when some now forgotten school pupil had christened him after a Fraggle. Even seven plus years later, Stuart still had the same sticky up ginger hair and, if asked, would swear blind it was auburn.

Stixx still remembered the first time he met Red. The first day at secondary school he found himself sitting next to him in chemistry class, eleven years old and feeling a little disorientated and lost in the big school after a small rural primary school. Nobody from his old school had wanted to sit next to him. The teacher was burning magnesium using a Bunsen burner, which pre-dated his own pyromaniac phase of his life by a year or two. Stixx remembered feeling a sharp pain in his foot, maybe even accompanied by a small *yelp*. He had looked down and saw Red was under his desk with a compass stabbing through the leather of his brand new school shoes. 'I'm doing my own experiment,' he'd told him.

Crazy little shit!

Red now had his lucky silver hipflask out. 'Hair of the dog?'

'That's what you have the morning *after* you get smashed, idiot. Get your drinking facts straight! So I am presuming you're aware that there are now murder victims cluttering up our

21

village? Anything you want to get off your chest before I call the police?'

'My MILF lover will happily provide me with an alibi as per usual. I believe we were watching *Murder She Wrote* re-runs as per usual for a Thursday night.'

'Perhaps you could plead insanity at the trial. Get to share that bunk bed with Peter Sutcliffe, like you always wanted.'

'Two people have died, Stixx! You need to treat this with the serious gravity it deserves.' Red didn't manage to keep a straight face for long. 'Who knows how many other dead bodies there might be anyway? All those old people here with no close relatives. They don't get many visitors, and it could be weeks before the neighbours notice the smell. That woman who lives next door to you could be dead as a fucking post... with all her blood sucked out and shit.'

'Blood sucked out?'

'You're such a Luddite, Stixx. I can't believe you don't even have a PC in your bedroom. This isn't the dark ages!'

'What can I say? We're not rich and live in a council house like you.'

'You're such a prick.' Red reached into another pocket and brought out his iPhone. 'Check out the headlines.'

Red scrolled down the tiny screen: *VILLAGE BLOOD SUCKER KILLS TWO. POLICE NET TIGHTENS OVER VAMPIRE KILLER. TWO DEAD BY VAMPIRE RITUAL KILLER SAY POLICE,* the headlines screamed.

'It's all over the news, man. They reckon the police were trying to keep it on the down-low about the vampire stuff, but it leaked out anyway. The rumour mill now has it that Devlin Jones, married father of three, was up there doing the horizontal twist, with a very gay Irish fella called Patrick Kilkenny. Then some crazy *Twilight* loving fucker came over to make up a threesome and tore their throats out when he couldn't get it up!'

'What the hell paper do you read, Red?'

'It was on my favourite internet forum, *dirtymilfs.com*. It's gospel I swear!'

'So are we going to the pub or what?'

'Have you got your holy water and a cross?'

'We could order garlic bread when we get down there.'

'Good enough.'

Stixx deposited Red's mess of chip papers in the bin and they headed down the stairs. The guest floor corridor was overflowing with boxes and bags full of electrical equipment. The three remaining rooms had been snapped up by the press. They saw the bearded Diego queuing outside the one bathroom.

'Hey, Veronica, if you don't hurry up in there our room isn't going to smell too fresh if you know what I mean. There is a waste bin in there that's looking awfully inviting,' he was shouting through the door. He shrugged when he noticed them. 'Shouldn't have eaten that second burrito, I guess.'

They headed out of the front door and followed the promenade. Stixx thought the estuary looked pretty with the half-moon reflecting off it. Far across the bay was a dark silhouette of rolling hills and mountains of The Lake District. Thicker clouds were creeping slowly in. 'Maybe we should have invited him to the pub too. Diego seems like a fun guy. He'd probably want to let his hair down after all that human tragedy reportage type stuff.'

'Mate, could you sound any gayer? Six beers and you'll start opening your mouth. Next day I'll log on and there will be the headline: STIXX PUTS HAMSTERS UP HIS BUM.'

'Funny man!' Stixx growled and pushed open the swing door into *The Noble Man*. 'I only put one in my underpants as well you know. I was like six years old!' The blast of a thousand voices and stale air met them like an old friend.

'Got to love this place,' Red said barging his way past people to the bar.

The Noble Man's interior was all dark oak and brass, a traditional village pub with stone walls adorned with vintage photographs depicting the promenade, the pier and the village over the ages. Lots of creepy faces, like ghosts looking back at you.

'And how are the umbilical twins tonight?' Jeff, the ruddy-faced barman asked. He had a heavy Liverpool accent, but he'd been in the village for at least ten years and could call himself at least halfway local.

'You know it by now. Two snakebites guv'nor,' Red told him.

They took their pints and looked for somewhere to sit. The main bar room was rammed with people, far more than normal. There were a lot of non-local faces. 'Journalists,' Red hissed under his breath.

'Over here.' Stixx spotted one of their favourite corners had free chairs. They managed three pints in the first hour without breaking a sweat.

'You know, what I don't get is why anyone would want to pretend to be a vampire.'

Red swigged back half his snakebite. 'Well the guy is either a massive *Twilight* fan right, who has somehow lost the plot, and thinks it's all real and if that's the case then we are looking for a pale kid with terrible hair like you. Or he's a disgruntled fan of vampires, who loves his *True Blood* and wants the world to know that sparkly vamps are not and never will be the real deal. That guy is going to be more difficult to find. It could basically be me.'

'That narrows it down loads,' Stixx said, just tipsy enough to be warming to idiotic conversation.

'Anyone with just terrestrial is probably innocent, barring the fact they may have free TV top boxes. Could be that wannabe vampire is the patient type. He waits to the end of each *True Blood* series, and *WHAM!* He buys the box-set and watches the whole thing in one night. Goes out the same night and kills two guys on O'Halloran Hill. Case solved!'

'Apart from the bit where he or she is actually caught!'

'You're right, could be a she. And talking of shes, have you noticed the hot chick yet?'

Stixx sipped on his snakebite. He knew who Red was referring to. Queuing at the bar for a chance to order was a young woman who instantly fell into Stixx's category of drop-dead gorgeous. She wasn't overly tall, and had dark blonde hair streaked lightly with punkish reds. Smart, but still hinting at a little rebellion under the surface. Stixx thought she might be the same age as him, in the ball park of late teens. She was wearing a white blouse that showed off her ample curves without resorting to explosive cleavage, and skinny black jeans that hugged her hips like glue.

Cute little ski jump nose too.

'Do you want a refill?'

'You stammered there, Stixx. I heard a distinct quiver in your voice. You're not going to try and talk to her are you?'

'Refill?' Stixx said a little more sternly.

'Calm down!. Composure. Think Errol Flynn on speed and go get her. And then bring her back over here 'cos she really is well fit.'

Stixx got to his feet and walked over to the bar, trying hard not to stare constantly at the new girl like some kind of serial killer. He needed a line, something witty. There was a gap opening at the bar next to her as someone carried drinks away. The pub gods were smiling down on him.

Stixx estimated there were two people to be served before her; he had a small window of opportunity to play with. He fumbled in his pocket for some change and chanced a glance back at Red for Dutch courage. His best friend was grinning like a loon and stuck two fingers up at him. *Not very helpful, Red!*

The blouse looked even greater close up. And her perfume smelled fresh despite the stinking atmosphere of the pub.

'Are you peeping at me?' She was looking straight at him. Her voice had a bit of a Home Counties twang to it.

Posh.

'Err, no. Just doing the usual... getting, you know, drinks and stuff.'

'Yes, love, what will it be?' Jeff and his big mouth ploughed right into his moment.

She smiled and turned away. 'Some more of that yummy house red I think, Jeff.'

'So are you new in the village? Haven't seen you in here before,' Jeff carried on. Stixx stared at him, willing the barman's head to explode like in *Scanners*.

'Me and my mum just moved in yesterday onto Hill Road. Can't believe people started getting killed off at the same time. We'll probably end up as prime suspects.'

'Well, don't you watch Midsomer Murders,' Stixx butted in. 'Jeff probably did it.' That's right, he thought, I'm a lot funnier than *you*, Jeff.

She turned back towards him smiling again. 'I thought only old people watched that rubbish.'

'Old people and the unemployed... that's not me, of course. I have a job. I'm in retail, in fact.'

'Yeah, Stixx here is the best shelf stacker in the county. Another snakebite?' Jeff said reaching for a glass.

'Two as well you know,' Stixx said giving him his evil eye. 'And it's not true what Jeff said, I don't stack shelves. I'm much more part of the engine room of ASDA, a very big cog in that particular mouse wheel actually.'

'A very big something,' Jeff mumbled under his breath and started to serve another customer.

'Jeff is best ignored. He has an ASBO you know. It's a miracle they even let him run a pub,' Stixx told her now Jeff was out of earshot.

'You're a bit of a funny guy, aren't you? Sort of funny ha ha,' she said to him.

He was melting inside. 'So you're not a journalist?'

'No, why?'

'There's a lot of strange faces in here tonight... not that you have a strange face. It's just we're pretty sure lots of people in here are dodgy journalists.'

'Thanks pal!' It was bearded cameraman Diego at the bar next to him, looking half-cut and with spittle in his bushy beard. Stixx hadn't even noticed him coming in.

'Ah, didn't see you there, Diego. No offence meant really.'

'You're dead right anyway. You couldn't find a dodgier bunch than the motley crew in here. They'd pick the scabs off a dead dog if they thought there was a story underneath. You should watch your step.' He wandered off, looking a little unsteady.

'Thanks, I'll remember that.' Stixx shrugged his shoulders at the new girl. 'What's your name anyway?' he asked. 'I'm James Stixx, but everyone just calls me Stixx.'

'Nice name, like a seventies rock star or something. I'm Faye. Faye Burns.'

'So, do you want to join us? My friend over there, Red, looks a little like a Fraggle, but I promise you he won't sing.'

'Yeah, alright. I don't know anyone here anyway.'

'Just like a drink hey... I mean in a good way, not the AA, I'm an alcoholic way.'

'Stop being so nervous already!'

Stixx was blushing as they pushed their way over to Red.

'So you've obviously got a boyfriend haven't you? Just to put poor Stixx out of his misery here,' was the first thing out of Red's mouth. Stixx looked around for a weapon to impale him with.

'I've got a boyfriend called Alan, actually, a teacher. But he's away at the moment in Ghana,' Faye shouted over the din.

'And while the cat's away...' Red went on.

They settled down and started to tell each other their potted life histories. It turned out that Faye had already found her soul mate. 'I know what you will think, but he was my geography teacher. Me and Alan were never together at school or anything seedy like that. If anything I came onto him after the graduation ball,' she told them. Stixx stared back, nodding, his tiny heart doing swan dives, melting into her green eyes. It felt like having a winning lottery ticket go through the wash and then getting eaten by a dog for good measure. Stixx half-wished she was a journalist now.

'The gap year didn't work out. I was going to go to Africa to work with Alan, and then I broke my ankle playing a stupid hockey game and there were other problems getting my visa. Then Mum wanted to move 'cos of my dad, and brought us here of all places.'

An hour of drinking later and Stixx was feeling more mellow and basically drunk.

'Why here?' Red was slurring his words.

'Well, I didn't pick it. I mean I've got nothing against Royston Vasey, it seems a really nice village and all that. No, Mum came here as a child with her school and remembered loving it, stayed in an outward bound place somewhere.'

Stixx's eyes lit up. 'Lake District Outward Bound Centre! It's been closed down for ten years at least. It's nothing but derelict buildings and woods these days. There's even an old swimming pool. Me and Red used to play in there all the time when we were kids. The trees are still full of rope swings and tyre bridges, although mostly they're all rotten and treacherous now. It's just down the road, at the end of the prom.' He pointed his pint towards the window.

'Calm down, crazy!' Red whispered.

'Can we go and see it?' Faye asked.

Stixx frowned. 'What now, in the dark with some homicidal bloke running around?'

'Or a real vampire,' Red corrected him.

'Don't be a pair of pussies. I think the three of us can look after ourselves. And besides, I do need some fresh air and a smoke.'

'So basically what you're saying, Faye, is you want us to risk our lives, illegally walk through private property in pitch black woods, so you can get fresh air and have a drag of nicotine? All the while hoping an actual bona fide murderer doesn't manage to sneak up and start drinking our blood?'

'Yes, Stixx! Are you a man or a mouse?'

Chapter 5 – The Watcher in the Woods

'Christ, I can feel my balls shrivelling into my abdomen,' Red cried, as they walked down the last stretch of promenade. A long row of tall Victorian houses dominated on their left. Sitting above trellised gardens, and mostly split into semi-detached homes, they boasted the best estuary views in the village. Greystones' one three star hotel, The Poppyfield, was one of them, next to, of course, yet another old people's home.

'I wish I'd brought a coat. Are you warm in there?' Stixx said, looking across at Faye's red duffel coat. It made her look a bit like Little Red Riding Hood.

The promenade ended abruptly with a wall and a gate. To the right was a path carrying on ahead along a concrete concourse which paralleled both the beach and the high wall of the old outward bounds centre. However, instead they went through the gate into an overgrown grounds for the old centre, flanked on one side by a looming mass of ancient trees, each indistinguishable from the other in the darkness. Ahead was the old training centre building, a large detached edifice and courtyard that hadn't been inhabited since the centre closed.

'...And so you're sure you want to be doing this? We could catch last orders you know?' Red was moaning.

'Come on, what's the worst that could happen?' Faye said.

'If I didn't know you better, I might be a bit suspicious of a comment like that,' Stixx said a little incredulously.

They passed a faded *'KEEP OUT – PRIVATE'* sign. What had been an expansive lawn circling the building, was now thick with uncut weeds and ankle turning ruts. 'They'll manage to sell it one day, and then this will all be luxury apartments,' Stixx offered

'...or another old people's home,' Red cut in.

Over the rise of The Hill, on the far side of the main centre building was a smaller structure. It was fifty metres away and sandwiched between the high wall and the start of the tree line. 'It's too dark for the woods, but we'll show you the pool,' Stixx told Faye.

'We've got to be nuts to be doing this!' Red grumbled behind them, spinning around every few paces, and shining the torch wildly around. 'If you see anything with fangs, just fucking tell me, okay!'

'So did you and your cronies hang out down here a lot? Making dens and traps, and talking about girls?' Faye teased Stixx

'Yeah, pretty much I guess. One Halloween we even re-enacted Vietnam. Five of us firing every rocket, banger and air bomb we had at Red in those trees. God damn nearly set the whole place on fire. They got the fire engines out and chased us out with police dogs,' Stixx said, feeling vaguely nostalgic at the memory.

'You should be aware, Stixx here was a bit of a fire starter back in the day,' Red said. 'I remember that big fireworks fight. That village copper Flint sniffed us out that time hiding out in someone's back garden, creepy bastard that he is! Clip on the ear and cautions all round.'

'You guys are bat shit crazy, aren't you?' Faye giggled, and started reaching to open the swimming pool front doors.

'Those doors are locked, come on we've got another way in. All that stuff was years ago. We just go to the pub now like normal adults,' Stixx told her, and wondered how convincing he'd sounded. 'And of course it's much easier to meet new people in the pub and lure them off somewhere dark and quiet, if you know what I mean.' Stixx's teeth were glinting in the torchlight.

'Well you know I've got a mean kick in the bollocks if you two do try anything,' Faye announced, and Stixx didn't think she was kidding.

'Well, in Stixx's case, I hope you packed a microscope!'

'Shut up, Red!' Stixx barked, and led the way through a hole in the corrugated plastic at the side of the swimming pool.

The pool room had a domed plastic roof, and smelt far worse than Stixx ever remembered. It had been two years at least since he'd last been inside and in the near darkness he could make out a large debris field surrounding the swimming pool. He shone his iPhone torch around and saw that the usual foot of stagnant water in the deep end of the pool had turned black with lichen, bacteria and general rotted rubbish. Around his feet lay everything from used condoms to a hundred empty beer cans and bottles. Stixx looked up at the opaque plastic walls and for a second thought he saw the shape of a person on the other side. He was about to shout something, but he adjusted the light and couldn't see it again.

Trick of the light!

'Got to say guys, this is a nice place you got here!' Faye was off exploring.

'Trust me, we kept it a lot cleaner,' Stixx said, still looking at the wall.

'Youth of today, totally fucked!' Red called over from the changing rooms at one end of the pool. 'And I'd give this end a wide berth. Either someone has sacrificed a cat, or had a dodgy barbecue – truthfully it's hard to tell, but it's definitely very meaty and stinks.'

They wandered over anyway, Stixx poking the remains with his foot. The dead animal was the right size to be a cat, and felt stiff and sticky when he tapped it with a shoe. The wooden walls and floor were covered with burn marks, *the pyros of the next generation,* he thought.

'I hope it died of natural causes,' Faye offered.

'Like your cock, Stixx,' Red said, and moved into the changing room across the short hallway.

There were more beer cans and a wet jacket, which Red eagerly checked every pocket of. 'Stop looking at me like it's weird.'

There was a loud smack on the roof, and another one, the echo reverberating around the plastic dome. 'What the fuck was that?' Red whispered. Everyone froze.

'Where's the back way out?' Faye asked, her face pale in the torchlight.

'One way in, one way out, and doors are all double bolted. Let's just go,' Stixx said, moving.

They all ran for the broken hole as the sound came again: heavy bangs on the roof. Stixx pushed through the gap first, ready to see something waiting, mouth open. Outside it seemed darker, and in his rush he knocked the torch function of his iPhone off.

'Come on!' Faye said, pushing at his back, Red close behind. They ran over the uneven icy ground, the wind whistling through the black trees, hiding a killer. The scratching and banging on the roof sounded out again, fainter now they were outside. 'Wait!' Faye shouted. 'Stop running.'

They did as they were told. 'Up there on the roof,' she said pointing. 'It's just a tree branch, look.'

Stixx looked over the swimming pool roof. Faye was right, the wind was making a sagging limb of a tree thump down on the roof, like a giant wooden hand. 'Christ, I thought we were all going to die.'

'Fuck this, I need a drink. I'm going back for last orders,' Red told them. 'Anyone coming?'

'I need to get home, my mum is going to be getting worried,' Faye said apologetically.

'I'll walk you,' Stixx said. 'It isn't safe out here on your own with all these tree branches around.'

'Okay, you walk her and I'll just go this way and get killed by a pissed off vampire. No, that's great,' Red said, and stomped off.

'Catch you later, Red.' Stixx turned to Faye. 'I think that tree branch spooked him a little. Now if you live on Hill Road, I know a short cut. Can you climb walls?'

They climbed down onto the concrete causeway that paralleled the beach. One hundred metres along it, Stixx showed her a steep narrow path. 'This village is going to get me fit,' she said, before they were both too out of breath to talk. Stixx wanted to talk about the boyfriend again but thought it would probably kill the moment.

'This is Hill Road. Imaginative name!' he gasped, as they stood catching their breath under a street light.

'And so easy to get to. I can't wait to use that short cut all the time.'

'Sorry about the swimming pool. Guess it wasn't as much fun as it sounded in the pub.'

'No, it really was fun, Stixx. Just sorry your friend got the hump like that.'

'He's fine, just a drama queen some of the time. So which way is your house?'

'Just over there, I can do this last bit without getting eaten by Dracula, I think.'

'I want to walk you...' he began to say, when a police car drove slowly past. There were two grim-faced policemen staring at them and he didn't recognise either.

'I think I'll be safe. Catch you tomorrow okay, Stixx. I've got your number.' She gave him a hug and a peck on the cheek.

He stood in the shadows and watched her walk into her house. Stixx's cheek tingled and fizzed, and he thought perhaps this was what love felt like.

Chapter 6 – The Graveyard Shift

'Ah, young love,' Rex said as he drove the patrol car past the two teenagers.

'They shouldn't be creeping about those dark paths. Don't they read the news?' Thomas answered, and craned his neck around to look out the back window of the patrol car. They'd been drafted in from the town for night patrols with an open book on overtime. Thomas only had three years in the job, compared with Rex's hundred or so. The pretty goth-looking girl was opening the front door to a small modern house. The thin lad had just disappeared; probably back down the beach path to get eaten by the vampire nut job. 'Do you think we should double back and drive down to the coast?'

'Thomas, Thomas, Thomas, what are we doing here?' Rex was clearly heading for O'Halloran Hill lane, now that the scenes of crime had cleared it to be opened again. Rex was a sergeant and could do basically whatever he wanted.

'Well we're driving around this shitty little village trying to stop a nut job from drinking anymore blood and killing all these fine citizens.'

'Wrong. What we are actually hoping is that he gets his chops around one of these country yokels ASAP. 'Cos you know from what I'm hearing, DI Hastie and his crew of suited Nazis have more issues with the investigation than a twenty stone woman under an up-turned canoe. That hunchback Hastie's already thrown one telephone out of his office window, and when some dumb probationary constable asked him if he would sign off his probbie book, he fed it into the nearest shredder. Kid actually started bawling!'

'Victor Two One for an update?' the radio fizzed to life.

'Control from Victor Two One, all okay here. O'Halloran Hill sector,' Thomas answered. Control wanted updates every fifteen minutes to keep everyone safe. There was a killer out there, after all.

Rex changed gear and they proceeded to climb the long steep lane that led up The Hill. The car front beams were on full, illuminating the ragtag clusters of trees marking either side of the track. The breeze blowing the thin branches around was unnerving Thomas, who kept expecting someone to suddenly appear. A thin drizzle of rain coated the windows, skewing his vision further.

Rex was still in full flow. '...no, what I am saying is we need another victim. Not saying we want that victim to die, but it looks like we at least need some blood to be spilt. Then we can swoop down off one of these patrols and catch the guy out. Or girl for that matter. I mean who the fuck knows? We could be looking for a chick with a giant steroid induced clitoris!'

Thomas looked up to his right, and read the sign, *THE RIDGEWAY CONVALESCENT HOME.'* It was now just a derelict site: a husk of an old hospital building – a giant irregular shape, with wings and balconies which sprung randomly in every direction. It was easily the largest building in the village, set halfway up O'Halloran Hill, with no doubt an impressive view of the bay in daylight. Thomas had seen the place a few times, and heard that it had been an asylum for the mentally insane in the early 1900's. In more enlightened times it had been turned into a convalescent home for rich people with private medical insurance, a place where people could enjoy a mud pack in peace after a serious illness or operation. It had gone bust eventually and lay empty for over ten years, no doubt waiting for a developer with big ideas to come along and save it.

'Perfect place for a psycho to hang out at night don't you think?' Rex said, while pulling the patrol car through the open gates and into the wide courtyard. There was a flash of full beams from another vehicle: another patrol car already parked up. It drove forward until parallel with them.

'Great minds think alike hey!' shouted Greer through the driver's door window of the other patrol car. He was travelling solo tonight and it smelled like a Chinese takeaway inside his vehicle. 'Say this place is creepy as fucking shit! And it's boarded up tighter than Fort Knox by the looks of it. This is going to be a long night, man. I'm going dizzy driving around this village.' Greer was the only black man in the constabulary, a big

Caribbean man, with an even bigger sense of humour. Any racism rode off his back like water off a humpback.

'What are you thinking, a little hide and seek?' Rex asked. The hide and seek game for town cops was an unsanctioned way to amuse bored coppers on long dragging night shifts. Very often it involved a patrol car hiding somewhere along an agreed route, and utilising any means necessary to disappear. It had been known to use sleeping residents' driveways and garages. Anyone caught out always had the universal catch all phrase, *we thought we saw a person trying to break into your house.'* If only the public knew the half of it.

'That's the best idea I've heard all night. Give me forty-five okay, 'cos I need to grab a bite and get some coffee. See you back here for kick off.'

'That leaves us enough time to have a good poke around anyway. See if we can get Thomas here to shit his pants,' Rex told him.

Greer spun his wheels on the gravel and took off while Rex drove the patrol car forward and parked up. Outside the rain was getting heavier. The wind was icy cold. 'Let's do some of our own exploring,' Rex said looking a little wild eyed, showing Thomas the crowbar he had in his hand.

'Now, you are aware that's not strictly legal?' Thomas said, turning his police torch on.

'Shut up Serpico, and just follow me.'

Thomas fell in behind, his fluorescent jacket already leaking. The walkways around The Ridgeway seemed to zigzag everywhere. Thomas tried a few of the doors, each one feeling like it had been screwed tight with bolts from the inside. 'This way,' shouted Rex up ahead. The guy was on a mission. Above were at least another six floors and not even a glimmer of light. Thomas looked behind and couldn't see the courtyard or the patrol car.

'Hey, Rex, my Airwave terminal just red-lighted, meaning we don't have a radio signal. We should go back.'

'It's fine, we'll get the signal back on the other side. Stop being such a pussy!'

Thomas followed Rex's wavering torchlight, trying not to slip on the walkway slime growing out of the ancient iron gutters that criss-crossed the walls. No one had looked after the place for a long time.

He thought they must have walked at least two hundred metres when they finally reached the far end of the building. They shone their torches down the stone steps and scanned across what must have once been a grand garden area. It was now an impenetrable tangle of weeds and mud. This was where the rich had come to sit on benches around finely manicured lawns, playing croquet and the like, when the weather had been kinder. The garden was bounded by ten foot walls, beyond which fields stretched to the summit of O'Halloran Hill and the car park where the men had been killed the night before. To the right, Thomas could see the thick woods stretching all the way down to the estuary. The village in the main was hidden by the building behind them. 'Have you been here before, Rex?'

'Not for fifteen years or so,' Rex said, drawing lightly on his roll up cigarette. The burning end cast an orange glow over his craggy face: deep black lines that made him look a hundred years old. 'There was a suicide job I went to here once: a woman called Louise McVey – she must have been fifty, going on sixty. Her family had all chipped in and sent her to The Ridgway, a no expenses spared trip. They'd found her passed out in one of those old Mark II Escorts in her garage back in Birmingham. Her doctor had recommended this place, and in fact it turned out she'd actually visited and stayed in Greystones as a young a girl. The family said she perked right up just at the thought of coming here. This family had high hopes this would be a turning point in the old duck's life. She'd been depressed for years, but this was going to turn it all around. Anyway, first evening she gets here, the staff recognise she's paid top dollar, give her the full tour. *Yes, Mrs McVey, you'll start your day with a lovely organic breakfast with all the trimmings, and then the world's your oyster. A swim in the pool, let our hunky Swedish masseur go crazy on your flabby back for an hour. Whatever you fancy darling!* She was still smiling they said, just wanted a good night's sleep and couldn't wait to start her four week break. The staff found her the next day. It looked like she'd tried hanging herself but the shower rail wouldn't support her weight. She was rather a big lass, you see. So she went for the next best thing, found the cleaner's bottle of industrial bleach under the sink. When me and the undertakers came to pull her into the body bag her stomach split open. That chemical had burnt right through her, you see. I must have had Louise on my boots for the next year easy.'

'You've seen some sick stuff, Rex.'

'Sick world, ain't it?' He picked the crowbar off the floor next to his feet, and jammed it into the wood of the boarded-up conservatory door behind them. The wood must have been half-rotten and opened easily.

'So, why are we going in here again?'

'Catch a vampire, what else!'

'Search teams and CID have already been in here, surely? They've gone through every derelict and abandoned place in a ten mile radius. There's nothing here, Rex. Not to mention we'd be blatantly trespassing on private property.'

'What are you talking about? Didn't you hear that scream inside? We're here to save life and limb.' Rex disappeared inside.

'Rex!' Old dry leaves crunched underfoot as Thomas followed Rex's torchlight. The air was damp and stagnant. Thomas noticed his Airwave radio had a green light and he tried to press the handset button to give a status update. The set just beeped when he pressed it. *Still no reception.* The light was lying.

'Yo. Wait up, Rexy!' There was a long stone tiled hallway beyond the confines of the conservatory, an endless dark corridor that his torch beam didn't even begin to penetrate.

'Up here!' Rex's voice was somewhere above him. Thomas shone his torch upwards, and saw his colleague leaning over a thick wooden banister rail waving. Thomas found the beginning of the winding staircase. 'Stop jumping ahead will you? This place is totally creeping me out. And, by the way, we are due to update control. They'll be sending Greer out to look for us at this rate.'

'Well, we did say we were going to play hide and seek. The whole village is covered in black spots. No way we'll get into any trouble. When we get to the roof garden we can give them an update from there.'

'Roof? Are you fucking crazy?'

'Is that any way to talk to your uncle?' Rex laughed.

The staircase went up three floors, and then they found themselves on a landing with hallways heading off in six directions. 'This place is just a crazy maze, we're going to get lost,' Thomas told him, shining his light over the giant oil paintings on the wall, landscapes covered by a thick layer of dust, left behind to rot.

'Doesn't matter, we just need to find another set of stairs. Anyway, if we don't find the conservatory again, then we have this for the purposes of egress,' Rex said showing him the metal bar again. 'Our heavy metal can opener.'

Thomas was disorientated by the time they finally found some steps leading steeply upwards.

They moved from one mini-landing to the next and Thomas felt it was like being stuck in a chimney. Long settled dust was disturbed by their presence, kicking up a choking cloud. Rex had got ahead again, and was noisily shouldering a locked door at the top. 'We're in,' his voice boomed and echoed down like a madman's.

Thomas helped push back the heavy door as it caught and grinded on the stone floor. There was a rush of cold air and suddenly he had a very high view of the village lights stretching out before him. Rex had brought him to a platform no more than ten metres square on top of The Ridgeway's roof. His torchlight flashed over an old rotted deckchair and iron table, now badly rusted and sagging over. 'Good job old Louise McVey didn't find this little picnic spot, or I'd have been all day cleaning up her pancake off the patio. Thank God for bleach!'

'You're a sicko, Rex. But heck of a view though.'

Rex lit up another smoke, and the pair of them idly ran their torchlight over the gardens and courtyards below, getting as close as they dared to the hundred plus foot drop. The patrol car below looked small enough to be radio controlled. Something caught Thomas' eye then, a movement he couldn't place at first. He moved the torch over the overgrown tangle of shrubs that lined the outer walls. There was nothing there.

'Jesus fucking Christ!' Rex hissed.

Thomas looked again, and saw the figure, just before Rex pulled him back from the edge and out of sight.

'Control, this is Victor Two One. Control... control are you receiving this? Suspect is on the grounds of The Ridgeway, in the courtyard, standing on the roof of our patrol vehicle. Do you receive?'

'It's a red light, Rex. No fucking reception!' Thomas whispered.

'Try your mobile, try it right now!'

'Nothing, mate. No bars.' Thomas was close to panic. 'We should barricade ourselves up here and wait for Greer. Wait for dawn if we have to!'

'He's not a bloody vampire for Christ's sake. He's only a nut job made up like one. Do you want Greer's blood on your hands? He turns up and that fucker jumps him, what the hell are we going to do from up here?'

'So we go down. Are you fucking serious?' In his mind he could see the image of the tall man with the gaunt face, covered in blood stains. He had been standing on the roof of the panda car like some statue, staring right up at them, not a stitch of clothing on his whole damned body.

Rex wasn't taking no for an answer. '...we go down, we keep trying the phone and the radio. If we do meet that guy, we kick his fucking head in and get on every front page of every paper in the country as full-blooded heroes. You wanted a decent example for your sergeant's board. This is gold dust!'

Rex jogged down the concrete steps making it hard to listen out and hear if he was coming the other way. *If the guy was a whack-job, then he was a very convincing looking one,* Thomas' mind raced.

Back at the top of the stairs where the six-way corridor started, they waited. Thomas tried to stifle a cough from the dust. He couldn't hear any footsteps.

'This place is locked tight, the guy's only way in is going to be via the conservatory door. We'll see him coming up the stairs a mile off with the torches. You got anything on that mobile yet?' Rex asked. Thomas thought he was starting to look scared.

'No bars. Where the hell is your phone anyway?'

'Bedside table. It's got a better signal for the village than yours as well. Bleeding sod's law!'

There was a crash somewhere below, perhaps on the ground floor. It sounded like glass breaking. 'That was definitely internal. He's in here with us now.'

'I've still got this,' Rex said waving the crowbar. 'Plan is we head away towards the other side on this level. We'll get reception on the way, and break our way out of a front door with this.'

Another crash. Maybe the floor below, Thomas thought.

'Let's go!' Rex barked. They ran down a long corridor which flowed through The Ridgeway like an arterial vein. Thomas nearly tripped on rolled up carpet, then did trip and fell down, skinning his knees and banging his head against the plaster wall. Ahead of him Rex and his torch disappeared. Thomas shone his light back down the corridor the way they'd come, half expecting to see a slavering vampire sprinting along the ceiling towards him, like in the movies. There was nothing there but swirling clouds of dust. Thomas stood and started running again. 'Hey, Rexy, wait up!'

Finding stairs he headed down, with no sign of any torchlight. Thomas started to take the stairs two at a time, floor after floor all the way down to what looked like a reception area – more furniture left to rot, and too many open doors and corridors to count. Thomas felt eyes on him, paranoia rising with nervous bile in his stomach. There was a wood and metal double door and the windows had bars across them. He heaved on the door handle, willing it to open. Any pretence of keeping quiet was long gone. 'OPEN YOU BASTARD!'

The door split outwards, bolts breaking out of the softened wood. Thomas felt the rush of the cold night air again. There was the patrol car, just off to one side, waiting for him. He didn't move though, didn't run forward. Thomas just stared into the grey face and those black, pitiless eyes.

Chapter 7 – The Stash House

'Wake up, you big lug.'

Stixx's eyes opened a slit as he noted the sharp pounding pain from somewhere deep inside his frontal lobe. A hangover was definitely alive and kicking. Blurry vision began to focus. It was very, very, early in the morning and Faye Burns was sat on his bed. Stixx attempted to summon a few words: a spry morning greeting. He grunted instead.

'Do I toss water on you?'

'...sink hasn't worked in years,' he said, sitting up with some difficulty and trying to focus a little.

'Your mum let me in. Wanted to check you were still actually breathing. I'm guessing you haven't seen the news today?'

'Err no,' he said and reached for the bedside tele-remote. The screen flickered and showed Border News. 6.32 a.m was not a logical time to be awake on a Saturday.

It did not compute.

Veronica Myers, the news reporter staying at the guest house was on-screen, standing with a serious expression next to the pier on the promenade. There were a heck of a lot of people milling around for so early in the day. She was using words such as *'multiple murders'* and *'the search for the missing police officer.'* At one point she said, ' *a senior police officer has said it was one of most horrific scenes he'd ever encountered.'*

'I think it was the two police officers we saw last night.'

He thought Faye looked a little paler than he remembered. 'What do they mean by horrific? Have they said anything more about the vampire stuff?'

'They haven't shut up about it. Have you seen Greystones? ...well obviously you haven't. The place is crawling with press, and people who just want to see what's going on. The place is crammed with journos, weirdos, and tourists. This guest house is going to get awfully popular!'

Stixx put his feet on the ground and tried to steady the dizziness. 'Thanks for checking up on me. That was really cool of you.' Bile jumped into his mouth, and he swallowed.

'You're naked under there, aren't you?' she quizzed him, as her phone went off with *Bitter Sweet Symphony*. 'Just Mum checking I haven't been murdered in the last five minutes.'

Stixx started hopping across his bedroom with a sheet wrapped around his middle, looking for the elusive pair of pants.

'...yes, Mum, I'm fine! Just at my new friend Stixx's house. No, Mum, he's not my new boyfriend... and no, his eyebrows aren't meeting in the middle, so he probably isn't the serial killer they're all looking for. ...no, really I don't want to get bitten in the neck. Besides, they would only be out at night if they were real ...just chill-lax will you?! I'll be in for dinner.'

Stixx really couldn't believe he had a beautiful goth-chick visiting his bedroom. He was physically stunned it was really happening.

'She's a worry wart.' The big, beautiful eyes back on him. Stixx was pretty sure this was the first time anyone remotely attractive had been in his bedroom.

Stixx manoeuvred jeans on, embarrassed by how juvenile some of his wall posters must be looking. The assortment of stills from *The Battle of Britain*, Spitfire, Mesherschmitts and the like, needed to fly into the bin sometime soon. This was not a bachelor crash pad that was going to impress the ladies anytime soon. Faye was wearing a black and blue *Green Day* long-sleeve top, and tight black jeans. The girl was hiding some amazing curves and he pondered if the perfume was wild strawberry, or something similarly fruity. 'Let me give you the tour,' he said just to stop himself staring.

They dropped down a floor and stepped round the heaps of camera equipment. The volume of cases, tripods, and loose wiring had doubled overnight.

'See what I mean,' she said. 'For every journalist you've got staying here, there's another ten who would love not to be sleeping in their vans tonight. You should buy more beds!'

As they passed the only bathroom, almost on cue a tall elderly looking man came out with a towel wrapped around his waist. He had a somewhat prominent hook nose. Stixx recognised him as a regular Christmas guest, who'd been coming to the guest house regularly for years. He must have arrived the evening before, and for the life of him Stixx still couldn't remember his name. 'I'm so sorry if you have been waiting. The water is not so good here.' His accent was thick. Stixx thought maybe Eastern European. The man disappeared into room number one. He was at least six foot three and had to dip to get under the door frame. There was a faded tattoo of a cross on his back.

Faye grinned at him and started jumping down the stairs. 'Come on!'

'Who's giving this tour anyway?'

Stixx's mum Margie was in the kitchen, blowing smoke from a cigarette out of the window. 'You've achieved a bona fide miracle. We don't usually see Stixx walking and talking before lunch at the weekend ...and him dressed as well!' Stixx could read a knowing look in his mum's eyes when she looked at him. A simple piece of telepathy that told him she was very surprised and happy for him to have a pretty female visitor, rather than just Red and his dirty feet.

'Yeah, well we couldn't have him lying around in his pit all day.' Faye had punk attitude. He pretty much loved her already.

'Do you want me to whip up some bacon, sausage, and eggs?' Margie dabbed out the cigarette and flicked it out of the kitchen window towards the gravel patio below.

'I'm one of those veggie weirdos I'm afraid, Margie. My mum was into *Greenpeace* and *Save the Whale*. I never stood a chance really. But I do dream of McDonalds most nights.'

'Well, I won't tell if you don't.'

'Maybe some toast?'

Stixx and Faye sat down facing each other at the small kitchen table. He wished they had kept moving instead of sitting down. His hangover brain wasn't giving him much to say.

Dumb brain cells!

So... you're a fan of Green Day?' He threw it out there.

44

Faye screwed up her nose and gave it a twitch. Stixx thought that was pretty cute. 'Modern punk is pretty special sometimes, gets your blood going. Are you a fan?'

'Oh yeah!'

'So, what's your favourite track?'

'Well, err... the one that had soldiers in the video?'

'Stixx, you aren't very good at fibbing are you? You'd make a really rubbish poker player.'

'I'm a very good poker player, actually.'

'Here's your toast.' Margie sat down a plate in front of Faye with one hand, and with the other dropped off a plate piled high with fried eggs, bacon, sausage and beans for Stixx.

'Thanks, Mum.' Stixx was one of those people that no matter how much saturated fat went in his mouth, he never put even an ounce of weight on. He was a naturally skinny string bean.

Mrs Phillips bustled her way into the kitchen, her beady eyes straight on the new girl. 'So are you Stixx's new lady love?'

The little Irish tinker.

'Please forgive the hired help. We'd sack her if she wasn't so cheap,' Stixx cut in. His cheeks were burning.

'You haven't met my family yet. You have no idea!' Faye winked at him.

A while later they were walking up one of the many paths on O'Halloran Hill, a rutted, well-used trail through the woods. They had to tread carefully around smooth limestone, wet mud, and exposed tree roots. Walking on The Hill was one of Stixx's favourite things in the world. Usually it gave him the peace and quiet to think his best thoughts. Stixx imagined this was a far better introduction to the village than the pub and a trip to an abandoned swimming pool.

'So you and your mum have picked your time to move here. One hundred years of nothing, and now we're the murder capital of Great Britain!'

'Just like the Lost Boys, hey?'

'What do you mean?'

'You really need to keep up with my film references,' she giggled.

'Just keep them coming!' They climbed over a large wooden stile and dropped into a frosty green field. The gradient climbed steeply towards a fresh tree line and the summit of O'Halloran Hill. There were assorted grubby sheep milling against one of the dry stone walls – a few briefly looked up and then went back to their bored chewing.

'It doesn't feel real you know,' he said. 'I mean I didn't actually know any of the people who were killed. Maybe I'd seen that Patrick around the village with his family a few times, I'm not even sure to be honest. What I mean is, the fact they're dead and mutilated or whatever, doesn't seem real. Any minute now they're going to catch some creep who's been running around pretending to be a vampire, and it's all going to be over: just another story for down the pub.'

'Jeez, so you can string more than two words together. I'm impressed!' She smiled the million watt smile again and a tingle buzzed its way up the back of his neck. 'But what if it isn't over, Stixx? There's this monster out there. It could literally be anyone. It could be you, it could be me, it could even be Red. There could be a real vampire out there, have you thought about that? With all their weapons and training, one policeman's been torn apart and the other is, let's face it, probably sucked dry!'

'Have you seen our local policemen? The only skill they exhibit is stuffing donuts in their mouths! I don't think pepper spray and some thin weak-ass baton is going to cast fear into the heart of most serial killers. They were probably just caught by surprise.'

'But it's exciting though, isn't it? All that mystery happening right here.'

'I guess so.'

The trek up the steep hill stopped conversation for a few minutes, until finally they jumped another wooden stile at the top of the hill. 'Hell of a view!' Stixx wheezed.

Looking down they could see the ugly eyesore that was The Ridgeway. It was over half a mile away, yet still stood out on the green countryside like an ugly wart. The murder scene was getting a lot of attention, dozens of police vehicles ringing the building and the grounds. From their elevated position on The Hill they could see inside the courtyard, the police and forensic people in white overalls moving around, like tiny worker ants, literally taking over the asylum. Streamers of yellow police tape seemed everywhere, and nobody would be driving up the O'Halloran Hill lane anytime soon. 'So how many more people do you think will die before this is all over?' she asked him.

'Maybe nobody. Maybe they'll catch the sick fuck prowling around tonight in a cape and a pair of plastic fangs from the pound shop. It'll just end up being some creepy kid, I bet.'

Stixx turned away, and led them onto a wooded trail that led to the summit of O'Halloran Hill. The Ridgeway disappeared from sight, and he felt his breathing finally start to recover after the climb. Faye had some colour back in her cheeks, matching the red streaks in her hair.

'So we agree it could be anyone, although on good faith I'm prepared to exclude myself and you.'

'But why me?' Stixx asked, trying to sound mysterious.

'Trust me, if you can't even lie about knowing much about *Green Day*, I think I'd be able to spot if you were covering up a murder or four. I'm not going to say the same about Red, who is a creepy little so and so, you have to admit.' She was smiling what he was coming to know as her provocative smile.

'He would actually be flattered just to be called a creep. But he's my friend, I don't think he's guilty of anything other than downloading a lot of dodgy porn …anyway, how about your boyfriend for a possible suspect?' Truthfully, Stixx just wanted to shoe-horn him into the conversation. All he wanted to hear was that the cradle-snatcher teacher could be on his way to dumps-ville.

'Well, Alan is out of the country last I checked. That gives him a fairly concrete alibi I'd say. More to the point, I know Alan and he wouldn't hurt a fly. He literally would go out of his way to catch a bluebottle and release it back into the wild.'

'Sorry, but that sounds a bit serial killer-ish to me. And how do you know he is out of the country?' Stixx selected another path that branched off, taking them down the slope at the far side of The Hill, straight into the thickest of the woods.

'Well, I did give him a long, lingering kiss at the airport, and watched his plane fly away. And then there's all the love letters I keep getting with Ghana postmarks. I reckon you could safely scratch him off the list.'

Scratch his eyes out! Stixx thought. 'I still say he could be a serial killer,' he said quietly, ducking under the branches of a tree that had fallen over the path. 'Anyone who loves bluebottles surely can't be trusted.'

'Jealous much, are we?'

Stixx's cheeks went scarlet again and he walked ahead. The path passed in and out of the trees, and at one point traversed a near vertical field of shingle, which had the local name of *The Shillerbeds*. The adventurous-type could plant their feet in the loose gravelly rock and slide their way down on a mini-avalanche. It was fun if you were young, when bones bent rather than broke. Stixx decided to give it a miss, and instead they snaked their way down to the far side of The Hill. From there the path opened up onto a bridleway, wide enough for a 4x4 vehicle.

'So you dragged me over that big fucking hill, when we could have just gone round.' Faye was cute when mad. She lit up a Marlborough Lite, and Stixx wondered if smoking had ever looked so cool.

'Yeah, well. I thought you'd like the view up here!'

'I'd like my lungs back.' Faye took a long drag on the cigarette, and held up the packet. 'You want one of these?'

'Okay,' Stixx said. He didn't smoke anything other than pot usually, but he didn't want to do anything even halfway negative to put her off him.

They smoked for a while, staring aimlessly into the woods. Dead twigs fell every thirty seconds or so, adding to the general restless rustle of the leaves in the chilly wind. The woods could be eerie if you stood and listened for long enough. Stixx caught sight of a grey squirrel, but just as quick it disappeared in the thick brambles that weaved around many of the old crusty tree trunks.

'So it's one o'clock and I can't see a picnic hamper. There's a rumbling and a grumbling,' Faye said rubbing her flat tummy.

Stixx offered her a mint from his pocket and Faye pulled a face. He wondered if she had her belly button pierced. 'Well before we go back, do you want to see something cool, and slightly illegal?'

'Listen to you, *Mr Intrigue* all of a sudden. Lead on McDuff!'

'Well, you're not to tell anyone anything, okay?'

'My lips are like a bathroom tile - *sealed!*'

It took them another fifteen minutes to exit the woods, and to follow the quiet single lane tarmac road that followed the line of The Hill. Eventually it snaked off towards the coast and the next village along: the small and innocuous village of Silverdale. Stixx had no plans to go that far however, and took them through a tight gap in the wall and across yet another field. 'Not far to go, I promise.'

'If when we get there you kill me, I'll haunt you. You do know that, don't you?'

'What are you going to do, set Alan on me?' He was safe – she was smiling.

At the end of the field there wasn't a stile or any gaps in the stone wall. The top of the stone wall was lined with ageing barb-wire fencing, with a rusting green and red sign attached : *PRIVATE LAND. TRESPASSERS WILL BE PROSECUTED.'*

'An empty threat as always,' Stixx said, while dusting the mulch off a ladder he had hidden in the corner of the field. The ladder was wooden, and a few of the rungs had rotted out over time. He leant it on top of the wall and pressed down on the wire. Looking back towards the road he couldn't see any vehicles in sight. 'Come on, I've done this before.' He climbed over and jumped down onto the bank of wet moss on the other side. 'You'll be fine!'

Faye looked unsure of herself for the first time all day. There was a vulnerability there hidden beneath the confident attitude, he figured. For a fleeting second Faye looked a lot less the *Green Day* punk ready to take on the world, and more the teenager still trying to throw off the last vestiges of childhood. He moved forward to help her down, but slipped on the moss and fell on his backside. 'Those skiddies are going to stain. Your mum won't be happy!' Faye said, deftly jumping down next to him.

They went on through the private woods. No path or trail to see, but Stixx knew where he was going. At the edge of a clearing he held his hand up, just like he'd seen Willem Defoe do in *Platoon* when he hears the Vietcong nearby.

'That was a bit gay,' she whispered in his ear.

Nestled in the middle of the open space was a long rectangular greenhouse. It was as big as a bungalow, but old and broken down: the wooden frame was visibly sagging, and the panes of glass that weren't already broken had a thick film of green lichen coating over them. 'The Colonel used to love his fresh veg in his younger days, I've heard.'

'Who is the Colonel?'

'Well he's not the owner of Kentucky Fried Chicken,' Stixx smiled walking out into the clearing. He ducked under the doorframe and into the greenhouse. There was still a lingering smell of concentrated soil and peat in the air, even after all the years of neglect and the intrusion of the elements – the smell was ingrained. He walked down the central aisle, past the crude rough-timbered potting tables and benches. The pots still intact were full of grey, leached soil. Nothing lived here but the spiders in their webs. Just how he liked it to appear.

'Over here,' he beckoned to Faye. Her face looked like it had done at the top of the wall, a little of that uncertainty creeping into her pretty features. 'I thought you said you were sure I wasn't a serial killer!'

'Well, wouldn't it be ultra-clever of a serial killer to pretend not to know *Green Day*, and then lure the poor innocent new girl to his secret hideaway?' Faye might have been joking, but was still hanging back in the entrance to the greenhouse.

'Miles from civilisation in the middle of the woods – could be a neat slasher film?' He took a step towards her. Faye didn't flinch. 'And at the end Alan could be the serial killer!'

'Well I can't see any fake fangs, and the sun's still up. You can't be much of a vampire.' They were a metre apart.

He made to jump forward to try and scare her. Faye brought her leg up and the next thing he felt was an uncontrollable urge to curl up on the floor and die.

'SORRY! I didn't mean to do that. You jumped at me… I was always doing that at karate when I was a kid. They called me Rover, on account of me always going for the balls. The blokes all had to buy cricket boxes to save their nuts!'

'That explains why Alan hasn't got any testicles,' Stixx managed to squeak out. He was aware his face had probably just turned scarlet.

Later, when his balls had just a dull ache, Faye sat on the ground next to him. 'You could have rubbed it better at least,' he said.

'But you never asked.'

He wondered if she was kidding.

'So, why are we here again? Big horticultural fan, are we?' She was changing the subject.

'Pot.'

'What?'

Stixx struggled back to his feet and shuffled over to the far end of the greenhouse, pushing back one of the tables and kicking away some leaves on the floor. There was a trapdoor. Lifting it, he slowly descended down the wooden steps into the small cellar. 'I think they used the room to store all the fertilisers and stuff for the plants.' The air was thick with the smell of marijuana.

'Jesus Stixx, you've got an entire cannabis factory!' Faye looked at the blue fluorescent lamps, shining down on the sprawling cannabis plants which smothered half the room.

'The Colonel owns so much shit that he must have forgotten this place still has live electricity. I've got a full hydroponic set up – *The Full Monty!*' he said proudly, pointing towards a heavily overloaded multi-socket on the wall. 'I set it all up five months ago. My lovelies just need a little food and water every other week.' The cannabis sprawled out inside the confined space making it look more like a jungle than a cellar.

Faye stroked some of the leaves. 'You must be making thousands!'

51

'It's deceptive. Once it's dried it'll be more like hundreds, rather than thousands. But at least Red and me don't have to mess with dodgy dealers. It cuts out the middle men.'

'Small town village drug dealer hey? So, you were going to tell me about the Colonel anytime soon?'

They heard a noise, the growl of a diesel engine. 'Shit, we need to get out of here,' Stixx said. They ran back up the steps and Stixx slammed the trapdoor down in a hurry. Through the dirty glass he could see a grey Landrover coming into the clearing. 'Duck down!' he hissed. 'We need to get out the back way.'

The voices came nearer. Two men stood outside, moving towards the greenhouse. He recognised one of them straight away as the village sergeant, Flint. It didn't look like he was in his uniform either.

'…your dad should sell off this land, you know. It's not like he's going to be coming down here anytime soon to tend the tomato plants. How many years has he been locked away in that mausoleum that he calls a house? I've lost count.'

'What my father does or doesn't do with his land is no concern of yours, sergeant. I only brought you down here to show you the cellar. God, I hate fucking kids!' The voice was gruffer and lower than Flint's. Stixx figured it to be the Colonel's son, Myles. He was a thick-set lump, who was generally thought of in the village as a bit of a thug, but one born with a silver spoon in his mouth. Stixx only knew him at all from the days when he got five pounds an hour working as a beater on one of the estate's many pheasant shoots. Stixx had got to walk through the woods beating a stick on a pan and shouting a lot. He remembered Myles getting his kicks from pushing the kids around, like the bully that he was.

'Come on Faye, we need to get moving.' They started crawling through the dead leaves and dirt towards the greenhouse doorway. They needed the cover of the building to make a run for it.

'…this is the last time I follow you into any secret cellars! If I get a criminal record, you are so dead!' she hissed.

'Wait.' Stixx couldn't help himself, he was holding his hand up Defoe-style again. The men were walking around to their side of the greenhouse. Only the grimed up window panes were saving them from being discovered. *They were in trouble.*

'So, why haven't you caught this freak yet? Detective skills getting a little rusty?'

'You always were a little creep Myles, do you know that? So where is this trapdoor?' They were almost at the entrance to the greenhouse.

'...in the cellar, I told you! Some little cretin has set up a cannabis factory right under my father's nose. We will want results with this one, Flint.'

'The vampire case gets priority over whatever crap you want to show me.'

'Come off it Flint, a flat-foot like you isn't going to be on any murder cases. They have people with brains and investigative skills for that sort of thing, I imagine. As my father likes to say: you're nothing more than a glorified lollipop man...'

'Listen to me, you little fuck...' Flint hissed back. Stixx thought he had hold of Myles by the shoulder. 'Keep talking like that and see what happens.'

'I could... have... your... badge for this!' The man was struggling to get his words out. He sounded in pain.

'You and your father'd better tread lightly, Myles. These killings might just rake up more than you want. Pass that message on to your darling daddy later, would you. Perhaps while you're giving him his bed bath.' Their argument was outside the open door to the greenhouse. They only had to look down to see him and Faye now.

'I forgot the torch,' Myles said stomping back towards the vehicle. Flint paused, his broad back facing them. Stixx imagined Faye's mother would probably get a restraining order against him: the village druggie. But then, like magic, Flint moved away, his phone ringing in his hand. He was whispering and mumbling into the handset. 'I'll be right there, sir!'

'You'd better hurry up Myles, I have places to be.' Flint was walking back towards the Landrover. Myles was in the back searching for the torch, no doubt.

'Stay low, and run straight!' Stixx told Faye. He started to sprint towards the tree line, Faye just behind. Pulling himself around the trunk of an oak tree, he dropped to the ground and pulled her down with him. Behind them, Flint and Myles were walking into the greenhouse with the torch. *They'd actually got away with it.* 'Come on, let's go!'

'Are you not worried they are going to arrest you for the cannabis?'

'Flint is too lazy to get any proper forensic evidence. He'll probably just bag it up and throw it in the nearest bin. Everyone knows he's lazy as shit!'

'Here we go!' Faye cursed, looking down at her phone. 'My mum is doing her nut. Walk me home would you, Romeo?'

'It'll keep me safe, I suppose.' Stixx glanced at her as they crossed the field again, both of them covered in dirt and cobwebs. He was pretty sure he was in love.

Chapter 8 – The Romanian

'So what about the Romanian?' the text read. He replied quickly. It was late and Stixx was sprawled on his bed. Outside the attic window there was a sliver of moon visible behind the banks of dark grey cumulonimbus cloud. Stixx half-watched some bad golden oldie Burt Reynolds film, waiting for his mobile phone screen to light up again.

He'd taken refuge in his bedroom since walking Faye home and eating some of Margie's left-over stew, trying to avoid the scrum of journalists that seemed to have taken over the guesthouse. His mother had allowed a lot of them to double up in their rooms, making the place fuller and noisier than it had ever been. They were running at way over their legal capacity, and charging four times the normal rates, for everyone, that was, apart from *The Romanian.*

The phone screen lit with his screen saver of Faye. He spent the last hour answering all her questions about the Colonel. He'd told of the legend: that he'd been some kind of decorated military genius back in World War Two, a very rich decorated military genius, who after the war had inherited a huge slab of land around Greystones, including a massive mansion set in a thousand acres of prime field and woodland, populated with deer and more fat pheasants than one man could shoot in three lifetimes. He also told Faye the man owned leases on half the shops in the village, not to mention countless houses which he rented out. The guy was a millionaire many times over. Not that all that money had bought the great Colonel much luck.

Stixx had managed to cram the Colonel's misfortunes into a very economical nine text messages. His index finger was tenderised from all the typing. He started by telling her how, somewhere around 1950, The Colonel had been riding in a hunt, hot on the heels of some flame-haired, chicken-thief fox. His horse, probably a top of the line racing stallion, had jumped a fence. Unfortunately, the great military mind had not counted on the flock of sheltering sheep hidden on the other side. Somewhere in the carnage of ruined sheep, the Colonel found himself crushed under the weight of a half-tonne horse. And sometime later, when the other huntsmen had prised his legs out from underneath the beast, he found he had a spinal injury that put him into a wheelchair for the rest of his life. But the unlucky gods hadn't quite finished with him, not by any means.

The village loved to gossip. Stixx half-remembered some drunken night in the pub when the Colonel had come up in conversation. Apparently, in the 1960s the whispers were of young men visiting the manor house at all times of the night. The gossips said they were rent boys, well paid to carry out all manner of illicit and illegal acts with the infirm Colonel. Supposedly that gossip had changed direction again when he married a cousin: a sweet, round looking woman on his mother's side, and someone who had already been caring for him for years. From the messages he was receiving back from Faye, she was loving every single bit of this information dump, and Stixx wished he had brought it all up sooner.

He told Faye the cousin had died in childbirth trying to squirt the degenerate Myles into this world, and sometime after that the Colonel hid himself away completely, becoming a recluse in his own mansion to this day. Fresh rumours became thin on the ground, and it was only Myles who was ever seen in the village representing his father's rather expansive interests. Stixx imagined the Colonel to be a little like Citizen Kane, not that Stixx had ever managed to watch the film all the way through.

Faye seemed to love every sordid half-fact and rumour he could dredge up out of his memory banks. *'So what about the Romanian?'* The message had come after a break of half an hour. He'd imagined she must have fallen asleep, or the village's bad mobile phone reception was delaying things again.

'What about him? Just a guest who comes every year. Only reason he got a room was cos he booked it ages ago,' he typed back.

The phone finally flashed back with a new text. Stixx wondered if he should ask her to send a photograph, or at least ask her what she was wearing. Her message read, *'I mean don't you find it odd that when the village has some vampire impersonator running round ripping throats out, you have a guest who sounds like he's out of a Dracula film?'*

Been coming for years. He's on same floor as loads of media people and they haven't batted an eyelid,' he texted back.

'Maybe he hasn't spoken to them. What's he doing here all on his own year after year anyway? I smell fish.'

'*...something fishy!'* the next text corrected.

'What do you want to do about Romanian? Don't think Flint be very interested or any of other coppers '

WE INVESTIGATE!!!'

'*?*

'This is chance of lifetime. Coming up to Christmas... we've got time on our hands... could crack case and save some lives. Come on! Could be fun, teammate!'

'*?*

Stixx was puzzled. All he wanted right now was a nice picture of some cleavage. Now she wanted them to go all Sherlock Holmes. He wasn't going to get any pictures, he knew it. *What makes you think we can find this guy when whole police force out there drawing blanks?'*

'You very negative for a Sagittarius.'

'What can I say... I'm not very religious! Not saying it wouldn't be fun or that I'm not up for it. Just don't know how we'd do it, that's all.'

'The Romanian!!!!'

'Faye what are you wearing?'

Stixx laid his head back on the pillow and stared up at the green fluorescent stars he had plastered on his ceiling. Eight years they had been up there and they didn't have much glow left in them. Disappointingly, the phone refused to light up with a graphic picture, and he found himself finally drifting to sleep.

'Wakey wakey!'

Stixx knew the voice. *Got to be kidding!*

Faye was stood over his bed. Sunrise sunlight was streaming in through his thin curtains, casting an orange hue around her. She was the evil morning angel!

'Do you want me to pretend to close my eyes so you can get dressed?'

Stixx pulled back the covers. 'See I'm already ready for action.'

'You've still got your clothes on… and your shoes I see. Is that normal?'

'Normal is as normal does.'

'You're weird, you know that?' She was grinning though, so Stixx thought she mustn't mean it. She handed him a cup.

Five minutes later, with fresh coffee in his stomach, he felt half-alive at least. The red digits of his clock mocked him with the time, 7.22am. 'So let me get this right. You want us to harass the poor guy who stays here every year without fail, and just loves walking on the beach and taking photographs?'

'For all we know, he's been coming here a hundred years and doesn't even show up on photographs!'

'You are the crazy one, you do know that? Totally nutso!' When he said it he saw a little reaction from Faye: the smallest hint of discomfort that flickered over her face and was gone.

'We should make a pact…' she said, all smiles again, '…a promise to get to the bottom of this whole damn vampire thing before the police, the media, or anyone else – me and you saving some lives. What do you think? And don't say I'm crazy again!'

Stixx was getting a tingling feeling up his neck. It was delicious. 'I say I'm in!'

They sat at the top of the attic stairs. Stixx loved the feeling of their thighs touching on the narrow stairway. They didn't have long to wait. Faye held up her compact mirror over the banister rail and watched Burt the Romanian come out of the guest bedroom. He walked straight into the bathroom just vacated by the hairy cameraman, Diego. 'Nice timing there,' Stixx whispered.

Once the landing cleared, they made a dash for it. Stixx grabbed the round ceramic doorknob and twisted. 'Locked, but I have this!' he whispered frantically, holding up a duplicate key. In his bedroom Stixx had copies of every key for every lock in the house, having previously been a little key obsessive as a child. Already he felt like the great detective. The lock turned, clicked, and they almost fell into the room.

'You do the drawers and I'll do the bags.' Faye sounded excited and borderline deranged.

Stixx did as he was told but expected Burt to come bursting back in, accusing them of stealing his stamp collection or whatever. When they'd first moved into the guest house, his mum had cut a deal at the village's pseudo antiques shop to take a bulk order of ageing dressers and wardrobes off their hands. She'd saved a bundle, and after they were delivered had spent the next week painting the faded and chipped woodwork with white enamel gloss. Now, after ten years, most of the furniture was chipped and faded all over again. Stixx opened the top clothes drawer and began sifting through piles of very washed out, grey underwear. 'So what are we looking for again?' He looked at Faye with a quizzical expression.

'You know… vampire stuff!' she said shrugging, and opened up a reading glasses case from an open suitcase against the wall. 'Sometimes serial killers like to keep mementoes, like a ring or an earring. You never know.'

The old clothes smelt musty and old, much like Burt, Stixx thought. The only significant thing he managed to find by the time he'd finished the bottom drawer was a small silver cross on a chain. If Burt the Romanian was a deluded vampire-wannabe, then he wasn't too fussy about his neck attire.

Faye had satisfied herself that the suitcase was clean, and now had Burt's briefcase emptied over the double bed.

'Are you kidding me?'

'Quickest way to be sure. I don't think it has any secret compartments,' she said knocking her fist on the red leather panels.

Stixx heard a tell-tale double click from outside the bedroom. It was the latch in the communal bathroom being pulled back. Burt was on his way back already.

'Let's get under the bed,' Faye pointed, and then her face dropped. There was no more than a three inch gap under the bottom of the bed. 'FUCK, SHIT, WANK!'

'The wardrobe, and hurry up!' Stixx opened the door, grateful that old Burt didn't own more than a handful of things needing hangers. Stixx pushed the three shirts, two pairs of trousers and one sweaty-smelling duffle coat to one side. He hopped inside first, with Faye a millisecond behind. The bedroom door was being pushed open. Stixx struggled to hold the wardrobe door closed with just the end of his fingernails. 'If he wants to get dressed we're fucked!' Underfoot the old floorboards groaned and creaked.

Stixx could see Burt through the crack in the door he couldn't close. Burt's skin was still wet over his bare sloping shoulders. He had wisps of grey hair on his sunken chest, and a strange distended belly button. Burt dropped the towel from his waist onto the carpet. Stixx averted his eyes from the old man's buttocks.

'What's he doing?' Faye whispered in his ear. Her hot body pressed against him in the confined space.

We must do this more often!

He craned his head forward to see what was going on with Burt. A half second later he pulled his head up sharply, the image of the so-called vampire killer laying spread eagled on top of the towel was seared onto his retina: one hand holding a lit cigarette lighter, while the other held what looked like a small, tired chipolata.

'He's making a fried hand shady by the looks of it!' Stixx whispered back.

'What the fuck is one of those? Let me see!' Faye pushed forwards, the wardrobe slowly but inexorably tipping forward and crashing onto the bedroom floor.

Stixx's vision swam in and out of focus. Burt's penis was dangling over him, far too close for comfort. 'We can explain?' Stixx told it.

'Just a... termite inspection,' Faye said from somewhere under the ruined wardrobe. She was giggling wildly.

'Diz is not acceptable!' the penis seemed to be saying.

Chapter 9 – A Bad Night

They had drifted the rest of the way through Sunday. Their indiscretion with the wardrobe had been explained away with help from Margie Stixx.

After five solid minutes of what could only have been Romanian swearing of the highest calibre, Burt had come back to planet Earth. Margie had somehow traversed the language barrier and sold the idea that he and Faye had not been on some madcap mission to spy on his erect nakedness, and in fact had been doing some overdue investigation into woodworm in the furniture. How Burt had ever bought that, Stixx had no idea. But old Burt had almost appeared radiant when Margie offered to slice his bill in half and throw in a few vintage bottles of red wine. With all the journos and their open cheque books, they could definitely afford it.

Faye had thought the whole thing hilarious, of course, and worthy of instant posting on Facebook.

'Wouldn't that be giving the game away? What if he reads it?'

'Does Burt have Facebook, do you think? Don't worry. I'll just make it sound like a sex game gone wrong instead.' She winked at him and Stixx was happy for her to do whatever she wanted.

He had started to think that he should kiss her soon, but halfway along Hill Road, Faye had started talking about Alan again and killed the moment: Alan the paedo-teacher, who really should be struck off and locked up with all the other nonces. *Why couldn't he just get eaten by the vampire?* Stixx wondered.

'He's on the satellite phone at 2pm our time. It feels like I haven't heard his voice for so long, even though it's only been one week. Sometimes, I feel I can't remember what he looks like – my memory just playing tricks on me. It drives me crazy, you know!'

'He drives me crazy too,' Stixx answered, tuning out.

'What?'

'Nothing!'

Faye left him near her house, and seemed far more interested in making nice with her absentee boyfriend than making any firm plans for the next step in their new enterprise.

He kicked a stone across the road, very nearly hitting a news van driving in the direction of the latest murder scene on O'Halloran Hill. Stixx wondered how all this news coverage would change Greystones. Already the place got a lot of tourists in the summer for the pretty estuary and woodland walks. Was there going to be sickos and gore-hounds arriving now, if Mrs Phillips was right, all wanting to visit the famous kill sites? And how many *sites* were there going to be by the time the guy was caught? Someone could make a fortune selling tee-shirts and memorabilia. Stixx thought he should talk to Red about it. Perhaps they could set up a business together and he could leave his work in a dead-end storeroom.

He pulled out his mobile and dialled Red. '*Red is not available right now. He is with your mother again,*' was the familiar answerphone message. He'd probably been up all night playing *World of Warcraft*. A creature of habit, he would try him later.

Heading back to the guest house, Stixx could feel the Sunday glums starting to kick in. The downstairs internet killed a few hours. The murders were getting as many Google hits per day now as Katie Price's breasts. Margie made him a nice roast chicken dinner, but made the cardinal sin of reminding him of things he was trying hard not to think about.

'Have you got work tomorrow?'

'Yes.'

'I really like your new friend.'

'She's got a boyfriend in Ghana.'

'I think you two would make a pretty couple. Cheer up *Les Misérables* and come and give your old mum a hug!'

Stixx retreated to his bedroom and busied himself giving the place a facelift on the off-chance Faye might drop in unannounced, perhaps spend the night even. He fired texts off to Red and Faye, then watched as his mobile phone steadfastly refused to light up.

Outside the sun was already down. It was 6pm in darkest winter and so, of course, it was pitch black. The news quickly got boring and it was obvious the police didn't have any fresh leads to boast about. They were considering a 10pm curfew around the village, *for the safety of all the residents.* Good luck with that one, he thought. Stixx turned off the TV and lay on his bed, staring at the stars on his ceiling again.

Alone!

He wanted to get off his bed and close the attic window. A chill breeze was coming through and he couldn't get comfortable. Stixx knew he had to move but every muscle in his body felt relaxed and ready to sleep. The breeze was persistent and chilling, and became accompanied by a strange scratching noise. At first he thought the arm of the old window was catching and grating on the frame. But that didn't seem quite right. There was a tapping, a rhythmic noise that couldn't just be the wind. Stixx half-opened his eyes and took a look.

In the darkness he couldn't make it out at first. Slowly he picked out the features one by one: a crooked nose was pressing against the glass. There was an ugly mouth of shadows and teeth, still like a statue. A pointy tongue flicked out, and Stixx felt himself scramble out of bed and run towards his mother's bedroom.

'RUN, RUN, RUN!' he was shouting, the words coming out like gobbledygook.

Margie's bedroom walls were wet. There was a curtain flapping and billowing, all torn and shredded. The wallpaper wasn't pastoral whites and flowers anymore, but spattered with clunks of blood-stained meat. Pieces of Margie seemed to be everywhere, even squeezing between Stixx's bare toes. He staggered back into the attic hallway and felt for his phone, finding nothing but empty pockets. The vampire was there silhouetted in the doorframe of his room: fat and sweating with a pig-like face. It moved towards him – a lizard on thick legs. There was nothing human about him, *not a single thing.*

Stixx tried to run down the steep attic stairs and fell. A bone broke, but he wasn't sure if it was his arm or his shoulder. 'IT'S HERE! IT'S HERE!' he shouted to the landing, thumping steps coming down the stairs behind him. He was going to die now.

Stixx staggered forward, legs now not wanting to function properly. Reaching out, he banged his fist on one of the guestroom doors. There was nobody coming out to save him, or even to distract the thing bearing down on him. The fat lizard man wanted to tear his flesh and drink hot platelets from his veins. Stixx nearly fell again, trying to turn his body for the next flight of stairs. The world was all moving in slow motion.

The blood sucker, the monster with the mouth of endless overlapping teeth, was watching him at the base of the attic stairs. Stixx expected it to fly at him at any moment. It was playing with him, he knew that. There would be no happy ending, just torn flesh and pain.

In the darkness he flung himself at the front door, feeling for the latch from memory. Any second he expected a cold reptilian hand on his shoulder.

How long before the teeth?

In the darkness there were rasping breaths: deep and dirty, like rotten bellows. He pulled the front door towards him and went out onto the stone steps. Stixx imagined that the great bay windows would explode, that the monster would come through the old glass and wooden frames and tear into him.

On the road outside the guest house he tried to run, his bad arm feeling like it was dying, broken muscle and bone turning into putty. Footsteps were echoing loudly off the tarmac and houses behind him, not his own. Stixx craned his neck to look back and saw the thing striding forward to take him. In one clawed hand it had the head of the hairy cameraman Diego, eyes rolled back, white eyeballs catching in the moonlight.

The world was ending.

There was a light then, a jeep tearing its rubber tyres in the rush to get onto his road. Stixx was blinded by the whiteness, squinting to see through it. 'OVER HERE!' Stixx shouted, over and over.

He heard a sound, a familiar and wonderful voice. 'You need to get out of the way!' Faye shouted back, and drove the jeep straight over the lizard, squeezing it flat.

Then Stixx woke up.

He sat up in his bed, his body hot with sweat. The attic window was closed and locked. On the duvet his iPhone was flashing. Stixx grabbed at it, feeling terrified and trying to calm his breathing. There was no sound other than the natural creaks and settling tones that the old guest house always had. *I hope you're ready for more?'* the message read.

'Horrible nightmare. Scared!' he texted back instantly.

She rang him, soothing him. 'You have nothing to be scared about.'

'I dreamt he was a lizard man.'

'He's just a man, Stixx.'

Soon Stixx was asleep again, his phone clutched in his hand.

Chapter 10 – The End of Work

Stixx trudged from the train station to work, kicking ice blocks off the pavement. Any semblance of a mild winter was now falling away.

It was bad enough that the sun went down at 3.30pm every day, now the temperature was regularly heading south of zero degrees, making walking anywhere a full-blown health hazard. Somebody had fixed a Santa climbing a ladder to their outside window. There was a ring of fairy lights blinking around the frame. It warmed the heart, he supposed.

Being in the locker room at work made him melancholy, bordering on despondent. There was no place in the world he wanted to be less than at ASDA. Even the name was like acid in his mouth. Every day in the warehouse was like another day in a life sentence: the lucky ones got a noose and a short drop. He wanted to be with Faye – adventuring, investigating, and falling out of wardrobes.

'I know what you did,' a familiar weasel voice said from behind him.

Stixx turned towards Sebastian, the wannabe management drone with his fetish for bicycles.

'I didn't draw you getting anal-type pleasure from a bike, if that is what you're insinuating, Seb.'

'You just incriminated yourself there, James!'

'Fat Les told me earlier,' Stixx lied, brushing past and getting out of the changing room. He left Sebastian looking frustrated: the come-back quip eluding him, along with any Columbo-esque skills.

'I'll be checking that with Les,' he shouted at last.

'Whatever, fuck-face!' Stixx said under his breath. Fat Les hated Seb almost as much as he did. He would be happy to tell a small fib on his behalf.

Stixx started his work on the warehouse floor. The ancient free-standing industrial heaters were making a less than useless dent on the bitter cold. His breath plumed out of his mouth, and the ASDA issue warm winter coat was not doing what it said on the tin. He needed more layers and headed off towards the clothing skip. His watch was only thirty five minutes on since he last looked. Another bleak seven hours stretched out before him across the warehouse moors.

At the far back area of the warehouse were a line of four skips, for cardboard, plastics, glass and clothing. Fat Les was already there ahead of him. Even in the cold he was managing to stand on a ladder, bend over the skip and expose his hairy Welsh arse crack. 'Can't you put it away,' Stixx shouted over to him. 'There are woman and children down here going blind!'

'They should think themselves lucky. I tell you, people pay good money down the docks at Pembroke just to run their fingers over these bristly buttocks. Say Stixx...' he said quieter, eyes checking for eavesdroppers. 'Do you have any of that rather nice, home-grown stuff with you today?'

'Unfortunately, Les, my own warehouse was raided, so to speak. So it's not going to be a very merry Christmas, I'm afraid.'

'Sorry to hear that, pal.' And Stixx thought he genuinely meant it. Les was the only decent person in the whole store, in his opinion: a gentle, Welsh, marijuana-smoking whale. He got him up to speed on Seb. 'Fucker's out for blood, and probably out to avenge the honour of his bicycle as well.'

'The big nonce won't be getting any joy from me,' Les assured him.

Later Stixx headed into the toilet to check his handiwork, and saw already the toilet door had been scrubbed clean and re-painted. There was also a new notice, laminated and in bold red print. *'GRAFFITI BY STAFF MEMBERS WILL NOT BE TOLERATED, AND IS A DISCIPLINARY OFFENCE – BY ORDER OF THE MANAGEMENT.'*

Stixx took his permanent black marker out of his pocket and wrote, *'and Seb's cavernous anus'* underneath. It wasn't smart, it wasn't clever, but for five minutes at least, Stixx basked in the warm glow of this mild rebellion. He also figured that Faye would approve.

At 12 o'clock he went for an early lunch. The savoury vending machine was looking particularly barren today. The one remaining unnamed sandwich had the appearance of either corned beef or old spam. Stixx decided to take a pass.

'You know you could just buy something downstairs. It is a supermarket, you know!' It was Genie, the three hundred pound slab of council estate wisdom. She ate her microwave burger like a walrus chewing a bull dog, chewing a wasp: lots of tongue and dribble.

Stixx nodded and went to get the lonely sandwich just to spite her. It did taste like spam. He tuned out the other gossiping till workers, and half-watched the wall mounted TV and the news. The murders were all over Border News, but it seemed like the BBC had already forgotten about it. Nobody had found the missing police officer. The lack of new victims or police breakthrough meant that other fresher tragedies and carnage moved in to take their place. Stixx thought if things didn't change soon, the journos would be shipping out of the guest house as well, if they hadn't done so already. After his half hour was over, he left Genie tucking into a giant cake and headed back to warehouse floor.

As he passed the bosses office he heard big boss, Bob call out, 'A minute of your time, Stixx, if you don't mind.' He knew straight away he was seriously fucked. Bob was a small man, with petite round-rimmed glasses. All brains not brawn. He was the main manager of the ASDA store. Stixx had spoken directly to him perhaps once before and that was only to say hello. Bob ushered him into his office with an oddly effeminate wave. If he wasn't getting fired he would be surprised.

Inside the office Stixx's heart plunged another mile down when he saw Sebastian sat to one side of Bob's desk. He had a smile that he wished he could strangle off his face. For a second he wondered if this was how the vampire felt when he found someone to bite.

'Sit down, Stixx,' Bob said, moving past Seb to the main seat. 'I've been hearing some disturbing reports, unfortunately. It would appear that somebody has been writing homophobic remarks about Sebastian here in the warehouse male toilets.'

'I don't have any issues with Seb's sexuality,' Stixx said.

'I'm... err, not actually gay,' Seb interrupted. 'This is straightforward bullying!'

'Okay, bullying then,' Bob said, a little flustered. 'Do you know anything about the remarks that were written in the toilets today? And also the picture from last week?'

'What picture?' Stixx asked.

'Come on, Stixx, you know exactly which one.' Seb had red flared cheeks and ears now.

'Describe it, can you?' asked Stixx grinning.

'There was a picture of Sebastian on his bike, with an appendage... a male member. It was quite shocking!' Bob said.

'That does sound quite gay to me,' Stixx shrugged. 'Are we sure it's not a little homophobic as well?'

'How can it be homophobic when I'm not gay?' Seb had a beetroot face.

'Whether it is homophobic or just plain bullying, it doesn't make any difference. It is definitely graffiti and it's costing the company money to clean it up. Do you know anything about this, Stixx?' Bob continued.

'No.'

'Is that your final answer?'

'Yes... and I hope you're going to be interviewing everyone on the warehouse floor, not just me!' was the line Stixx decided to take. Seb was smugly passing something to Bob. *What the hell has he got?*

'Unfortunately Stixx, it would appear Sebastian has uncovered some rather disturbing evidence. Do you recognise this?' Bob pushed the document his way. It was a handwritten accident report he filled in six months ago when he'd fallen off a ladder and cut his knee open. It was signed James Stixx at the bottom. There was also a digital photograph of today's graffiti. It didn't take a rocket scientist to see that the handwriting was the same. He had been an idiot to use lower case.

'Oh right,' was all he could think to say.

A few minutes later Stixx was walking to the exit, a small bag of possessions having been hastily put together. He'd been suspended for a week, although Bob had warned him that there may still have to be criminal action, and almost certainly he would find his wages docked the money for the paint, not to mention missing all the Christmas double pay for public holidays. Les had been sympathetic. *Just smoke some blow and forget about it,* had been his advice.

Stixx could see Seb standing next to the store's big Christmas tree at the exit. 'What do you want?'

'Bob asked me to make sure you didn't steal anything on your way out. Can I check your bag, please?'

Stixx shoved him with both hands and Seb fell into the Christmas tree. The ten foot spruce went over in a glittering heap on top of him.

Stixx jogged through the exit and didn't dare look back.

Chapter 11 – Night moves

Stixx managed to make it all the way home without being arrested, although he imagined life in the family ASDA had just come to an abrupt end.

What were dead-end jobs anyway, if not disposable? he thought, chewing his way through one of Margie's average Christmas stews.

'So what are you going to do with yourself now you're back in the dole queue?' Mrs Philips asked, squinting her Irish eyes at him. 'Not up to no mischief I hope, with that killer out there gobbling up people.' She was filling in for his mum with the guest dinners. Margie had disappeared for a few hours, Christmas shopping in town. She'd already decorated the guesthouse and twenty year old tinsel hung over most of the doorframes. There was a six foot plastic tree with semi-functional lights in the guest lounge. It was the 20th of December.

'I'm up to nothing!' Stixx said, meeting Mrs Phillip's beady stare while chewing the fat out of the stewed beef. The blank screen of his iPhone was also staring at him from the kitchen table. Faye had not messaged, or spoken, to him since last night's nightmare. Stixx wondered if he'd managed to scare her away finally, or if Alan the dick in Ghana had told her not to see him anymore. He'd sent her four text messages telling her about the Seb situation and he was considering sending a fifth.

The screen lit up. Faye was ringing, not texting. 'I've got to go!' he shouted, tossing his plate into the sink and practically running out of the door.

'You know there's a curfew! Police say nobody should be out after ten. Did you hear that, Stixx?'

No need to be hanging around, he'd meet her at her house. He pressed the green button on his phone. 'Hi, it's me!' he said too loudly.

'I know, I rang your number. What have you been doing, Stixx? You sound sort of out of breath.'

'Just eating too fast. I've been texting you all day.'

'Sorry, I had to go and see my dad with my mum. It's a bit of a road trip and I left my phone behind,' Faye said.

Stixx didn't really know much more about Faye's dad other than he was 'ill' in some way and wasn't with Faye's mum anymore. He would ask her about that later.

'You had me worried. There's been some interesting developments with the vampire stuff while you've been away,' he told her, trying to actually think of one. '...for one, the police have a ten o'clock curfew.'

'I heard that on the radio. What else did you hear?'

'Okay... not much else. But we still need to keep investigating, don't we?' he asked hopefully.

'Of course we do, we're barely getting warmed up honey. You didn't think I would leave you in the lurch, did you?'

'No, of course not,' Stixx said, gulping a little. 'I'm on my way around to your house now. Forget that curfew. I got a really good feeling about tonight.'

'See you in a minute then.'

Stixx felt the happy buzz up his neck again as he marched up the promenade. He looked across at the estuary's still waters. Whatever was going to happen was going to be pretty special.

When he reached Faye's bungalow she was already waiting outside, wearing her usual red coat. *If Little Red Riding Hood was ever a rock chick, then she would look like this.* 'Have you got any tattoos?' His mouth asked the question before his brain had chance to stop it.

'Just one, but no way can you ever see it. That was a very random question, even for you, Stixx.' She smiled and gave him a hug.

'Well, I'm a very random person. Shall we decamp to the pub and come up with a battle plan?' He knew he was way out of his depth with this girl, but he was going to give it his all. Pure nervous adrenaline was fuelling his every word.

'Agreed!' Faye said, and then surprised Stixx by holding his hand as they walked. *This was new.* Her black fleece gloves were fiercely warm.

Red was in the pub waiting. He was sat alone at a table beside a bay window, a pint of Guinness next to a few empties.

Stixx had a shudder of guilt that he hadn't seen his best friend in days, at Christmas of all times. Usually no more than a day would pass before one of them was at the other's house, with a bad horror DVD or some unfinished business with an Xbox game. Now for days he hadn't given Red a second thought. Faye was this amazing exotic creature who dominated his waking thoughts. The world was all bright colours and possibilities when she was around.

'Are you having a senior moment or something?' Faye prodded him, putting a pint of snakebite in front of him.

'What?'

'You were staring into space looking like a guppy trapped in an air bubble, mate,' Red informed him.

'What? I'm clearly thinking hard here,' Stixx said, feeling the burn on his cheeks.

The three of them sat around the round table and sipped at their drinks. Faye seemed to have persuaded the landlord Jeff to make her a white concoction. *The first cocktail I've ever seen drunk in the village..*

'So what's that?' Red said, pointing at Faye's drink. He was still being less than friendly. If there wasn't an elephant in the room, it was at least a good sized hippo.

'It's a white zombie: Cointreau, coconut cream and rum, with some rum, rum and more rum. Mostly it's rum!' Faye said, sipping again.

'Well it looks like zombie gizz if you ask me!' Red sounded a little drunk.

'Nice one there, mate,' Stixx intervened. 'My friend is as always the charmer, especially when he's had a skin full.'

'It tastes more sweet than salty, ' Faye said unfazed, offering to pass Red the drink. 'I do quite like zombies you know… the films, I mean. I used to love those old George Roman films as a kid. Nothing like a video nasty when you're thirteen years old.'

'George Romero you mean,' Red said, a tisk sound on his lips. 'The guy made scary old zombie films but with something to say. Like the one where the zombies go shopping. It says a lot.'

'That zombies like shopping?' teased Stixx.

'Yeah, that people like shopping… and, you know, zombies do too. American ones anyway!'

'That was pretty profound stuff you came out with there, Red. A bit of an intellectual hiding in there, I can see. Although myself, I think vampires are sexier,' Faye said, doing a good job at holding a straight face.

'Are we talking *Twilight* again here?' Red was not a *Twilight* fan. The high water mark for him was watching pirated VHS copies of the original *Fright Night* over and over.

'We are not talking *Twilight*, we're talking *True Blood*. Vampires should be sexy and lustful and dangerous.'

'Vampire porn you mean,' Red offered, taking another slurp of his Guinness.

'Nothing wrong with that,' Faye winked and actually got Red to turn a little red: putty in her hands.

'Well, I don't think the present vampire nutty-type we have in Greystones is going to turn out to be particularly lustful or sexy,' Stixx said. 'In fact, to my mind I think he'll end up being some sad-sack disappointment, who probably looks like Robert Pattison's butt crossed with a goat.'

'More of a shark than a goat, Stixx,' she said. 'He, or they, are killers. Three sturdy blokes ripped to shreds most likely. A policeman missing and probably dead. We're going to have to be careful.'

'We? You mean you and Stixx don't you?' Red hissed, sounding grumpy.

'No, I don't. All three of us can do this thing. You know, like the three musketeers!' Faye was doing her killer smile again.

Red looked a little blank, possibly it was fear. It was hard to tell with him. 'You mean, I can come along as juicy bait?'

'Exactly!'

Red looked suddenly happy with the idea. He was such an unpredictable lunatic, thought Stixx. 'So how do we go about doing this thing? Isn't there a curfew from ten?' asked Stixx.

'Well, I don't think many people will be sticking to that one.' Red pointed out the window. Already there were torches on the beaches: groups of the village youth off on their own awfully big adventure.

'Oh yeah! Not enough police to stop them all. That's good for us,' Stixx said, getting excited as well. 'So are we going out to join the party?'

'Definitely!' Faye said, banging her fist on the table. 'But you've both got all that local knowledge. We don't want to just go out and join the herd. We want to get ahead of the game.'

'Well I think I can help us with that one,' Stixx said triumphantly.

Thirty minutes later and they were all sat eight feet off the ground in a tree, on one of the main trails on the western slopes of O'Halloran Hill woods. 'Well it beats that stinky swimming pool, I suppose,' Stixx said, shivering uncontrollably and getting grumpy. 'It's the best I could come up with factoring in Faye here, with heels bigger than Red's knob. I had local knowledge of this tree so I thought we could all just sit in it!'

'To be fair,' Red's voice drifted down from somewhere high above. 'That would make those heels pretty darn big! Hey, does anyone know if vampires climb trees?'

'Only shiny ones do, I think,' Stixx shouted up. Faye had been silently sulking for a while he thought, or had possibly frozen to death on the branch they were sitting on.

Looking ahead there was a gap in the frosted canopy of the trees, showing that beyond the trail the hill slope fell away dramatically. Stixx could see the shore far below and the faint moonlight reflecting off the estuary waters. The viaduct crossing the estuary was just a thin string line over the water from this distance. There was a tiny portion of beach visible too, with the faintest strobe of red and blue lights. The outnumbered constabulary was down there on the mudflats and quicksand, getting the run around from kids. It seemed like everyone was thinking this was the coolest thing since Brad Pitt met Angelina Jolie.

'So here we are... up a tree.' Faye finally chose to speak, and sounded a little pissed off. 'My bum is numb as fuck!'

Stixx's jeans also felt damp and clingy where his body heat had managed to melt the thin layer of ice around his knobbly perch. 'We should have some more of that sparkling conversation. Take your mind off your bum.'

'But not your mind off it, hey, Stixx!' Red called down. He sounded like he was somewhere near the top.

Stixx shone his iPhone flashlight upwards and spotted Red's dirty trainers. 'It really would be a shame if you fell.'

'So anyway, if this vampire guy is for real, what powers do we think we're up against here?' Red shouted too loud.

'Well…' Stixx began to say.

'Wasn't talking to you, buddy. I want to hear Lady Burn's take on this particular conundrum.'

'I'm no lady, but my dad once said I could pass for posh in a good light. Well let's see… say you had these so called supernatural, super-type powers. You could fly maybe, or certainly jump up and down houses without a scratch. Great night vision of course, which means that if this guy running around the village is for real, we literally would be sitting ducks up this tree!'

'Somehow, I feel confident that's not going to happen,' Stixx chipped in.

'Well, flying, jumping and seeing are all probable. I reckon we can add in super-strength, which might be the one attribute this loon may hold, judging by the mayhem he's managed to unleash on her majesty's finest already,' Faye went on.

'So maybe the guy lifts a little iron in his mum's basement and eats too many egg yolks. Maybe he'll have a coronary before the police get to him?' Red shouted unhelpfully.

'So, vamps sleep all day and stalk all night, or so legend goes. You know if we go by Dracula, they're pretty romantic souls, too. Maybe there's a girl in the village who he's put under a spell. Someone helping him out, so he doesn't get caught.'

'You're going off-track, Faye, we were talking super-powers here,' Red's discombobulated voice was starting to grate.

'Alright, Red, so if you had all those powers what would you be doing right now?' Stixx asked, his tone hinting that he might like to shut up.

'You know, the usual… chewing on Prince William's neck while Kate circled us, dancing a naked fertility salsa.'

'You are…' Stixx started to say, when there was a crack of dry twigs, crisp and close by. There was a rustling above and

Stixx guessed Red had just gained more altitude. The sitting ducks suggestion was now very real. *Either make a lot of noise or stay dead silent?* Stixx's mind raced.

'I think it's a deer or maybe a rabbit...' Stixx tried to reassure Faye. She was looking worried. The flight or fight reaction was spreading through him: a wave of adrenaline. He was sure it was nothing really. Then the noise came again – a distinctive crunch of frozen twigs practically next to the tree.

Too heavy for an animal.

Stixx strained to see through the blackness and he felt stupid to have allowed them all to get carried away with this childish hunt. Too many movies with Red – *Charley Brewster* had a lot to answer for!

Faye gasped and he saw a figure at the bottom of the tree: a shadowy silhouette looking up at them. Stixx expected that any second it would leap at them with teeth and claws. He jumped first – for Faye: a crazy gesture, a chance for her to live on. Perhaps she would visit his grave every year with Alan. Lay a wreath.

Shed a tear.

Stixx dropped through space towards the shape below, misjudging the angle and glancing off to one side. The shape was solid, hard and rigid. Half-winded, Stixx grabbed out at a leg and made the figure overbalance. Stixx wanted to shout to the others to run, but the breath wasn't in his lungs. They struggled and rolled over. Stixx felt barbarous tree roots scratching over his back. Something hit him on the right cheek, and then again: a small but heavy fist. Suddenly he was crushed, a great weight on top of him. *Would it be quick?*

There was Faye's voice. 'Get off of him, FUCKER!' She was snarling defiance. It was decided – they would go into the next world together.

'You locked me in that toilet, you bastard Stixx.'

FUCKING MARCO MARX!

He wasn't going to die. Stixx felt another punch and his brain fizzed out for a second.

'Marco!'

'...five hours... in that... toilet... you bastard!'

Faye had grabbed Marco around his neck and was choking him. Stixx escaped Marco's grip and rolled off to one side.

Stixx struggled to get his breath back. 'What the hell are you doing up here, Marco?'

'You locked me in that toilet, you bastard!'

Stixx was on his feet and moving away from the little Down's terror. 'Steady now, Marco. Drugs don't work – did you never hear that one?'

'I've got to punch you again!'

Faye was touching his face. 'No more punching little man, I mean it! Are you alright, Mr Hero?'

'You know, I'll live!' Stixx struggled to his feet. The truth was that Stixx didn't know what was bleeding and what was broken. He just knew he hurt all over. It was the first time he'd ever been called a hero as well.

'What are you doing in the woods wee man? We thought you were frigging Dracula risen from his grave!' Red said, finally climbing down out of his perch.

'I was with some friends on the beach, but they told me to wait behind a tree and I didn't see them again. I came here to find them. I saw you all up a tree from miles away.'

'What, can you see in the dark? We were invisible!' Red's voice was indignant.

'No, I could see you just fine.'

Faye's soft warm hands were dusting the debris off Stixx's shoulders and arms. 'So, do you often lock Down's Syndrome kids in train toilets?'

'It's more a talent for me than a vocation,' Stixx shrugged.

Chapter 12 – Marco Marx

When all the swearing, spitting, and general stropping had finally dissipated, they walked out of the woods as one group. Marco offered to shake Stixx's hand, which his dad had taught him was the right thing to do after an argument. Stixx said that he'd prefer it if he was hung from the tree by his hands instead, but then the new girl told him off and they'd shaken hands. Marco said sorry a lot when they'd got back to the road and street lights and saw that Stixx had a big bruise on his cheek. His coat was ripped up as well. Stixx didn't seem to mind because the girl was holding his hand.

They all walked him to the cottage he lived in with his dad. Definitely no vampire was going to mess with them tonight. Marco felt happier than he could remember in a long time. Even when he asked tentatively if they could all go out again and look for the vampire they didn't say no, or make fun of him, like a lot of his other friends in the village seemed to always do. He told them that they'd definitely find the vampire tomorrow night, and that he had even seen some tracks they could follow in the woods. The girl had said that was good, and that they would definitely do that.

The cottage was small compared to the monstrous grey stone edifices that flanked it on either side. His dad had often talked about knocking their house down and building upwards to match them. He'd even had permission from the council to do it, but without Marco's mum being there anymore, the idea had been left and forgotten about. They didn't even need the room anymore – nobody ever stayed there other than him and his dad.

'See you, Marco,' Red shouted, as they left him at the front door. It was only Stixx who had been at primary school with him. Red came to the village later, but Marco didn't mind him either. He had ginger hair, and he had sometimes heard people shout nasty things at him too. Marco thought he was a good guy, if a bit loud sometimes. Marco wondered if his dad was still awake.

'Bye!' he shouted. 'I'll see you tomorrow, okay.'

Marco only got the key from under the plant pot when they were out of sight. *Be careful with that*, his dad had always said.

'Dad, it's really cold in here,' he called out when he got inside. He must have forgotten to put the heating on again. His dad was sat in his favourite armchair facing the television. The volume was down low on some antiques show, along with the lights. Marco was used to his dad mostly sleeping there. He said his bed had a lot of bad memories sometimes. On the patterned carpet he noticed his tumbler of whisky had fallen over. That always happened when he fell asleep. 'Sleep tight, Dad,' he whispered. Marco thought he would bring a blanket down later and cover him up.

Marco went up the creaky narrow stairs and pushed open the bedroom door covered with Manchester United stickers. He didn't even like football that much anymore, but the stickers wouldn't come off. The room's contents were basically tipped onto the floor, piles of chaos. Clothes weren't in drawers anymore, but lying in layers on and around the cast iron, blue painted radiator. Toy soldiers of various shades of green and brown were heaped like ant hills next to a shoddily grey painted fort in the centre of the room. There were dinky cars, lots of them: a traffic jam that ran across the room and under his single bed. He had fraying posters of *The Never Ending Story* on the wall, which was his favourite film on account of the giant flying dog.

Marco sat down on the desk at the corner of the room and flicked on his Play Station 2, loading up an Ice Hockey game. He wished his dad would get him the next model, but these days he seemed to have less and less money to spend. Too many bills were coming into the house, and too many things were breaking around the house that needed fixing. Marco wished his mum was still here. He worried dad was fading out, just getting sadder and sadder every day. Whisky had slowly become his best friend and Marco wasn't sure if he even left the house most days.

Marco's mum had been called Lily. One morning, three years ago she had been making sunny side fried eggs in front of him in the kitchen. Then she fell – tripped, Marco had thought for a second. The tipped over fat from the frying pan burnt her chubby arm bright red. He remembered Lily twitching, her feet tapping out a funny rhythm, making the cream slippers jump and skip on the linoleum floor. Her eyes had been open: a wet stare like the fish eyes on display at the village butchers. His dad had tried to get her to wake up, but couldn't make her.

Sometimes when Marco had a bad dream about it he'd wake up shaking, sad his mother wasn't there to comfort him. Often in the dreams he would see his father screaming while he held her, and see a deep dark pit in the ground sucking the sound down. Marco would always fall into it, tumbling through the darkness. Somewhere down below was his mother, but he always woke up before he found her.

Marco turned off the game and stared at his faint reflection in the monitor screen. He didn't like how round and fat his face looked. He wondered what it would be like to be normal like everyone else, and not special needs or *Downsy*, with cotton wool in his brain. Then Marco remembered his dad must be cold downstairs because the heating was off. He found a spare blanket from the linen closet and creaked his way downstairs again.

The lounge was as cold as a fridge. His dad hadn't moved an inch on the chair since he left, his porcelain fingers still almost touching the knocked-over tumbler on the carpet. Marco bent down and picked it up before reaching around the arm of the couch to place the blanket over his dad. He noticed it then, a smudge on his cheek, brown-red in the faint amber light. He looked asleep, except his head looked all wrong: tilted over too far, like a metal rod with a kink in it.

Marco grabbed him by the shoulders, and saw the other side of his face – a gaping canyon where his dad's neck should have been. He had a second mouth, a flesh-cave bordered by wet-flecked tendrils of gore, big enough to push a fist inside. Marco staggered back, his legs going rubbery and limp. He fell against the cold gas fire, feeling the dull sting spreading over his lower back. His dad's eye on the ruined side was open, looking at him like a bloodshot marble.

Staggering away and dizzy, Marco found the telephone. He knew the numbers, the three digits you used when you needed help.

'Hello, what is your emergency?' the voice asked him.

81

'My da…' Tears choked out his words.

After the phone call he waited by the lounge door, not even caring if that thing was still in the house with him. He'd covered his dad with the blanket.

'Marco is it?' said the first of two police officers at the door. One was Asian, and the other a fierce looking female. The pair of them looked scared and edgy, and held guns in their hands. Marco could tell they didn't trust him, that they would hurt him if he wasn't careful. He showed them to his dad, and soon his whole house was full of police, more people than had ever come to visit. Marco was asked to sit upstairs in his bedroom. The policeman outside his door wouldn't even speak to him.

'Hello Marco, I'm Detective Inspector Hastie!' A hunched man with a voice like gravel was in his room now. He'd seen him before on the television, talking about all the other people that had been killed. 'I'm the one who's in charge of getting to the bottom of all this. I'll get the officer here to get you a glass of water if you want. You must be feeling very bad right now.'

'Yes.' Words were still sticking in his throat like chewing gum. He watched the inspector pacing around his bedroom, twirling an Airfix model of a B-52 bomber that hung from a string near the window. His dad had helped him stick it together and paint it when he was eight years old. Marco gave a little sound, a half-sob.

'Marco, how did you get those marks on your hands?' The inspector was looking down, his green eyes boring into him. Marco felt like he was drowning and turned away.

'I had a fight with someone.'

'Marco, I'm going to caution you now. You have the right to remain silent Marco, but I must warn you that anything you do say can be taken down and used against you in court. Do you understand that, Marco?'

Marco nodded, but then the inspector explained it again and helped him understand he had to tell the truth. That not saying anything could mean he would get into trouble later. Marco didn't want to get into trouble. 'I had a fight in the woods…' Marco started to say, but then realised he didn't want to get his new friends into trouble. He really didn't know what to say.

82

'We need to talk more at the police station. Is that okay? We'll get someone that can sit in with you – an appropriate adult.'

'What about Dad?'

'We'll take care of that. You need to come with us.' The inspector nodded at the police officer standing behind him.

Marco felt lost. Down the stairs he tried to look through the doorway into the lounge. Already there were three people in white suits around where his dad sat. One was on his knees crawling, looking for something. Marco felt as if he was floating, that it couldn't be real.

The front door opened without him touching it. The Asian officer and his friend were there, one for each of his arms. Holding him firmly, not painfully. Lights flashed in his face. People were out there on the street taking photographs. Someone shouted, *Why did you do it, freak?* Marco didn't know who said that. The flashes were coming faster and faster, and made him feel sick. He felt the Asian officer push his head down so he would fit into the police car. His couldn't feel his legs anymore. He wanted to be with his dad and wondered if he'd ever see him again: whether he'd ever go home again.

'Marco Marx?'

'Yes,' he said, looking blankly at the female officer.

'That's a bit of a funny name.'

Marco didn't reply, distracted by a man running alongside the patrol car taking more pictures.

Chapter 13 – The Morning After

'So, why isn't the door open?' Stixx said, pushing on the thick oak double door that was the main entrance of the local Parish church. 'Aren't these places supposed to be like twenty-four seven? I think it's definitely in the bible!'

Faye had woken him up yet again that morning, and now stood there hands on hips in a stripy black and white top which hugged her figure so tightly it should be illegal. Stixx was kind of wishing the door would open around about now so he'd stop looking like such a useless dork. No doubt boyfriend Alan would have a smarter solution than just rattling the iron handle.

'There's more than one way to skin a cat,' she said, wandering off around the church. From school he knew it was one of the oldest buildings in Greystones still standing, built in 1854 according to the stone carved numbers above the door. It wasn't the biggest of churches by any means. The walls were limestone like most of the village buildings, from stone dug at a defunct quarry on yet more Colonel land a few miles away. It had a single bell spire which had recently had an upgrade and joined the information age. The bell was now computer controlled and rang hourly during the day. Stixx thought probably this was because all the willing bell ringers were now up in the cemetery.

Around the corner he found Faye six feet off the ground, at the top of a rusty drainpipe with one of those border-line deranged grins on her face. An upstairs window was an inch ajar. 'The house of the lord should never be closed. Besides the police will be too busy with Marco to pay much attention to us,' she called down. A few minutes later she let him in through a side door.

She was right to a point, thought Stixx. Although he imagined there were still plenty of uniformed bobbies knocking around who weren't detectives and chasing killers. It would only take one neighbourhood watch granny and there would be a patrol car arriving in no time.

'Come on slow coach, what are you waiting for?'

Stixx followed and found himself for the first time having second thoughts about his new friend. He started to wonder just how crazy she was?

The small room had a row of choir boy white blouses hung in a row on the wall. He didn't even know the village still had a choir. 'Come on, we'll open the main door and pretend it was open all along.' Faye was off again, walking into the main body of the church. There was clank of iron as she pulled the bolt back on the double door.

Stixx padded after her, the air off the flag-stoned floor a number of degrees colder than it was outside. Their breath plumed in the air like cigarette smoke and Stixx shuddered with the chill. The numerous stained glass windows barely cast any light through the general morbid gloom. The air was almost gritty and tasted of dust.

'So, why are we here again?'

She gave him the look. That faint wrinkle line on her nose that made her look cute and possibly dangerous. 'We are here for the purposes of research and assimilation of information, James.'

'Assim-a-what?'

'We are here because this is the oldest public building around. There could be something useful, like a clue, that's going to help us. I mean it's not like you can just go on the internet and expect to Wikipedia vampires and Greystones, and find all the answers.'

'Well we could try that. It would be warmer for sure,' Stixx said frowning.

'I already tried that. Vampires don't exist obviously, and there was nothing I could find on the net about any history of vampires being in the village before. If there was, don't you think it would have been in the papers already?'

Stixx thought of Marco, now locked up in some jail cell about to be charged with mass-murder. The newspapers all had front page stories about the arrest – photographs of the poor sod being driven away by police and looking terrified out of his tiny mind. They didn't say what had happened to his dad exactly, although the inside of the house had been described as yet another gory scene. They were painting Marco and his dad as an

85

odd-ball couple, loners who didn't have any friends in the village – saying that Marco was often seen out at all hours wandering the village and surrounding area. That pretty much described all of the village's youth these days. It made Stixx angry just thinking about it.

He and Faye were sure of Marco's innocence. Not in the 'sure, I've got definitive proof' kind of way. Sure in a way that you just are. They knew Marco Marx didn't kill anyone: that the real sicko killer was still out there, hiding in the shadows, waiting for his next move.

'Holy water?' Stixx said, fingering the font at the end of the aisle. It looked like a birdbath. 'Should we get a receptacle or something?'

'Two things, Stixx. One we don't believe there is a genuine, blood-thirsty vamp out there. And two, how do we even know that this is real holy water, that's blessed and all that other jazz?'

Stixx was frowning again. 'I'm willing to take those odds.' He drank the rest of his diet coke and then plunged the plastic bottle into the water. 'Be prepared is my new motto!'

'I thought your motto was *Snakebite rules!*' she said, punching him on the arm.

Hard.

They split up and began looking around the church. In one corner there was a display made by children from the adjacent primary school. It looked like they had been doing overtime on the nativity scenes. Christmas cards filled two temporary display boards. There was enough cotton wool glued there to insulate a small loft.

Stixx wandered on, looking up at the stained glass windows. Perhaps he could find one with a vampire on: a clue to a secret vampire cult and perhaps a handy signpost or arrow to the next clue, like *The Da Vinci Code*? Stixx checked every bit of glass and drew a big fat blank.

He saw Faye was looking at old photographs and descriptions along a side wall. 'Any joy?'

'Look at this,' she said pointing at some text. 'It says that the whole village was built on the site of an ancient Viking burial ground.'

'Does it?'

'No, not really, Stixx ...it does say that Greystones was once believed to have been an Old English settlement called Graegstan, and was used mainly as a place to store weapons.'

'Does that help us?'

'Nope, not really!'

'Can I help you?' A voice boomed out behind them making them jump. They turned and saw the hulking figure of the local vicar, Mr McClintock. Slightly stooped and now in his late 60s, he was still an imposing man of six foot. He loved his rugby league and was often seen on the sidelines of the village team encouraging them on. Stixx supposed the vicar had been a player back in his younger days. 'I'm very sure I locked those doors last night.'

'Well...' Faye said, rocking on the balls of her feet. 'These old doors, you just can't trust them I reckon.'

'I'm not sure I entirely believe you Miss, but as the church hasn't been covered in spray paint tags I'll give you both the benefit of the doubt. It is Christmas after all... you know last summer some youth spray painted all manner of obscenity on my pulpit.'

'That is not right!' Stixx said, and tried to look like he meant it. It was probably Red.

'Although really I know I should be calling our local police,' the vicar grimaced. 'But part of me is hoping you're keen to join our dwindling congregation... or perhaps even our choir?'

What was that, *blackmail?*

'We're only here for research, I'm afraid,' Faye soothed. 'Our teacher has set an essay question for the holidays, worst luck. The topic is the history of where you live... so we were looking here in your history section for a few titbits. These old photographs are really interesting,' she went on, pointing at a Victorian era black and white photograph of Greystones' promenade: people on the beach in strange full-length swimming costumes, and suited bowl-hatted people with enormous baby buggies strolling about. They reminded Stixx of the pictures in the local pub.

'Well, these are all from my own collection, you know. I put them up for general interest reasons. Not that there's much of that these days, I'm afraid,' the old vicar said sadly, drawing a line through the dust on a frame with his hefty finger. 'I have more back at the vicarage if you'd like to see?'

Stixx made a face at Faye, an attempt at negative telepathy. Faye wasn't listening though. 'We'd absolutely love to!' she squeaked.

The vicarage across the road wasn't much better for dusty air than the church had been. Mr McClintock might have been a man of God, but he was also a man living alone, and obviously a bit of a hoarder on the side. They'd passed his front room on the way through to the kitchen and Stixx only glanced, but he was sure it was packed to the rafters with old newspapers and what looked like engine parts. Every corner of the lounge-diner seemed stacked with assorted open boxes of miscellaneous rummage sale-style rubbish. It looked like he was just moving in, but the truth was he'd been the village vicar for almost forty years.

'I'll be a minute finding what I'm looking for. Do you two want tea?'

Stixx again mimed a *no* face towards Faye, and this time it worked.

'That's alright Mr McClintock, we're not thirsty.' The vicar shuffled out of the room and went to search for his elusive photograph books.

'What are you doing?' Stixx was close to having a strop.

'Scooby Doo-ing,' she said, just as the vicar appeared back in the room. He really did move quietly for such a big guy, Stixx thought. McClintock had two large leather-bound photo albums in his hands.

'These are a couple of my best collections. My own photographic record of the village, and people as they have come and gone. I find it's important to have such aides to your memory as you get older. You'll know that yourself one day. Everything has become so electronic these days. I think it's easier for things to get lost that way. Everyone seems to get a new phone and computer every year. People just don't keep things as safe as they used to.'

Mr McClintock opened the first album and the three of them spent the next hour leafing glacially slowly through it, while the vicar supplied his potted commentary. Stixx found it interesting for around the first fifteen minutes. There seemed to be an awful lot of pictures of the choir boys. 'Do you mind if I look at the other book? It's just we're a little short on time,' he had said finally.

'Not at all,' the vicar said, patting Stixx's leg twice. Stixx found it worrying and wondered about the choir boys again.

Stixx fanned through the second photo book, not really looking carefully: pictures of village fetes blurred in with endless artsy landscapes of trees, cliffs and storms... and storm damage. The washed up boats with holes in the bottom looked kind of interesting, but didn't really get them anywhere. He stopped flicking, went back a few pages and then stopped.

There was a picture of a group of people in a room, drinking beer and laughing. From the decor he guessed it might have been the 1980s. The brown wall-paper and terrible haircuts gave it away. There was a ghost, a fairy, a punk, a cowboy, and there in the centre was the good sergeant Flint dressed in a full Christopher Lee-style vampire costume.

'One of the Christmas parties at the Colonel's manor house. 1982 if I'm not mistaken. Those were indeed the days.' McClintock sounded a little wistful. 'The annual Christmas parties stopped once his son Myles took over. Nobody liked him very much it would seem.'

'So, did Flint like being a vampire?'

'Oh yes, he dressed up like that every year.'

Chapter 14 – Sunset

For a few months each summer Greystones buzzed with tourists. In the winter – bar the usual blip at Christmas when migrated offspring came back to visit their parents – the village had no pulse.

It flat-lined.

Walking onto the promenade with Faye, Stixx saw more strange faces than he ever did even on the hottest days of summer. The media were back in force and his mother's guesthouse was bursting at the seams with journalists paying through the nose for basic amenities. Every other vehicle he saw had a media insignia and oversized antenna on the roof.

He spotted television journalist Emma Murphy with microphone in hand and a cameraman outside the Spar Shop. They'd sent the big guns now there had been an arrest. Emma looked like she was after passers-by for comments about Marco's incarceration, although she didn't acknowledge him and Faye. Not grown up enough for the BBC, Stixx figured.

They walked out along a pier that went to the edge of the estuary water. Fifteen years ago it had been shorter and surfaced with cobblestones, before it collapsed into the sea over the course of one particularly stormy night. It turned out it had been filled with soil the whole time. The pier of today was an altogether more solid construct and had smooth tarmac to walk on.

The figure waiting for them at the end of the pier was trying very hard to look handsome and dashing. Red was gripping the railing and turning his head so the wind caught his ginger hair, looking away from them towards the distant Lake District hills. The sands below had coarse tufts of grass poking through. Frost made it all look dusted with icing sugar.

'You could be a model for a men's wear catalogue, Red,' Stixx told him. 'Specialised gimp suits for the younger male!'

'Well, everyone's entitled to an opinion I suppose,' Red replied, flicking his ginger fringe out of his eyes, 'even mentally retarded people.'

'Boys, boys, boys! ...and Stixx,' Faye interjected. They spent a while chewing the fat at the end of the pier. Red was sure they should be thinking outside the square, although Stixx corrected him that it was, *'outside the box, dickhead!'* Eventually they had a plan: a new plan, that didn't in any way involve sitting in a tree freezing their *cojones* off.

'So we're going to do this?' Stixx said, just noticing his hands were sticking to the metal pier railings.

'Yes, we are!'

Faye was a warrior.

*

Stixx led the way, he knew it well enough. The house he took them to was a neat, detached cottage on one of the quieter cul-de-sacs in the village.

The grey dwelling sat on a rectangle of land. The front garden was a well tended lawn bordered by leafless plants, which he guessed could be roses, but equally could be anything. Margie always used to make him help in the garden as a punishment for being naughty. Regardless of that, he couldn't care less about horticulture.

'So that's where the fucker lives – what a positively gay little cottage!'

'Are you bashing gay people again, Red? Have you ever heard of a little thing called transference, ' Faye said, her voice hushed as they crouched in the shadow of the trees, on one of the hundred dirt paths that disappeared into the woods surrounding this part of the village.

Stixx scanned the windows they could see. He figured that Flint must be on a late shift. Most Fridays and Saturday he would work late, no doubt rostered that way to attend to the local drunken violence that was few and far between in this backwater. At best he might pop back to the house for his tea, he guessed. 'We should come back when it's dark. When all the lights are out and we're sure he's not in there waiting for us.'

'It'll be pitch black by 4.30. Let's do it then,' Faye told them, and turned away.

They killed the rest of the day at Red's house. Stixx could tell Red was getting a kick out of taking a genuine flesh and blood female back to his parent's house. It was completely unheard of for Red to get the time of day from the local girls in the village, not since he was caught setting up a video camera in the women's changing room of the local swimming pool. If the sum total of Red's standing with the female populace was added up in a single all-encompassing word, that word would be *'PERV!'* The four word extension being, *'...he's a right PERVERT!'*

Red's mum greeted them from the kitchen wearing an unflattering green apron. She always seemed to wear that whenever Stixx visited, either baking or eating. She must have weighed in at twenty-five stones easy. Red ignored her and her offers of cake, and led them up the stairs to the first floor. It was a small house in comparison to the sprawling guesthouse: a three bedroom semi-detached house on a small strip of unloved soil and concrete.

'You know this room just smells wrong, don't you, Red?' Faye said immediately and made a show of holding her nose.

'I think it must be the socks. I pray it's the socks!' Stixx added, stumbling past the heaps of abandoned clothes on Red's bedroom floor towards the window. 'For Christ's sake this better open!'

The next four hours passed quickly enough in a haze of *Super Mario Racing* and a seemingly endless conveyer belt of pies and cakes from the large lady downstairs. To begin with Faye had been dead last in all the races, but by the end she was leaving him and Red in a back-wash of bombs, banana skins, and rocket propelled grenades. She was smart and a quick learner – two things Stixx knew about her already. Eventually the sun slid down under the line of the window and Faye rang her mother for at least the third time that afternoon.

'It's time,' she said after she'd hung up the phone. Stixx got goose-bumps on his arms.

'I'm going out,' Red told his mum. She was in the lounge next to the kitchen now, with plenty of pastries in easy reach while she watched back-to-back soap operas. Red's dad, a fitness freak who ran every morning on the beach before working at the local bank, had died of a heart attack. The poor sod had died instantly whilst cooling down from a swift five miler. It had been Red who found him face down in a pool of orange juice. The ample insurance policy meant that Red's mum would never have to work another day in her life. Comfort eating became the new job, and one she was very good at. 'Don't be too long. And be careful with that thing out there. Don't you do anything stupid, do you hear me Red?'

Outside it was very dark and bitterly cold. Fresh clouds were masking the moon and the feeble street lights barely cast any useful illumination. Red jangled a bunch of keys in his hand. 'We need some tools, I think.'

Further along Red's cul-de-sac there was a row of five lock-up garages. Red had the last one, inside of which he kept his BMX, the 1970's porn collection inherited from his dad, all complete with 1970's hairy muffs, and other assorted worthless junk. Before it became too much of an overcrowded mess they'd often gone there to smoke dope. Red put the key in the rusty lock and lifted up the door. 'Frigging light's busted, I forgot,' he moaned, bumbling into the darkness before flicking on a weak torch.

'I hope he has something better than that,' Faye whispered to Stixx.

'You may think there's only rubbish in here, but I've got everything we need baby!' Red said, tearing cardboard. 'Fresh batteries!' After much further rooting, Red procured Stixx and Faye two more torches with batteries.

Stixx found his torch was so old and decrepit that he could effectively turn it on and off by simply rattling it a certain way. 'Top notch there, Red!'

The three of them tested the varying beams of their torches first in the garage, before pointing them into the small paddock opposite the garages. Last summer it contained a small Shetland pony that died during an unexpected heat-wave. Its rounded belly blew up with decomposition gases before anyone noticed. The undulating field contained nothing but dead winter weeds and thickets of wilted grass. 'What's that?' Red shouted, taking a step forward. Stixx squinted, trying to combine his weak beam of light with Red's. He could see nothing but shadows in the grassy hollows. The back wall of the paddock was barely distinguishable from the night sky.

'There's nothing there, Red,' Faye said, when the three of them were standing close to the old paddock gate, breath pluming in the air around their torch beams. 'Let's just go to Flint's like we said.' Stixx thought he heard a hint of uncertainty in her voice.

*

He stood still, not feeling the chill on his pale porcelain skin. He could see every detail in the dark. Night was as day to him. For a moment he enjoyed being able to see his stretching, flexing hand so clearly, as if it burned white.

The nails were long and blackened by dirt, more like talons than anything really human. Flicking his eyes upward, not moving even a shudder of muscle, he watched the three figures in the gloom at the other end of the field. They could look straight at him and not see him camouflaged as he was by stillness, like a lizard on a rock. They were coming to him.

One was tall and thin; he wanted to be the leader but the sweet smell of fear was starting to ooze out and he was happy to let the girl climb the fence before him. Already the other boy was in the field, edging blindly towards him, his red hair burning in the darkness. He'd seen him before: it felt like it had been a long time ago.

An age.

Memories seemed no longer constant in his mind. They faded, pulsed and fluttered around like the wings of a butterfly. Such things no longer had a gravitational pull within him. He was a creature of instinct, living only for the night: the veil of red coming down, closing him off again. The tingling was starting in his face, spreading across his cheeks and entering his teeth — the delicious yearning. Every part of him knew that when he finally moved he would rip and tear. He would drink the boy up, and then his friends as well.

The three of them were halfway. Any second they would see his pale skin pressed against the rough mortar and stone of the wall. He knew he wasn't invisible, that trick would only come with more blood and time. The red headed boy was just a few tantalising metres away, shining a torch beam so close the dull edge of the light touched on his bare foot.

94

He *leapt forward, saw the red-headed boy freeze and fall backwards. He was moving, scrabbling to get away like an animal on all fours. Four long strides and he stood over him, reaching down with talons.*

'Don't kill me!'

The other two were coming quickly. He was aware of them, so obvious and clumsy in their movements. So predictable! The gangling boy tried to jump on his back. He hit him mid-air with a lash of his arm, a slash of his nails. He heard the air leave the boy's lungs and watched him fall in a gangling heap. The girl stepped forward hurling her torch at his head. He moved just a fraction and it glanced harmlessly off his hairless head. He grinned at her, considering who he was going to devour first for this insurrection.

The red-headed one was halfway back to the paddock gate, imagining he was safe. He followed him; great strides halving the distance in seconds. The boy was almost at the top of the wire fence when he effortlessly reached for his leg and pulled him back down into the paddock. The red-headed boy's head crunched badly on the frozen soil. There was the bitter smell of blood in the air, running in rivulets among the icy glass and cracked ground. The boy was still, not moving. He craned his mouth down to lick his pulsing neck. He wanted to feel that jet of blood, to taste the iron on his lips.

There was a dull pain, then another spark, so far distant inside him that it barely registered. The red-headed boy had woken and slammed a half brick down on his foot. He plucked the weapon from the boy's hand, and smashed the crumbling mass down into the side of his head. He was back to sleep in an instant, blood now filling the air like a fine mist. He planned to make this quick, pulling the boy up off the ground by his hair — a limp dead weight. His jugular was flickering and pulsing, he could see the beautiful red cells through the skin. Lowering his mouth towards it, he cast his eyes up for an instant.

They were coming again, the fearless girl and her gangly protector. Full speed and without hesitation. He knew they would need his full attention, even if only for an instant. He predicted they would run at him straight, without thought or stealth, but at the last moment — as he prepared his hands to strike and tear their throats out — they switched places, split away from each other and ducked to tackle his legs. The gangly one tried to rugby tackle him. So primitive! He succeeded only in pushing him back a few feet, his legs staying firmly upright. He punched down on his back: rhythmic hits, breaking up the boy's back muscles. He squealed and sagged. The girl was quicker, lashing out with a boot she caught him between his naked legs. Pain again, sharper and more vibrant this time. He bent over and felt his legs weaken. She had hurt him, reminding him what pain was.

'...fucking freak!' she was screeching at him.

There were new lights shining over the field. The house lights behind the paddock were coming on, one by one, lighting up like Christmas trees. On the road below the line of the fields there were blue lights approaching accompanied by a siren screaming into the night. He turned and jumped halfway up the fence, then jumped again. People were looking out of windows, perhaps noticing him. He ran, leaving the three in the field. He would come back for them. He would come back for them all.

They wouldn't see him coming.

Chapter 15 – Paparazzi

'How is he doing? Do you know?' Stixx continued to badger the nurse who was painstakingly cleaning the two dozen or so grazes and abrasions that now covered his body. There was a police officer on guard outside the private hospital room far away from the normal wards.

'I don't know. You'll have to ask the doctors when they come.' She was a heavy-set Jamaican woman who was all business. There was no point arguing with her.

Faye's mum turned up, sounding posh and panicked. If that's how Faye will look when she'd older, then there's nothing to worry about.

'Anyway, Mum this is Stixx. He saved our lives back there,' Faye said, introducing them.

'Amanda.' There was also a hint of husky smoker's rasp about her voice. 'Good to finally meet you. Faye has been talking about you non- stop. Those cuts really do look a bit nasty!'

'Just scratches,' Stixx said. Out of the corner of his eye he was sure Faye was looking away, perhaps blushing.

'I'll get you some coffee. It looks like it's going to be a long night. The police will no doubt have a lot of questions for you two.'

'Thanks, Mum,' Faye said, sounding a little tired. She turned to Stixx when Amanda was out of the room. 'You know I saved your ass really. I just wanted you to make a good first impression.'

'I aim to please,' Stixx smiled.

It had taken some persuading over the phone to stop Stixx's own mum, Margie, descending on the hospital. Stixx told her he wasn't injured and would be home soon. Stixx thought she sounded a little off, a little angry or tense. Not exactly herself. Margie said she hoped the police would shoot the vampire soon and have done with it. And that he wasn't to go out at night again. She said she would speak to him later and it was important.

Stixx thought about Red. He should have been out of the operating theatre by now, but was told he hadn't regained consciousness yet.

Faye disappeared out of the room for a minute, returning quickly, hands waving swirling gestures. 'It's a fucking madhouse in that waiting room, journos and film crews everywhere! They're dressing up in white coats and hunting for us one of the nurses told me!'

'What's the big deal with us, exactly?'

'Wake up, Stixx. We saw that thing and lived. Of course they will want to talk to us. They will be going mental for this story!'

'But what about Red?' he said, cringing as his bruised muscles screamed murder as he sat up on the bed.

'Mum thinks he could be bleeding internally.'

He looked at Faye. On the surface of it they both had come off lightly compared to Red. Faye's face was untouched, but like Stixx she had plenty of grazes and bruises on her arms and legs. By the look of it her pale skin marked up easily. Earlier he witnessed Faye taking her shirt off so the nurse could assess her injuries. Before chivalry made him turn away he'd spotted the little white lines marking her inner forearm. She'd self-harmed once upon a time, that much was obvious. However, Stixx knew this wasn't the night to start asking upsetting questions.

'Good evening, I'm Inspector Hastie,' a growl of a voice said from the doorway. Hastie stood owning the space. He had a badly receding head, retaining no more than a monk's rim. Still, it brought back flashes of the vampire and Stixx felt a little unnerved. Hastie wasn't a big man though, and apart from his cruel eyes he looked every bit a normal human being. He walked with an awkward gait.

Hastie closed the door and Stixx noted the inspector looked somewhat hunched in his posture.

Definite back issues.

He was accompanied by a younger plain clothes female detective with a clipboard and a thick pad of paper. Stixx figured they must be statement forms of some variety.

'The only reason you're both not in cells right now is that one of your friend's neighbours heard all the noise and looked out of his window. Ordinarily I would keep you separate to take your statements, but there is an issue of time, not to mention lack of room at this delightful hospital,' Hastie continued. 'So, what can you tell me about what happened earlier tonight?'

'I can tell you that the thing that nearly killed us all isn't some short ass Down's kid, that's for sure. It's time you let that poor fucker out!' Stixx cringed a bit after he said it, spotting Faye's mum hovering in the doorway behind the officers.

'Mr Marx has already been released. It wasn't that hard to eliminate him as a suspect. The blood on his knuckles was a match for your DNA, would you believe? You're on the database by the way James, for your little spate of fire starting a few years ago. And by my count that makes two beatings you've had just this week!' Hastie had something of a laser beam stare. Stixx didn't like it.

'So the little fucker never talked. What a hero!' Stixx told him. Faye's mum looked like she was reconsidering that good first impression.

'Moving on to the business at hand...' Hastie said, leaning in. His face was inches from Stixx's own, his breath smelling faintly of stale liquor.

'What about Red? When can we see him?' Faye interrupted.

'Your friend Stuart Richardson is going into a medically induced coma, I've been told. He will survive it looks like. We will give you updates when we know them ourselves. I'm sure you can see him after you've made your statements, if that's what you want to do. But first, we need some fast details about tonight.'

'We found the fucking devil!' Faye's statement made everyone jump. Later she said she thought the man must be wearing contacts, because his eyes glowed red when they caught moonlight. She said he even might have been an albino because he was so pale and hairless – like something from the film *Nosferatu*, which Stixx had never heard of.

Mostly it was Faye who did all the talking. At the end Hastie had just one more question. 'Do you think it is possible the person you saw in the field was actually a vampire?'

'Do you believe in the boogieman, Inspector?' Stixx answered, less bothered by Hastie's stare now.

'Would you be a good boy and just answer the question, James?'

'Yes,' Stixx said. 'The guy could be for real, or he could be some weirdo who's just very good at pretending. But I will tell you this, he will take some stopping alright!'

'That's for the police to worry about James, so no more vampire hunting, okay? Or next time someone will get killed!' Hastie nodded to his subordinate, who flexed her cramping hand. 'I'll see if you can see Stuart after my officers have seized all your clothing for forensics. Don't go washing your hands either. Who knows what treasure is hiding inside those dirty little finger nails? And be warned, you two have stirred up a hornet's nest of media interest that won't go away anytime soon. Brace yourselves, you're about to be become famous.'

'Or infamous,' Stixx whispered to Faye, as the two detectives left the room.

Later, police radios crackled as Stixx, Faye, and her mum, were escorted by a policeman towards the intensive care room where Red was in his coma. 'Do we have level two clear? We are on our way up now... did you copy?' This copper was a little jumpy, Stixx thought.

'I don't think they work so well in lifts,' Faye said, pointing at the radio clipped onto the officer's florescent stab-proof vest. The terminal had a blinking red light. The lift was taking an eternity to go up the two levels.

'It's airwave, not a radio. Encrypted, you know, to stop people eavesdropping,' the officer curtly replied. Stixx thought he sounded like an angry type, although, as he'd not met him before, it could just have been because he sounded Scottish. The officer pronounced each word individually, as if sucking them like a lozenge.

'Usually this works a treat,' he said bashing the black airwave casing with a thick digit, '...oh, fuck!'

The three of them walked out of the lift straight into a media scrum. Stixx counted seven journalists, most with a camera or microphone in their hands. 'James and Faye, can you tell us about the vampire killer?'

Stixx was trying to think of some clever reply but all the flash photography made it hard to focus. Three other police officers ran up the corridor and started pushing the line of journalists back. 'They gave us the slip. Fire exit entrance!' one of the policemen shouted.

'Miss Burns, was it a real vampire that attacked you?' a particularly sweaty looking man with a pot belly and huge digital camera shouted as he was pushed back around a corner of the corridor.

Faye looked at Stixx, and sighed. 'So, let's just go and see Red.'

They seemed to have picked up at least five minders now, burly police officers watching their backs. He and Faye stood behind a glass window looking in at a room where numerous wires, drips, and machines, all seemed plugged into Red. There was a ventilator going into his mouth, helping him breathe. His hair had been shaved and a thick gauze bandage covered half of his head. Red's heavy duty mother was in the room, filling a chair near him and clearly weeping. She didn't even notice they were standing on the other side of the glass.

'He's stable now, we are quite satisfied that the bleeding in the brain has been stopped. Of course it is too soon to say whether this will have long term implications. We'll cross that bridge...' the doctor trailed off. 'We can't let you in the room, but you can see him from here.'

'How long will he be asleep for?' Faye asked.

'The coma aids with the healing process. I can't give you exact time frames tonight. It could be days, or weeks.'

'He'll be gutted if he sleeps through Christmas!' Stixx said. Faye groaned next to him. The doctor looked nonplussed and glanced towards the police officers. He wondered if the doctor was thinking Stixx and Faye had caused this, and that they were suspects. Stixx wondered if perhaps Hastie had been thinking the same thing on some level. The doctor wandered away from them. He had other patients. It was a busy night, no doubt.

'So, what do you think?' Faye said, quiet enough so the police officers couldn't hear.

'I think we need to get out of here and figure this out. Perhaps consume some alcohol.'

'Well, there have been worse plans, I suppose. Get better soon, Red,' she said to the window.

'Guys, are you able to take us home now?' Stixx said to the five officers, still standing like silent sentries watching them.

The one from the lift said, 'My advice is that once we start moving, we don't stop until we get you in a vehicle. We'll punch a hole through the journalists if we have to!'

They threaded through to the rear of the hospital, shown the way by a helpful nurse with a swipe card which opened all the doors. Finally, they went through an industrial-sized laundry and out via the morgue, both in semi-darkness. Stixx counted a dozen closed body freezers and wondered how many would be occupied. There were probably victims of the attacks on ice in there. It gave him the creeps.

'It seems like I'm in this place every week,' the lift officer said. 'Trust me it's a lot less scary during the day,' he said, cracking a crooked smile.

The double doors opened and they were outside. A police van had its sliding door open. 'They'll take you from here,' the officer said, turning away.

As they drove out of the staff entrance, Stixx could see the patients car park below filled with media vans and television crews.

'Getting into your houses tonight might be interesting,' the police driver shouted. 'If needs be we'll just ram-raid our way through.'

Stixx looked across at Faye. She appeared quiet and lost in thought. He wondered what exactly they had started.

Chapter 16 – Brodie's Final Blog

Frederick Brodie pulled his hand out of his boxer shorts and looked for something resembling a tissue in the cluttered space around his computer.

The couple on the screen had also just finished, and now the cameraman wanted the viewer to see what a mess the stud had made between her legs. Brodie clicked the small *x* in the corner and closed that screen, along with the ten other pornographic spam pop-ups that had appeared during the last ten minutes. Now he felt guilty, *which was just great!*

He checked the time – 7.37pm. It was nearly time to catch the train. He'd eaten, his 'overnight' bag with his equipment was all packed, and he was just about ready for his adventurous night. All that was left was to finish the entry of the online blog he'd started before being stupidly distracted by the MILF with the huge jugs. Brodie cracked his knuckles and power typed the last paragraph:

'So it is with some trepidation that I venture to this village where there has been so much chaos and death this past week. But, constant reader, be assured I don't do this without some precautions. I will be armed, perhaps not to the teeth per se, but with a few sharp stakes, (real) holy water, and a damn good hunting knife for good measure! I'm not entering into this venture lightly. For if there are, in fact, vampires in this world, then surely there must also be vampire hunters. Wish me well, and I will update you on all turn of events in twenty-four hours' time.'

Checking his watch again he slammed shut the door of the bedsit apartment he shared with nobody but an ailing goldfish called Mr Chips. He was relatively new to the world of blogging. For the past four weeks he'd been sharing his inner workings, theories, even recipes with... well, at least fourteen people, if the website people counter was correct. It was a start. It was, in fact, the most positive thing he'd done with himself in years, other than moving from his elderly parents house into the bedsit. He was getting by on benefits, handouts from the government, faking trying to get a job because frankly they were all dead end and awful. Of course at twenty-one years old this couldn't go on forever, and eventually he would have to accept working in some yogurt packing prison with a load of dead-headed skanks, or perhaps shuffling around with the council refuse collectors like an extra from *Night of the Living Dead*, crawling around on his hands and knees prising reinforced chewing gum off pavements.

That had been his thinking, anyway, until he started the blog. The world had opened up before him with new and exciting possibilities. And okay, there wasn't going to be instant success, stardom, women and money to roll in. But he had a voice and world-wide views. He could build something from the ground level upwards and be a real cutting-edge investigative journalist without having to worry about bosses or even having a journalistic education. This was the new information age after all, where internet was king. So it might take years, but under the bonnet he was a patient type of person, he told himself.

Then two mornings ago he had woken up and thought, *sod it, I'll just catch that vampire instead!* It had been a genius idea, and he'd spent the last forty-eight hours amassing all the correct utensils and tools required to carry out such an enterprise, whilst entering almost half-hourly updates onto his beloved blog. At least three new people had subscribed to his blog, and every one of them was no doubt waiting with baited breath for his next move. It was an amazing feeling to be at the centre of something so real and exciting. It made Brodie giddy just thinking about it.

An hour later Brodie was stepping off the train in Greystones. He hefted the solidly packed rucksack over his shoulder and set off down the icy station ramp to the main road. It had been a few years since he'd last been here for cream teas with his embarrassingly old parents, and their quiet prodding and nosing into his life as it was then. In truth he'd never been particularly enamoured with Greystones – such a tourist trap in summer, with cars and people everywhere. He much preferred the quieter villages further up The Bay; the ones that nobody else loved. Part of him wondered how much this commercial little village was going to cash in on the vampire once he was finally bagged and tagged.

The Greystones Vampire Museum perhaps?

Brodie deliberately chose not to walk the conventional route along the village promenade, instead taking a series of roads that led towards the top of the village. He had forgotten just how far up that was and was already substantially out of breath and uncomfortable with the rucksack straps digging into his shoulder. Under a street light he caught sight of himself reflected in a car window. Frankly, he looked fat, there was no real point denying that anymore. Too many Big Macs, cheap takeaway pizza, and beer. He made a promise to address the issue properly, on a date yet to be determined. Perhaps a New Year's Resolution.

There were pleasant looking Christmas lights in a lot of the windows he passed. Some people seemed to have taken it upon themselves to go crazy and had filled their entire gardens with illuminated snowmen, Santas, and in one case a life-sized sleigh complete with huge glowing reindeer, not to mention a million and one Christmas lights. Nobody here was worried about electricity bills obviously. He made a mental note to bring this subject up in his next blog.

Frederick felt he was being lulled into a false sense of security. He needed to remember he was alone out here in the elements, and there was a killer who probably didn't give two shits about the yule-time season and the BBC's festive television programming. He wondered if now would be the time to dig out one of those sharp stakes for protection. It was true that at school he'd never really been even slightly successful at fighting, but he was older now: he had his man's strength. Brodie was sure that if it came down to it he could get one of those wooden spikes through a psycho's ribcage with no bother at all. It was just a matter of *visualisation*.

Brodie paused a moment to catch his breath and get his bearings. He was somewhere at the top of the village, next to a number of newish looking cul-de-sacs on the main road that went all the way past Far Greystones. The place he wanted wasn't that far. Brodie pulled a Dictaphone from his pocket and started speaking.

'The time is 8.12pm on the 23rd of December 2012. This is a verbal record of Frederick John Brodie for the online blog, Brodie's World dot com. I can see the graveyard now. I am aware from previously visiting that there

105

are a number of large tombs on the grounds. This must be the best place to start... oh, fuck it!'

After having not seen a soul the whole walk up through the village, Brodie was frustrated to find the ideal place for his own investigation to start – the village's main graveyard – was full of teenagers. There were enough torchlights in the darkness to suggest that the number of people amongst the graves hit double figures. They were even playing music, some sort of death metal rubbish. Brodie didn't even bother going through the iron gate, and kept on walking. He knew there was a curfew on and surely the police wouldn't be far away with all that noise.

It was time for a new plan.

It was too dark to go into the woods so Brodie instead stuck to the road which led towards Far Greystones. He figured if there were teenagers on the loose en masse, then it would be best to take a few paths less travelled. Therefore he decided he was going to walk the mile to Far Greystones and then walk on the beach back towards the village. The rucksack weight wasn't feeling as bad, and besides, the exercise would be good to clear his mind and help him think. He had all night to play with, after all.

He reached into the rucksack and brought out one of his stakes, liking the feel of the heavy polished oak in his hand. The local hardware shop had supplied him the off-cuts and he had carefully sharpened the ends into jagged points. Surprisingly sharp, he didn't doubt that with enough blunt force it would sail through any vampire's chest. He just hoped that if it was real that it wouldn't then combust into flames or shower him in goo like in the movies: that there would be at least some evidence left to show the authorities. Frederick thought he would handle the fame, the money, and the prostitutes, with real dignity. Perhaps he could even start a vampire killing cult, he fantasised. *Where there was one vampire, there must be more!*

There was nothing to see in Far Greystones but a cluster of houses, all with curtains closed and the murmur of televisions through their lounge windows. Brodie trudged on, taking the time to eat a nut bar to keep his energy levels up. From this side O'Halloran Hill rose above him like a tangled blackened mass, full of bird sounds and groaning branches swaying on the sea breeze. It was starting to freak him out, so much so that he took the first path he could see onto the shingle beach.

Opening the rucksack, Brodie thought it wise to break out the serious protective gear. There was a string of garlic which he hung around his neck and a high-pressure water pistol that fitted securely into the belt of his jeans. It was full of holy water – he watched the bemused priest bless it right in front of him. It was the perfect anti-vampire weapon, according to the vampire killer websites, as good as sulphuric acid on the skin of any night crawler. As a backup he had his sheathed hunting knife, which attached nicely around his ankle. Brodie didn't think he'd need it, but in the event of close quarters combat it could be handy for a quick *slice and dice*.

There was a final item in the rucksack – a not-too-light steel rimmed crossbow. Brodie hadn't believed his luck finding it in his local antique shop. He had fired it once so far, across the room of his bedsit of all places. The bolt had buried itself so far into the plaster wall he couldn't pull it out again. Technically, the bolts the bow had come with weren't stakes, but who was to say that one of those missiles in the head wouldn't kill it stone dead? He decided to toss the rucksack away and walked down the beach with both the stake and crossbow in his hands.

The wind off the estuary was so cold it felt like his cheeks were burning. Frederick picked his way over the jagged pebbles and worked his way around the coast. Already it was after 10pm and he guessed this might be the kind of time that a vampire could make an appearance. He looked up at the small cliffs and decided to stick to the beach. Trying to do battle on the cliff paths would be dangerous in broad daylight, never mind the dead of night. Brodie stuck close to the waterline, feeling the wide beach gave him a decent measure of line of sight and therefore protection. His torch was a good one and he could scan it over the beach as he walked, like a powerful search light. Nothing was going to find it easy to sneak up on him unawares.

At around 10.30pm Frederick started to flag and needed a good sit down and a rest. Suddenly the thought of staying out all night in the winter elements didn't seem the wisest choice ever.

The crossbow felt like it weighed a tonne in his hands and he just wanted a good rest. He was going to have to stash his weapons near the village and just get a taxi back to town. It was going to be expensive.

Around the next corner he saw what appeared to be an old limestone quarry of some description. He shone his torch around. There was graffiti on the face of the rock which read *Vardells*. Frederick had never seen the place before, but it looked kind of cool. He moved closer to take a better look. The number of discarded beer cans and circles of extinguished beach bonfires suggested it was a place where the kids liked to party sometimes. The cliff didn't look too hard to climb, there was practically a path running up the side of it. Halfway up, Brodie found a flat piece of rock and sat down with the crossbow in his lap. He would rest here; it was as safe a place as any.

The torchlight wouldn't last indefinitely so he turned it off. He could see hardly anything now, just the bare outline of the curving beach and the faint reflection of the moon off the still estuary. It would have been delightful if it wasn't so damn cold. Frederick put his head towards his knees and closed his eyes for a second.

A noise woke him, the clicking of stones bouncing down the quarry face. He blinked, unsure how long he had been asleep. Frederick checked his watch and saw it was after midnight. *Probably over an hour then*, he calculated. More pebbles were falling, skittering past close to where he was sat. One hit his shoulder, the sharp pain bringing him fully awake. He scrambled for his torch and shone the light upwards. A figure was moving down the rock face towards him. It had naked dirty skin, and was hairless from its bald head downwards. There was a snarl and other animal sounds coming from its mouth now. *Angry to be in the light*, Brodie's mind raced.

In a state of terror, Frederick forgot where he was for a moment, stepped into space and fell down the side of the quarry face. It wasn't a vertical fall, more an uncontrolled slip and skid down the rock face. He hit the base awkwardly and there was a crunch from somewhere in his hip. When he tried to stand a shooting pain made him double over. The torch was long gone, but the crossbow was glinting in the moonlight at his feet. Frederick madly scrabbled to pick it up, embracing the cold steel of the contraption to his chest. His fingers struggled to arm it with a bolt. The quarry wall was black but the shape was barely moving, taking its time. He tried to control his breathing while hobbling backwards towards the estuary. 'I'm armed. I will shoot YOU!' he shouted up at the thing.

His hip was seizing up with the pain. A broken bone was grating on his nerve endings.

Perhaps his pelvis was shattered?

The dark outline quickened, no more than a shadow now. Frederick pointed the crossbow. 'I will fire!' he warned again.

It charged him, running full pelt right at him. Frederick pressed the trigger and the bolt *pinged* off into the darkness – a terrible miss and no time to reload. Turning, he dropped the crossbow and hopped blindly towards the freezing estuary water. Somewhere he'd read that vampires couldn't cross running water. He'd certainly seen it in a Hammer *Dracula* film once. Splashing out he turned back to shore only when the water was waist high, holding him as if in a frozen vice. Gasping for air he tried to scan the shoreline: there was no sign of the vampire. It had vanished. He was safe, if now freezing to death.

He knew he needed to stay in the water though. He felt his ankle for the knife, but somewhere in the craziness it had fallen off. There was still a single stake in his pocket. Weighing it in his hand Frederick was a little less sure of himself. He'd got his story; he just wanted to go home. 'HELP!' he bellowed down the beach.

A splash over to his right sent a tingling fear back through him. Frederick moved further into the water, the depth now forcing him to tread water.

More splashing.

The cold was overcoming his fingers and the stake slipped out and disappeared into the black water. His teeth chattered uncontrollably and he set off to swim across the bay knowing he had next to no chance of making it. There was another eruption in the water, closer still. Frederick spun around 360 degrees trying to see the thing pursuing him. There was a domed head half-submerged in the water, barely visible in the terrible light. It was drifting effortlessly towards him. Frederick wildly tried to kick it away.

Sharp taloned fingers were digging into his sides, making him scream out. The domed head was out of the water and the vampire was trying to get teeth past his clothing and onto the skin of his neck. Frederick tried to beat his fists against it, but he was out of his depth in the water and quite helpless. His limbs moved as if in slow motion from the cold. He felt his neck open up and hot blood jet out into the bitter water. Frederick Brodie could do nothing but watch the faint, watery moon mock him as the last light faded from his eyes.

Chapter 17 – Breaking and Entering

'There's fricking journalists shining lights at my bedroom window again!'

Stixx read Faye's latest text on his mobile and rolled over on his bed. There was no chance of them being able to do that to him. His bedroom was three storeys up at the back of the guesthouse and looked down to a network of neighbours' private gardens. Margie had decided to turf all the journalists staying at the guesthouse out into the street before he got home. Stixx figured that if she hadn't done that, Veronica, Diego, and the rest, would have been hounding him all over the house. The place was empty bar the Romanian, Burt, who was still in bedroom with a very broken wardrobe.

'So?' The screen on his battered Nokia lit up with the question.

Stixx mulled it over. Red was in a coma, but he tried not to think about that. They'd all nearly died back in the field and he tried not to think about that too much either. There were parts of him that felt so numb that he wasn't really afraid anymore. He knew Faye wasn't likely to back down – backing down didn't seem to be in her make-up, in any way, shape or form. Stixx knew he liked her a lot, more than liked. This whole mystery ride and investigation had turned into something special. It was like they had some higher purpose now, and it sure beat stacking supermarket palettes for a living! Stixx felt they were really onto something; something that nobody else was seeing, not Hastie or the journalists, or anyone else in the village.

'We carry on what we already started,' he texted back.

During breakfast the next morning the front door was knocked on with three rhythmic thumps. 'Don't answer that! Just those journalists up to their tricks,' Mrs Phillips said loudly, from the kitchen table she was sharing with Stixx and Margie.

'No it's not. It's a code!' Stixx told her, and jogged to answer it. He pulled the door open in such a rush that it hit the wall behind and left a dent. Faye was stood there looking windswept and interesting. 'Are you... going to invite me in?' she panted.

'Don't tell me you're a blood sucker too?' Stixx grinned, pulling her inside and slamming the door when he saw at least two cameramen running up the guesthouse steps towards them.

'Fuckers chased me all the way here. Bunch of losers!' she said loud enough for them to hear.

Back in the kitchen Mrs Phillips was making more tea for her and Margie. Stixx thought they'd take it intravenously on a permanent drip if they could. 'We're going to wrap presents.'

'Is that what they call it these days,' he heard Mrs Phillips say when they started on the stairs, adding the mad cackle she saved up for all her best lines.

'So, presents?' he said to Faye. 'You know what? In all the excitement, I've kind of forgotten all about Christmas.'

'You know it's Christmas Eve today, don't you?' Faye said, walking into his room and visibly cringing at the smell. 'I think we'll have a window open in here. What is it with boys and their odours?'

Stixx noted his bedroom had again turned into a tip without him even trying. Faye was wearing her red coat again. *Little Faye Riding Hood*, his brain ticked over. 'Any ideas?'

'Well, I didn't fancy trying to do Christmas shopping with five thousand journos following me like lost puppies. Luckily...' she said, tipping her bag of neatly wrapped presents onto his bed. 'These are some I made earlier. Earlier being when I couldn't sleep because I kept having nightmares about fucking insects trying to drink my blood. God knows where that came from!'

'Can I borrow some of these for, say, my mum?' he said, picking up the various presents, shaking them and weighing them in his hands, none the wiser as to what any of them contained.

'That one is perfume. My mum has way too much of the stuff anyway. Her bedroom is like some kind of high price boutique these days. You can have it,' she said, handing him a pink wrapped parcel. 'What about Mrs Phillips?'

'After her last comment, I think she can forget it. And I guess Red is going to be good until the January sales at least.'

'Stixx, has anyone ever told you that tact isn't your strong point?'

'Well my maths teacher did once say I had a mind like a brass door stopper.'

'How very rude!'

They spent the next forty minutes talking over a plan of attack. From one of the empty guest rooms they could look down and count five media vans and twenty plus journalists now all hovering expectantly for another appearance. A flash caught their eye. One of them was taking photos of the window. 'A front exit is definitely off the menu,' Stixx said.

A few minutes later they were stood in the raised back garden to the guesthouse, on the sloped lawn that on one side was bordered by the side wall of the lorry garage. At the end of the garden was a high dry stone wall which curved around the end of the garden. There were two elderly trees down there, both sick with disease, giving the bark an ugly orange rash. Stixx climbed up onto the derelict rockery at the far end and pointed to a slate slab set halfway up the wall. 'Use that to step on.'

Stixx climbed higher, brushing away the attentions of a colony of woodlice that seemed awfully happy to see him.

'So who lives on the other side then?' Faye asked from below.

'Nobody that's going to notice us,' he promised. 'I've got it covered, trust me!'

Stixx ran across his neighbour's lawn, holding his head low. He imagined he was a special ops soldier for a second, although he suspected the reality would be a lanky goon with some deep-seated coordination issues. Stixx ducked lower still when he saw the television was on through the window of the bungalow. Mrs Higgins was a widow and her son only visited her occasionally. The chair nearest the window was facing away from him, and at the top he could see a tell-tale shock of blue hair.

The poor old dear was alone on Christmas Eve.

He felt a pang of pity for her, and then gestured madly at Faye to catch up.

Out of the garden Stixx led them through a maze of passageways, paths, and cul-de-sacs, to get them into the woods and the trails leading back towards Flint's cottage. The ground underfoot was muddy but in the main, frozen solid. Their breath was pluming like dragon's steam. The route Stixx took wasn't direct, as he stuck to the seldom-used paths, trying to avoid the bulk of dog walkers and day trippers. 'Are you sure you really want to go through with this?' Stixx already knew she did, he was just making conversation.

'Stixx, your best friend is in a coma. That creep Flint knows more than he is letting on I reckon. It's as good a place to start as any.'

'I don't know what we expect to find, exactly.'

'Me neither,' Faye said. 'That's half the fun of it!'

They found themselves back where they'd stood with Red the day before, looking across at Flint's cottage from the tree line, and soaking in the black windows that gave nothing away. Stixx had already told Faye that Flint should be away policing the Christmas Eve fête on the village's playing fields. The fête was a popular event with visitors, attracted by the stalls of mulled wine, cheeses, and last minute stocking fillers. Flint always attended it, in Stixx's experience. After all, he was the supposed face of law enforcement in the village.

Stixx and Faye had been stomping their feet to keep warm for around twenty minutes when, finally, Flint appeared as if by magic, driving his patrol car out of his garage. 'Better late than never! What did I say?' Stixx said with a big grin.

They put their gloves on and pulled their hats down further over their ears, as if that was going to somehow make it harder for anyone to identify them. Stixx was banking on the fact that Flint's neighbours were elderly, and that perhaps half of them had been collected for Christmas by their sons and daughters. Stixx was nothing if not an optimist.

Walking slowly and casually they moved past Flint's garage and around to his back garden where there were no overlooking neighbouring windows. From here they had a good view back to the tree line. 'We can always jump the garden fence and make a run for it if we have to,' he told her, starting to lift up plant pots.

'What are you doing?'

'Looking for a key. People stash them under plant pots, don't they?!'

Faye smiled and pulled a bunch of keys and what looked like metal tooth picks out of her pocket. 'If you find a key tell me, but in the meantime I'm trying this way.' Five minutes later and Faye had the back door open. 'Not even a scratch!'

The smell inside the cottage reminded Stixx of his grandparents house. It was slightly musty and earthy, as if the air had gone stale. Flint's kitchen was the first room they walked into. It looked wholly unremarkable, right down to the chipped white mug drying next to the sink. Faye looked in the cupboards. 'He loves his tinned food, that's for sure. Was he ever married?'

'She left him, I think. Probably uses prostitutes now, or something.'

They tried their luck in the lounge next. Flint had a very old television, the size of a small refrigerator. He obviously wasn't a follower of technology. There was no sign of a computer anywhere on the ground floor. 'Must be a reader,' Stixx said, looking at Flint's bookshelf. 'Likes his Jeffrey Archer. No crime against that I suppose.'

There wasn't a cellar that they could find, so that just left upstairs. The cottage staircase was narrow, creaking, and uneven. It had a nasty floral carpet, worn out and probably from the 1960s.

'I bet he inherited this house and never changed a thing in it,' Faye said in mild disgust.

Upstairs was more of the same. Flint had a spare room filled with next to nothing bar a few badly tarnished tournament cups for chess sitting on a shelf. They were dated from 1984 to 1987 – The Greystones Chess Club Champion. *He really was a sad act,* Stixx thought.

'In here!' Faye shouted.

Stixx found her in Flint's master bedroom. On the wall above his bed was a life-size framed picture of Christopher Lee dressed as Dracula. 'Look, it's even signed,' Faye said pointing to a squiggle in the corner of the picture. 'Sergeant Flint clearly loves his vampires.'

'I'm not sure that one's going to stand up in court. Come on, you do the drawers again and I'll get in that wardrobe.'

Ten minutes later they had to admit defeat. 'Not even any decent porn,' Stixx said. All they'd managed to locate was a box of Hammer Horror VHS tapes under the bed which, looking by the thick film of dust on them, hadn't been looked at in years.

'Time to get out of here and regroup,' he said moving towards the landing. Just then there was a noise from outside – a car pulling up to the house. 'Oh fuck!'

Stixx started to look wildly around. He could already hear a key in the front door which, when opened, had a clear line of sight through to the kitchen and the back door. They couldn't get out without being seen. Stixx looked up at the ceiling. There was a loft hatch too small for them to fit through.

Stixx felt Faye pull him by the arm towards the bathroom. She had a finger clamped on her lips as Stixx tip-toed and tried not to make the old floorboards creak. He followed her into the bathroom and they stood in the old enamel bath behind a dirty blue shower curtain as rapid footsteps came up the stairs. Stixx was close enough to see sweat beads standing up on Faye's forehead. His stomach felt like it contained a swarm of butterflies taking flight. They were going to get hurt, arrested, or both.

Footsteps were now in the master bedroom, but there was no sound that suggested the bedroom door had been closed. It was definitely Flint. Stixx could hear him mumbling incoherent words to himself. Stixx guessed he probably had an imaginary friend to keep himself company. He looked at Faye, and she shrugged, mouthing one word, *'Wait!'*

They both flinched as the footsteps approached the bathroom, the fight or flight adrenalin dump practically making Stixx's head spin. Flint was in the bathroom. At any second the curtain would be pulled back. Stixx felt a dig of pain at the thought of not being allowed to see Faye again, which would probably be part of the bail conditions. Faye's mother would blame him, of course.

There was a jetting liquid sound and a heavy sigh. Flint was urinating and it stunk the little bathroom with a smell of ammonia. He seemed to take an age. Stixx could faintly see the sergeant's outline through the thin shower curtain, then a hand reaching behind the curtain, calloused, black hairs coming out of

116

thick pores in his fingers. Stixx saw all the details in slow motion. The hand groped for the shower tap on the wall, nearly touching Faye's arm as she leaned heavily into Stixx, terror plain on her face.

Then the water was on, streaming in rivulets over their clothes. Stixx started to hold his breath, the prospect of a naked Flint stepping into the bath with them too much to bear. Stixx was about to step out and give himself up, but then Flint was moving away, back into his bedroom and the door was definitely closing.

The next move was instinctive. Moving as fast as possible without making noise, Stixx imagined himself to be a cat, gliding the hell out of there. Stixx wasn't sure he breathed again until they were running full pelt across Flint's lawn and vaulting the wall as if it was nothing. Neither of them looked back until they reached the safety of the tree line again, already starting to shiver uncontrollably in their wet clothes. There was nothing to see but Flint's black windows again. 'He'll know someone was in there, we would have left wet footsteps all the way out!' Stixx blurted out.

'Who cares? Look what I found.' Faye was holding up a thick iron key.

Chapter 18 – Christmas Day

Stixx had been staring out of the window and waiting for the best part of an hour. Overnight the journalists had thinned down to one Border TV media van. Disconcertingly, it appeared to contain the former guests Veronica and Diego, and a fat guy he hadn't seen before. Stixx was sure that if he did walk out in plain sight, more journalists would return like bees to a honey pot. The phone had rung enough times that his mum had stopped answering it. Usually it was cash offers for an exclusive interview. Stixx didn't care about the money, even if he didn't have a bean to his name. He was sure Faye would agree with him.

'THEY'RE HERE!' he shouted, spotting Faye's mum's blue estate car turning into the road. 'Did you hear me?'

'Calm down,' Mrs Phillips said, waving a potato masher from the doorway. 'You'll do yourself a mischief before you've even pulled a cracker!'

It was Faye's idea they all have Christmas dinner together. Margie agreed without a second's thought, even if it had been less than twenty-four hours notice. Stixx was excited at the prospect, but also somewhat scared he was going to make enough social etiquette mistakes to make Faye's mum, Amanda, think he was a caveman. Although, to be fair, Faye had told him that actually her mum liked him just fine. Faye and Amanda were carrying presents, walking up the stairs to the guesthouse front door. The journalists were snapping off a few pictures at them, but they didn't seem fazed. Stixx took his sweaty palms to the hallway and expectantly stood behind Margie and Mrs Phillips.

'Merry Christmas,' Faye said to everyone, giving him a Christmas hug and a kiss on the cheek. It made Stixx feel vaguely light-headed and giddy, and he hadn't even consumed any of the champagne yet.

'I like the look of those presents!' was the best he could think to say.

Margie ushered them into the guest's dining room, which his mum and Mrs Phillips had given an extra Christmas shine to, with additional paper streamers on the ceiling and tinsel down the doors like silver and green tears. The only guest left, Burt, had declined an invitation and headed out somewhere in a gruff mood. Mrs Phillips's husband, Liam Phillips, was already in there, quietly staring into space as usual. Stixx knew he had some degenerative brain disease, like Parkinson's but with a twist. He once owned the fishmonger's shop in the village, which closed when he got ill and was sold to become a tourist gift shop. Stixx knew Mrs Phillips clipped his white beard every day and made him presentable to the world. Liam seemed like he was trying to form a word, but Mrs Phillips hushed him. 'This is my husband, Liam, who's not been all that well lately. But don't worry, there's nothing wrong with his appetite.'

Stixx made sure Faye sat next to him, as it always should be now, he thought. She seemed to like pâté as much as he did. In fact everyone seemed to be having a great time, despite Mrs Phillips insisting on playing her Christmas *Cliff Richard* album for background music.

'Is there any more news about your friend in the hospital?' Amanda asked.

'Not a huge amount of change. He's still in the medically induced coma and his mum won't leave his side. Apparently people in a coma can hear things and it helps them get better. I imagine Red is annoyed he couldn't make it here, though. He always did like to double up on Christmas dinners. I don't know where he put it!' Stixx smiled, but felt a small wave of sadness wash over him.

After the pâté starter, Mrs Phillips and Margie began to bring out the real Christmas dinner, which this year included a giant-sized turkey. If they hadn't ended up with extra guests, Stixx estimated the leftovers from that bird would have meant eating turkey every day until Easter. 'So what have you two been up to lately?' Mrs Phillips said in Stixx's and Faye's direction. Her squinting Irish eyes suggested that she knew they were up to something.

'Mainly, Stixx has been showing me around. He's got a great knowledge of the local history of the village, you know. And, of course, he takes me on all the best walks over O'Halloran Hill.'

'I've never known our Stixx to be so helpful,' Mrs Phillips said, a twinkle in her eye suggesting mischief. Stixx was relieved that her husband grunted for more wine and distracted her. That woman loved to make him squirm.

After a lot more food and a vat of red wine, they all moved in to the well warmed guest lounge for some present opening and Christmas television. 'You know our mums really do seem to be getting on,' he whispered to Faye as they peeked out of the bay windows.

'I think she really likes her. Since my dad...' Faye started to say. 'Well, what I mean is, usually she's often a bit lonely, so this is great. She needs a proper friend, not just me.' Stixx thought he saw some unhappiness hidden in Faye's pretty face. He wanted to ask more questions, but would wait for the right time.

'So what presents did you get then?' she asked brightening up.

'Well...' Stixx said, beginning to squirm again. 'They're just over here.'

As *The Great Escape* burbled on the TV in the background, Stixx somewhat reluctantly led her to the corner table where he'd piled his assorted gifts from his mum and other distant relatives.

'Are these all for you?' Faye said, looking far too amused for Stixx's liking.

'Yeah, that's right.'

'So you still like Action Man?' There was really no getting away from the fact that there was a lot of Action Man related merchandise on that table. There seemed to be something of a jungle theme: Action Man with a trendy khaki suit, a box with a boxy tent and another box with a jungle jeep in it.

Stixx wracked his tiny mind for a trapdoor. 'I... err... collect them. It's kind of a hobby,' he said finally. It was at least half-true.

'Really?' She was cute when she wrinkled up her nose. 'Well, everyone needs a hobby I guess.'

Stixx gave the festivities of the lounge long enough for their two mums to pour a third glass of champagne each, and descend into tipsiness. As the film droned in the background he suggested to Faye that they head downstairs to play table tennis.

'That is not very festive, Stixx.'

Stixx had net, balls, two bats and an old dining table in the cellar room opposite the downstairs private lounge. The table worked alright, although it was a good deal smaller than a real table tennis table. If the ball hit certain grooves on the surface it would shoot off in random directions.

'Our mums really should do this more often,' Faye said, once they were out of earshot on the concrete steps to the cellar. The air temperature was dropping rapidly; the cellar had the atmosphere not unlike the average crypt. Stixx pushed the half-rotten cellar door open and wondered if they might be better served going into the basement's private lounge and lighting a fire instead.

'I hope you have heating in there, pal,' Faye said from behind him.

Stixx flicked a switch and waited whilst the tired fluorescent strip light blinked into life. The cellar room had a mish-mash of assorted junk against each wall, including a chest freezer nearest the door. There was also a pantry that was seldom used off to one side, which mainly now collected dust and mice. He plugged an old air heater into the grimy socket and was blasted with cold air for his troubles. Faye was at one end of the makeshift table tennis table, weighing up which was the better bat.

'So, this is where you like to play? Who'd be an only child, hey?' She was grinning.

'Actually Red was often around to play, before that vampire thing beat the shit out of him.'

'Poor Red. He'll pull through, you know. He'll be back to no good before you know it.'

'The local video shop will probably go out of business without him around,' Stixx said, trying to impress Faye with his ability to tap a Ping-Pong ball up and down on his bat. 'So that old key you nabbed off Flint's key ring in the house... I've been thinking, it either opens absolutely nothing, or will open up one of the doors of the old police station.'

'Are you going to hit that ball or just keeping tapping it around like a fanny?'

'Faye Burns, you have a potty mouth!'

'It's my best quality. And in answer to the key question, we either use it to open up that police station, or we get in there anyway. I mean Flint was the village's only policeman forever right? Until downsizing or modernising or whatever the heck happened. So he's out, having to go back to that expanded central police station in town with all the other plebs. But his place doesn't officially close down for good until the end of January. There has to be some hope that whatever connection Flint has to what's going on in this village could be hidden in there somewhere, hiding in his locker or whatever, right under everyone's noses.'

'Well there has to be some chance, ' Stixx said, now slightly distracted by the fact he couldn't speak and hit the ball back at Faye. Like most things, she was rather excellent at table tennis.

Faye pulled the key out of her pocket, holding it up for inspection. 'I'm pretty sure this opens something useful. You can see from the teeth that it has regular use. Look how clean they are compared to the rest of the key.'

'You've watched a lot of *Murder She Wrote*, haven't you?'

'Still do,' she answered.

'You know what we should do now?'

'Hit the police station on Christmas Day?'

'I was going to say, smoke some dope.'

'Well, I suppose that wouldn't hurt either. It beats getting a hangover... and then we hit the police station!'

Stixx dug an old tobacco tin from underneath a broken work bench. 'This stuff is the shit.'

A few minutes later they were stood close together in the pantry, breathing marijuana smoke towards a vent in the wall. 'I hope this doesn't go upstairs,' Faye said looking particularly fine in the haze. The pantry had never smelled better.

'So what's the deal with you and your mum?' Stixx asked.

'What? That's a wee bit personal, don't you think?' Faye was looking a little glassy-eyed. Stixx wondered how likely it was they weren't going to get found out if they returned upstairs in a doped up haze.

'All I meant was, you never talk much about your dad. Did he run out on you and your mum?'

'Well, in a roundabout way I suppose he did,' she said, inhaling more deeply on the joint. 'My dad ran all the way out of his mind, in fact. You know I was a bit of a daddy's girl, always... are you sure you really want to hear this shit? I mean it's not exactly a story infused with Christmas spirit, if you know what I mean.'

'Hey, I want to hear it okay.' Stixx really did want to hear it. It sounded important to Faye, so it was important to him.

'Well you asked for it. My dad was one of those people who used to collect things. With some people it's stamps, or pottery, or thimbles. With him, he liked to collect religious artefacts. One of the first memories I have of my dad is him nailing crosses to the walls of our old house. He had bookshelves filled with nothing but bibles. Mum said he didn't start out religious. He just got that way over a great deal of time, months and years, really. He liked plenty of normal family stuff too, like going to movies and out for meals, and also playing in the park with me and my sister, Jazzy.'

'Who's Jazzy?'

'She was my twin. I don't mention her much. We were non-identical, two eggs, not just one egg split in half, you know? Well, Dad started to act odd, and wouldn't go outside anymore. The doctors said that he was mentally ill, that he needed medication to just get through the winter. Like he just had S.A.D., the seasonal defective disorder some people get. Except it wasn't just the winter and the meds didn't really change anything. Not even slightly.

'I guess we figured that one out the first time my dad stabbed my mum. One day at dinner, Dad was quiet like he sometimes was. Then he goes to the kitchen and gets this dirty sharp knife out of the sink and goes up behind Mum. She started screaming and it looked like he was trying to saw into her shoulder. He got sectioned for that one: a six month stint. Mum never wanted to press charges. They never do, do they?'

'Shit!' Stixx wasn't liking this story much. He shuffled his feet on the dusty pantry floor but kept eye contact.

'When he came back they reckoned he was cured. A few years went by, and they were kind of okay. Dad didn't work much; he was signed off as disabled and just got benefits instead. He had been an accountant, a pretty smart guy with numbers. But of course eventually he stopped taking his medication, said it made him think like a zombie. That's when he started with the crosses again, and saying that me and Jazzy had some kind of evil spirits hiding in us that needed to be gotten out. He started living in the cellar, not letting anyone in there. We'd hear all kinds of weird sounds, banging and scratching at all times of the night. Mum was holding off calling the authorities, thinking she would cure him with time and kindness, or whatever. One night we couldn't find Jazzy. It was one in the morning and she was nowhere in the house. The door to the cellar was open. We went down and there she was, sawn into five pieces. He said he'd saved her.'

Faye was crying, not small tears, but a welled-up tsunami of emotion. Stixx took a step forward to hold her, but she shrugged him off. She looked lost, her eyes glazed for those seconds before she blinked back into life. 'Sorry, I guess that story doesn't mix well with pot after all.'

Stixx leaned forward then, moving his head towards her, nearly overbalancing. He opened his eyes and saw Faye's face loom closer.

'What are you doing?' she asked.

'I wanted to kiss you. Sorry.'

Faye walked out then, and he heard her steps going back upstairs. Stixx stood in the pantry, a burnt-out spliff in his fingers.

Always the idiot.

Chapter 19 – Fire in the Hole

The village police station had been Flint's domain for the best part of the last twenty years. Stixx recalled that over the years Flint occasionally had an extra officer assigned to the station, but none had stuck there with him for long. Whether it was in part because the village was a dead end, miles from the town, or because Flint was such an obnoxious weasel, Stixx wasn't entirely sure.

Three months ago the local paper reported the proposed closure of all outlying rural police stations by the County Constabulary. It was part of some plan to centralise the police's response to emergency calls. There was a million pounds being invested in the hi-tech facelift of the central police station in town. All the rural bobbies would find themselves working from there, so if someone raised the alarm in Greystones it wouldn't be Flint getting there in minutes anymore: the town was a good twelve miles away by twisting country lanes.

It was a fact that by mid-January Flint was going to have to pack his bags and get himself over to the new building with all the other relics. Although the rumour was that he was just going to call it a day and retire on his fat police pension. His beloved village police station was to be sold off for development. Stixx hadn't really noticed any great protest coming from the other villagers about any of this. Flint was about as popular in Greystones as a barnacle on a fisherman's arse.

The police station itself was nothing special to look at. It was a detached grey limestone box, two storeys high, with the classic slate roof. Stixx knew the layout well from his pyromaniac juvenile days, from when Flint interviewed him on tape numerous times with a mortified Margie in attendance, acting as an appropriate adult. At the rear there was a small courtyard big enough for six police cars. There were no vehicles there now, though. It was Christmas Day and Flint was still at home – they'd checked that much before coming to the station.

'I wonder how many people have ever burgled a police station,' Stixx asked breezily, looking at the back door. He tried the handle.

Locked.

'Think of us as trail blazers, Stixx.' Faye smiled. She had the large key in her hand. 'Now where does this fit?'

It was 5pm and they'd made an excuse about wanting to walk off their Christmas dinner. They'd left their mums, and Mr and Mrs Phillips, getting merry on pudding wine and port next to the log fire in the guest lounge. It was pitch black outside and the pavements were treacherous. On the plus side they'd noticed very few pedestrians and vehicles anywhere near the police station.

Stixx hadn't mentioned the abortive kiss. And it seemed to him that Faye was either not bothered that he'd made a complete fool of himself, or perhaps her male friends made so many frequent passes at her that his effort was just instantly forgettable. Stixx didn't want to ask, because he didn't like the sound of the answer either way. He was sure he wouldn't be trying again anytime soon.

A car drove past slowly on the icy road, its headlights lighting up the side of the police station. They both ducked down behind the stone wall that followed the boundary, paranoid they'd be reported for lurking suspiciously. The car passed and they went back to walking around the building.

'I don't think this bloody key fits anything here,' Faye said, the frustration evident in her voice. They'd tried three doors on the outside of the police station, two of which had key codes and a small Yale lock keyhole far too small for the key they'd taken from Flint's house. A fourth door appeared unused, and was possibly boarded up from the inside. The key went into the hole but definitely didn't fit into the lock mechanism. 'Look at all the spider webs. The door is obsolete,' Stixx said frustrated.

'Big words on the loose again,' she smiled. 'Maybe we should get back to the guesthouse and rethink this a little?'

Stixx didn't like the idea of giving up, not least because he didn't have a single idea of where else they could go with this key or any other part of the investigation, for that matter. He feared that without making some progress, Faye would find hanging out with him a whole lot less stimulating, and would probably start phoning Alan the boyfriend again.

That wasn't going to happen.

'Right, I'm going up!'

'Up?'

'Yep, up there,' he said, pointing to the roof. Faye had a quizzical look on her face, but wasn't saying no.

Stixx climbed onto the wall at the end of the police station and used it as something of a launch pad to get a decent foothold a quarter of the way up the old iron drainpipe that ran up the side of the building. If it snapped it was going to be a painful landing. The pipe was freezing on his fingertips, covered as it was with a thin veneer of ice. He tensed his muscles to start edging up. It had been years since he'd last done anything like this and he felt very out of practise.

'Don't fall off, you plonker!' Faye whispered from below.

'Who are you calling a plonker?' Stixx felt his foot slip. He needed to talk less and concentrate more. With difficulty he pulled himself onto the sloping slate roof of the police station's side porch. He felt a couple of the slates move and crack as he moved over them, then one did slip off the roof and crashed down onto the parking area below. 'Are you okay down there?' he shouted.

'You missed me by at least an inch!'

He needed to get up to the next level of the roof, which was at least a six foot climb with no more drain pipe to use. Stixx dug his right foot hard against one particularly prominent limestone brick near the base and started climbing. If he fell he'd no doubt bounce off the porch roof and end up pancaked into the car park tarmac.

Stixx didn't exactly know what vertigo felt like, but if it was something along the lines of sheer, blood-curdling terror, then he was right there. Halfway up the wall of death he could see Faye below, if not exactly ant-sized at least small enough to emphasise to him he was now very high up. Stixx dragged himself over the edge of the roof and again could feel the slates moving under his hands. He patted his hand around to find a halfway decent hold, before he pressed all his weight down and heard the whole roof creak. At the back of his mind there was the cold, terrifying thought that there would be no way he was going to be able to climb back down and not fall off.

'Now what you going to do?' Faye hissed up from below. 'Shall I call the fire brigade?'

Stixx could see where he was going, even if Faye couldn't. On the other side of the roof, past the stone chimney, there was a small rectangular skylight. Or rather, Stixx remembered there had been one around seven years ago when Flint had last dug out a caution form to give him and Margie.

He slid himself forward over the apex of the gabled roof and saw with not less than huge relief that the skylight was still there. Stixx moved on his belly towards it, gripping the slates and dislodging more to crash on the far side of the police station.

'I wish I had a camera,' Faye said, having moved around to the other side to watch his progress.

Stixx examined the skylight. It was thick with green lichen and mould on the frame and the edges of the glass. It clearly had not been cleaned for years, and barely any light could get through.

He tried to get his fingernails under the sill, but it didn't budge. Out of other options, Stixx picked up a loose slate and smashed the glass. It was a noisy break, and he cringed at the thought of any neighbours or passers-by hearing him. Stixx looked down into the darkness below and tried to remember how long a drop it would be. There was no alarm sounding, although he knew he couldn't be sure about that until he went inside.

'Can't believe you just did that!' Faye's disapproving voice came up from below.

Stixx chipped away the worst of the glass and squeezed his body through the gap to start lowering himself down. It was one of the few occasions where he'd been glad to be skinny. He let go with his arms half-extended above his head, half expecting to break something in the drop. Stixx was amazed to land without major injury.

Blinder!

Stixx fumbled his way down the stairs and did his best to orientate himself in the darkness. They hadn't thought to bring his phone and the only torch Stixx had was lost or broken in the field where Red was nearly killed. He moved through what he was sure was the back office, painfully banging a knee on a desk. Eventually he found the back door that led to the rear car park and ran his hands around the rough wooden surface. Through trial and error he eventually found the catch to unlock the door.

Faye was standing on the other side like a statue. 'Aren't you going to invite me inside?' she said in a low, scary voice.

'Only if you bite my neck really hard,' he told her. She was pretty funny sometimes.

'I think we need to have some lights on, or we aren't going to find very much around here.' Faye found the light switch without too much trouble. 'I've always been good at seeing in the dark!' she said using the scary voice again.

'Okay, so we take our chances with the lights, and move room to room. It's still Christmas Day, so hopefully most of the village is vegetating in front of their televisions by now, anyway,' he said. It was the most sense he'd made all day.

They started in the room they were currently in, which looked like a very messy office for just one person. 'This must be where Flint does most of his work, I guess,' Faye said.

There were piles of incomprehensible police forms and handfuls of yellow and pink backed files littering the floor and desks. The files were all minor offences, like *Urinate in a Public Place.'* The room was almost chaotic enough that you'd think the police station had been burgled already. Against one side of the room there was a large wooden unit containing open pigeon holes for correspondence. It was obvious nobody else ever worked there as most of the holes contained a thick layer of dust. On the floor were cardboard boxes half-filled with yet more files, police books and other assorted junk. 'He's started to pack for the big move then?' Stixx offered.

Ten minutes later they both agreed there was nothing very interesting in the room. Faye had even managed to open two locked desk drawers with a butter knife. There was nothing to see but rock-hard blu-tack.

129

'Okay, this fucker must have a locker hiding somewhere!' Faye was on a mission.

They moved through the bare corridor and passed the stairs to the first floor. They found furniture stacked up in the back rooms. The old interview room that Stixx thought he remembered so well looked tiny. On a shelf in the corner was the double tape machine recorder, although layers of dust suggested it didn't get very much use these days.

The toilet was next door, adjoining a cramped changing room with three tall, heavily dented metal lockers. It wasn't hard to guess which one belonged to Flint. Only one was padlocked.

'Wonder what he's hiding in here?' Faye smiled.

The butter knife wasn't going to cut it. 'Give me a minute,' Stixx said, remembering the three foot long heavy metal battering ram next to the back door. 'I think the term they use for this thing is an enforcer. The cops on TV use them to open doors.' It wasn't exactly light.

With Faye's help they lifted it above the padlock, and then brought it down with enough force to send the shattered lock pinging off to the other side of the room in small pieces. Half the metal door of the locker bent out of its hinge, and the enforcer went all the way to the ground with a heavy *thump*, narrowly missing Stixx's right foot. 'That could have been nasty. Now, let's see what we have in here.'

The locker had three dark blue police polo shirts on hangers, along with a black fleece top. There was a pair of old police boots and an empty shoe box at the bottom. 'Jeez, this is rubbish. What's the point of even locking this,' Faye said reaching her hand into all the pockets of the fleece.

Ten minutes later they'd gone through upstairs as well, searching through the near empty, unused rooms. There was nothing but dead spiders and out of date community policing posters.

'So where's left exactly? We've been here too long already,' Stixx said, getting anxious. They'd been leaving all the lights on. *How long would it be before someone came along and knocked on the door?*

'What's downstairs?' Faye asked. There was a painted white door next to the stairs. Again the key didn't fit, but for once they were lucky and the door wasn't locked. Stixx and Faye looked down onto a set of concrete steps disappearing into darkness. 'What if... you know?'

'What if what?' Stixx asked.

'What if, you know... there's actually a vampire in a coffin, or something crazy down there? It is night time.'

'You know what I think?' Stixx said. 'I think that we've been here way too long already and need to get the heck on with this before we get caught.' And with that he started down the stairs. He figured that together with the roof stunt he must be looking pretty darn heroic right about now.

Or pretty darn stupid.

'Stixx, you have way longer veins than me. You know how tasty you're going to look?' Faye whispered from behind. She was coming down the stairs too. They found a string dangling in the darkness and pulled it. A bare bulb flickered to life. There wasn't much headroom, and Stixx felt himself instinctively ducking to avoid the cobwebs lining the ceiling. There were a dozen rusted upright shelves, with a mishmash of cardboard boxes on them. 'This must be where he keeps all the good stuff,' Faye said. 'Let's get digging!'

Stixx pulled a box down. It felt damp and smelled of rotten paper. 'Did you hear that?'

'What?' Faye didn't look concerned.

'Nothing, I just thought I heard something upstairs.' Stixx really was getting paranoid. He just wanted to get out of there, now.

'Don't worry, it's still Christmas Day. Nobody is going to come around here. Flint's probably in a drunken stupor.'

Stixx focused on his box again. It was obvious that Flint was no great detective. The box was full of yet more files persecuting generations of the village's youth for ground breaking transgressions, such as *Littering* and *Breach Of The Peace*. Other boxes on the shelves were much the same, cautions and on the spot fines. Loose statement pages littered the bottom of each box, left to turn to mulch. It was all ancient history.

'Check this out.' Faye's voice sounded loud and urgent, echoing off the cellar walls. Stixx navigated his way through a gap in the shelves and found her in the corner of the cellar. By her feet was a wide, heavy-set safe the size of a large washing machine. It looked like it probably weighed a metric tonne.

'It was hidden under some dust sheets. And look at this, the key fits,' Faye said ecstatically, sliding the key into the keyhole at the front. There was no tumbler on the safe door like in the movies, this was old school. The lock turned with a dull *clunk*.

'Jesus!' Stixx muttered. Up above his head he swore he heard something, a faint creak of floorboards. It was just the police station cooling down, he told himself. It was night after all, and he knew from the guesthouse that old buildings always did that. It was nothing. Faye was pulling out the contents of the safe onto the floor. *Perhaps they should have worn gloves?* Stixx pondered.

The safe appeared to have two things inside: a thick manila envelope and what looked like a box of chocolates. Faye opened the box first – it was full of photographs, mainly black and white. 'We've found a secret hiding in here I think,' she said beaming.

Stixx picked up a handful of photographs and started sifting through them. There was nothing remarkable in them, no people, just endless arty pictures of trees, hills and landmarks around the village. Faye's handful of pictures seemed to be mainly buildings, and Stixx recognised The Ridgeway convalescent home on Hill Lane. It must have been taken decades ago, when the place was still open. There were old fashioned looking white-hatted nurses on the manicured lawns, tending to patients. There was a car that looked vintage, and Stixx guessed it might have been the 1970s.

'What do you think the deal is with these?' he shrugged.

'Perhaps he just loves his old photographs. It's a strange place to keep them though. Anything in yours?' she nodded towards Stixx's hands.

Stixx flicked through more scenic black and white pictures, some of the promenade, fishermen and people walking on the beach, with the *The Noble Man* pub there in the background. There were three pictures of an old gypsy caravan, light-coloured, with a rounded roof. It was being drawn by a horse, along the causeway that led to the beach and one of the outlying farms in the area he recognised. He didn't recognise the driver though – a tall, gaunt figure all alone on the front seat. Inside the caravan there appeared to be the outline of another person, but it was too dark to make out a face. There were three more photographs, all very similar. Snap-shots as the caravan passed, Stixx guessed. 'I don't know what to make of these.'

Then Stixx saw them, photographs of animals strung up in trees: deer and rabbits, even a dog, cut open to show their guts. There were close-up pictures of their wide, bulging eyes. Stixx wasn't even sure if they weren't still alive during this mutilation. The pictures disgusted him, and he threw them to one side. 'Flint's a sick bastard!'

Faye tore open the thick envelope. As she pulled at the contents some of the papers slipped out and spilled on the floor. It was another police file, with a crumpled, yellow back cover. The date on the front was written in what looked like faded felt tip pen, and was dated 1980. The name on the file was Myles Heathers Jr. It was the Colonel's son. The offence was written plainly: RAPE.

The pages were creased and obviously well read. They saw the file was filled with statements from over a dozen witnesses. Stixx and Faye took turns skim reading some of them. He found what looked like a transcript of some kind of interview with the victim, a name he didn't recognise – Rachel Dowling;

'...*HEATHERS then pushed me onto the floor again. He had his top off, and he ran his fingers up my leg until he touched my knickers. Then he hit me again. I felt my nose break and I think I must have blacked out.*'

'I don't remember anyone saying anything about this in the village. This is totally fucked up!' Stixx said.

'And look at this,' Faye said. Loose in the middle of the file was a psychiatric report for Jr. Faye skipped to the end and read out, '*Myles Heathers would appear to suffer from a multitude of psychiatric conditions inclusive of schizophrenia, serious mood disorders and depression. There is also evidence of self-harm. However, despite these aforementioned conditions undoubtedly being of a serious nature there is nothing to suggest that he can be considered in any way unfit to stand trial, should that eventuality arise.*'

'Bad and mad, the guy is a total nut job!' Stixx said. The mention of self-harming made him think of the marks he had seen on Faye's arms, and he wondered if he should bring it up.

There was another creak upstairs, a little louder this time. Faye didn't even seem to notice.

'You know what this all means don't you?' she said. She looked excited, practically bubbling like she always did with a good idea in her head. 'BLACKMAIL! It means Flint was holding onto this as some kind of leverage. This file has been buried here for safe keeping. It must never have been anywhere near court. Flint had hidden it here in his little castle all to himself as something to hold over crazy Myles and the Colonel.'

'You think?' Stixx said. There was another creak above. 'Shit, are you hearing this? Let's just go, okay.'

They decided to keep the photograph box and the file, and closed up the safe. Stixx jogged up the stairs and went to turn the handle of the cellar door. It turned but the door didn't budge. He pushed against it. 'Something heavy is blocking it. Help me open this!'

Together they tried to push against the heavy door, but it didn't move an inch. 'Oh fuck!' Stixx shouted. He could smell it, the thick odour of acidic smoke filtering under the door. Something was on fire. 'We need to find another way out!'

'Wait! Let's block the gap under the door first. Buy some time!' Faye wasn't stupid. She knew as well as he did how bad this was going to get. Stixx used his jacket and wedged it into the small gap under the door. The stinking, caustic smoke was visibly seeping through the other gaps in the door. It was going to choke the life out of them if they gave it half a chance. They retreated back down the stairs. Stixx wondered if he should hug Faye, tell her he loved her perhaps? It was probably just what she wanted to hear as they choked to death.

'Window!' Faye spluttered. It was getting hard to speak. The cellar was quickly filling up with choking black clouds, spiralling around the shelves. Above their heads the building was roaring and crackling with small explosions. If the floor above caved in they were definitely dead. Stixx's lungs and throat felt like they were getting sandpapered. The heat was building up like a furnace.

Where were the firemen?

A small cellar window looked like it led out under a small surface grate. Faye started breaking the glass with her shoe. He took his own shoe off and copied her. The window was tiny. He didn't think they'd fit through. Stixx started kicking at the wooden frame of the window, trying to knock that out as well. Flaking red paint fell to the floor but the wood held firm. Above their heads the single bulb began to blink on and off.

Without warning, the ceiling at the far end caved in and suddenly half the room was on fire. Stixx felt as if his clothing was starting to melt and combust. The oxygen was almost gone. Stixx pushed Faye to get her through the window. Instinctively he knew that she would not be tall enough to push open the grate now above her head. They would both fry if he couldn't get out as well.

Stixx pushed himself up into the broken window, aware that his hands were being sliced by the broken glass all around the frame. Faye grabbed his shoulders and pulled, and he felt the glass cut through his jumper and into his skin. There was a dizzy feeling in his head, and he knew he was close to blacking out. Life didn't flash before his eyes; instead there was an endless black void opening up as his vision swam in and out of focus. He could hear Faye screaming for help that was unlikely to come.

Stixx suddenly found himself in a heap on wet, icy leaves. Smoke was pouring out of the broken window, venting upwards through the grate. The cellar room had turned into a blazing inferno. Stixx tried to stand, his legs betraying him. He tried again and reached above his head. He couldn't see – the world was all choking smoke and heat. He had his fingers through the gaps in the grate and pushed. It didn't move.

They were going to die.

Suddenly the grate lifted out from his fingers, as if by magic. Hands on him. Figures in the smoke.

The firemen, the firemen had found them.

135

Chapter 20 – Two Kinds of Trouble

'You look tired.' Stixx was looking at the police officer guarding the door to his hospital room, the same one as before. He was getting a bad case of déjà vu. The compulsion to cough rose up his throat again. Taking the rough hospital tissue paper away from his lips he saw more black-tinged phlegm. He was lucky to still be breathing, there was no doubt of that. His hands were hurting again. Earlier the nurse had taken an age to pick all the glass shards from his shredded palms.

The volunteer firemen from the next village had saved their lives. Despite having various fire retardant head covers, gas masks and the burning police station to contend with, they'd picked up the shouting from below the cellar grate. Stixx was told afterwards it had taken three firemen to deadlift the grate up, breaking the crumbling concrete and frozen earth.

Faye had been most affected by the smoke from the cellar. Stixx remembered watching, horrified, as the paramedics attached an oxygen mask to her face. For a few seconds it had looked as if she was losing consciousness. He had watched in horror, even while trying to hack up a lung at the same time. The thought that Faye could die, that he could lose her, still haunted him. There would have been no demon vampire to carry the blame this time.

But Faye had been okay. She had come around quickly, joining him with a chorus of coughs and splutters. As they sat in the ambulance he'd seen more and more police officers arrive. The road around the blazing police station had been closed and houses evacuated. This would undoubtedly be a memorable Christmas for the neighbours.

As the firemen fired their jets of water into the flames, Stixx noticed two figures standing motionless, silhouetted against the backdrop of burning red and yellow flames: Inspector Hastie and Flint. Neither had looked towards the fire, instead he felt they were staring at him, as he sat on a stretcher cocooned in the ambulance's interior light. They appeared like demons, untouched by the heat and the danger. The paramedic closed the door, and they were taken quickly to the hospital with police car escorts front and rear.

Stixx and Faye were treated for mild smoke inhalation. It was recommended that they both stay in the hospital overnight to be monitored. They were given separate rooms this time. Police officers hovered in the background constantly, and Stixx wondered then when the axe would fall – *when were they going to be arrested on suspicion of arson?* Although it hadn't happened yet, there was no doubt the police guard was as much to keep them locked down, as stop any press getting to them. They weren't just innocent victims anymore.

There had been a long wait where nothing happened other than Faye's mum, Amanda, turning up and calling Stixx, '...*a stupid fucking loser who needs to stay away from my daughter!*' Faye shook her head at Stixx, and he knew she didn't have the energy to argue his case tonight. They disappeared back into her room and the door firmly closed. Stixx felt so dog tired all he really wanted to do was sleep.

Margie hadn't been far behind, slurring her words even more than Faye's mother had. Tears were streaking her mascara, making her look like some kind of wild clown-faced banshee. 'Do you have a death wish, Stixx, is that what it is? What in hell's name were you doing in that police station? This isn't burning a rubbish bin, Stixx, people could have been killed. They will lock you up for this one. Are you ready for that, Stixx?' He didn't ever recall her being so upset.

'Take a pill or something, for God's sake, Mum!'

'If Faye put you up to this you need to let the police know. You've been changing since she came along. Don't think I haven't noticed!'

'Nothing has changed. Stop being so dramatic, Mum. Can you get me some water and something for us something to eat, please? Perhaps it will help you sober up as well!' Stixx felt bad saying it, but he just wanted some peace to think. Margie stormed out of the room, past the police officer who stood in the corner like a statue.

'Know any good jokes?' Stixx asked the policeman. The statue remained silent.

Like two ghosts, Hastie and Flint moved silently into the room, their clothes layered with soot. They looked like they'd just finished a shift down a coal mine.

'I'm going to bill you for this suit,' Hastie said, yellowed teeth flashing beneath black lips.

Flint stood next to the police guard. There was a rage there, bubbling below the surface. Stixx sensed he wanted to tear him apart, that all he wanted was a few minutes alone with him. It was all in the eyes.

'The good sergeant here is understandably rather annoyed that you've just turned his beloved police station into a burnt-out pile of shit. In fact, twenty years ago perhaps you may have found yourself unexpectedly falling down a set of stairs on a number of occasions. Fortunately for you Sergeant Flint here is part of a modern progressive police force, and you're likely to be leaving this hospital in a rather better state than you entered it,' Hastie said.

Behind Hastie, Flint made a noise not unlike a hissing snake, and spoke. '…but on the plus side, we have you bang to rights. You are going to do some hard time, Stixx. You're not a juvenile anymore. You'll be going to the big house!'

'Should I be asking for a lawyer? I didn't burn down your crappy police station, Flint! And you can stop eye balling me too. Everyone knows you are basically a pansy.'

Flint moved forward off the wall, and for the first time emotion flashed onto the face of the statue cop near the door – the emotion of deep alarm. Flint took a long step forward towards Stixx. One step was enough to cover half the room.

Hastie had his arm out though, calling his dog off. 'Easy sergeant, we've all had a rather long and fretful night here. Let's not give into base instincts. Not that I'm sure Stixx wouldn't deserve a little pain for all the mayhem he's stirring up.'

'I'm not scared of you, Flint!' Stixx held the sergeant's stare.

'No one here believes for a second that you didn't just break in and torch that police station, Stixx. You and your little bitch,' Flint growled.

'Say that again!' Stixx was on his feet.

'Cool your heels, Stixx. And sergeant, would you and the other officer mind stepping outside for a moment.' There was a pause where nobody moved. 'Anytime now would be GOOD!'

Stixx was alone in the room with Hastie. He moved closer, harsh brown eyes boring into him. He noticed the strip lights made his near hairless head shine, highlighting the dirt ingrained in it from the fire. He looked far more dangerous than Flint.

'So what do you have to tell me, Stixx?' Hastie whispered in his ear.

'Hey, man...' Stixx began. 'I can't say we weren't in that police station. I think that it is plainly obvious we were. But we were just looking for Flint for an update on the case. The door was open. There was some other fucker in there with us who locked the cellar door.'

'But, let me guess, you didn't see them, he, she or it, did you?'

'We thought we heard someone in the cellar. We went down there to see if it was Flint. The door locked behind us. Someone tried to kill us, no doubt about that! So are you really going to be arresting us for nothing?' He was banking on the fact the fire would have destroyed any evidence of the broken skylight and wondered how all this would play out in court.

What would jail be like?

The inspector was pacing the narrow room, a bundle of coiled energy. 'Flint wants you both arrested and remanded in custody. The expectation is you're going to be arrested. The whole village, no doubt, wants to see you get arrested. But lucky for you, I'm not everyone Stixx.'

'Next you'll be asking me to trust you. What does that mean, you're not everyone?'

'It means that those action-starved volunteer village firemen managed to get that fire out before the whole place turned into toast. That cellar door that you mention in that likely story of yours... there was a police issue battering ram wedged between the outside of the door and the wall. Someone did trap you down there it would seem.'

'Some fucker tried to murder us, you mean!'

'The question remains, why you were there in the first place?'

'Come on. I just want a good night's sleep, Inspector.'

'Yeah, I'm sure we all do.' Hastie had stopped pacing now and loomed in close enough to Stixx's face that he could count the open pores in the inspector's beaked nose. In a slow voice he said. 'At some point soon I would love to hear something resembling the truth uttered from that mouth. I'm not stupid enough not to know you and the far more intelligent Miss Burns are up to something. I can only assume that you're sinking deeper into some kind of kamikaze investigation of your own into these so-called Vampire Murders. I would strongly suggest you leave it to the professionals before you both end up down the morgue with all those other unlucky people.'

Margie returned to the room. Stixx thought he'd never been as grateful to see her as in that moment. 'What's going on in here, then?' she asked.

Hastie recoiled away, like a snake. A switch was being thrown back to being the well-spoken police officer. Stixx could also see Flint and the statue in the background – all eyes towards their leader. 'Well, the good news Mrs Stixx is that James here won't be getting arrested today. However, he has graciously agreed to help us with this latest investigation.' He left the room, his arm sweeping Flint with him. From the corridor he heard the inspector's voice bark again. 'Statements and forensics. You know the drill!'

'Jesus, Stixx!' For a second he almost couldn't recognise her. Margie leaned forward and hugged him. He couldn't recall ever seeing her so upset.

Hours later he found himself for the second time that week dressed in pale blue hospital pyjamas. CSI officers had descended on his room and taken every stitch of clothing from him. Detectives had followed with their statement forms, one going into Faye's room, again her mum closed the door before he could see if Faye was awake.

'Hey,' Stixx said to the now slightly sagging statue against the wall. 'I'm going for a wander. Follow me if you want.'

Stixx left the room leaving Margie snoring lightly on the chair in the corner. He passed Faye's room and nodded at the officer standing outside. Stixx figured that Hastie had wanted to keep a closer eye on him and kept the statue inside his room. They obviously didn't realise Faye was the leader of their gang.

Stixx wandered on, the statue trailing behind at a three metre distance. If that guy had said ten words to him tonight, Stixx didn't know what they were. *Perhaps he was annoyed to be working on Christmas Day?* He passed the nurses station, the lights in the corridor dim. Behind the desk there was an artificial Christmas tree with cheap white lights. They were nowhere near the Accident and Emergency. This was a quiet ward set well away from most of the public.

Out on the main floor at the top of the hospital he wondered if he was going to bump into a scum of press corps again. There was none to be seen. Stixx knew the way and kept walking, dropping a level using the stairs.

'I'll only be a minute,' he said to the staff nurse when he found the room. 'I only want to stand here.' The nurse smiled and looked awkwardly back to the police officer.

'Just one minute then,' she said kindly and walked away, the light tap of her soft heels sounding on the hard plastic floor.

Stixx looked through the wide window into the room beyond. Red didn't seem to have moved since he last saw him. His body was still full of tubes. He wondered what advice Red would have chosen to impart at this time. The photograph of the gypsy had been turned to ash in the fire, along with Jr's file from the safe. There was nothing left. Probably all Red would have said was, 'Let's get wasted and worry about it all tomorrow.'

Stixx turned around and started to walk back to his room.

We'll figure it out, mate.

141

Chapter 21 – The Return

The Border Television van bumped its way down onto the foreshore of the beach. The roof was littered with various antennas which made the vehicle resemble a cockroach in a certain light. At a distance the van was navy blue, but close up there was no hiding the creeping rust on the wheel arches and bonnet. Border Television was a cheap regional television channel, but one of the main terrestrial channels for the county. From the outset, the channel had been avidly following *The Vampire Killer* case.

The van rocked wildly as it hit yet another pothole on the beach track leading to the parking area. The car park itself didn't amount to much more than a semi-circular ring of sizable boulders with a clear view to the estuary, the railway viaduct, and the smooth wet quicksands reaching to the water's edge. On the horizon the sun was sinking slowly below the distant peaks of The Lake District, giving the twilight a faintly orange glow.

'So, who the hell thought it was a good idea to take this heap of rust and rivets down here?' Ricky shouted over the tappetty engine. Ricky, the sound guy on a good day, looked like a twenty stone tub of lard – pale-white, freckled, and with an outburst of dark red hair on his head: hair that was thinning on an almost daily basis. He was also Scottish and for years loved to recite the monologue from the end of the film, *Trainspotting* whenever he was drunk.

Up front, Diego the hairy camera operator was driving, his eyes squinting with concentration. The front air conditioning vents were stuck on hot due to some malfunction with the ailing van. Sweat glistened in his bushy salt and pepper beard, and there were stains under the armpits of his *Monster of Rock* t-shirt.

Since being asked to leave the guesthouse by Margie, they had been commuting to the village from a Travel Inn near the motorway. Tonight would be their last night on the story. The Border News Desk had finally lost all patience with the vampire story. They wanted the outside broadcast crew back at head office in the morning, ready for some more mundane day to day stuff like school fairs and New Year shop sales.

'What a waste of a good Christmas!' Diego mumbled under his breath. Apart from the fire the night before, it seemed like nothing was happening in the village anymore.

Nothing newsworthy, anyway.

'Why doesn't that fucking vampire just bite someone, already?'

In the back, Veronica Myers the reporter, sat scribbling her notes as they bounced into the car park. The back of the van smelled of oil and body odour, and was full of cabling, monitors and cameras. There wasn't enough room to swing half a dead cat. She couldn't believe she was still in this awful village when she could have been in the Seychelles with her executive boyfriend, even if she was sure he was going to dump her any day now. She was the wrong side of thirty-five and had noticed the crow's feet around her eyes getting worse. If there wasn't a recession she'd quite happily tell the fat bastards back at head office where to stick this stupid regional job.

'Is it true you once tore out Emma Murphy's hair extensions in a cat fight?' Ricky piped up. Ricky was only a *'temp'* sound guy on a short term contract with Border TV. Veronica and Diego hadn't worked with him before. He was even greasier than Diego, Veronica thought... *if that was even possible.*

'Heard you kicked that bitch's ass!' Ricky went on.

'Yeah, well that will teach her not to go cracking onto my fella again,' Veronica said. It was an out and out lie, of course. In the front Diego raised an eyebrow, but didn't say anything. The actual truth was that Veronica had once been fired by the all-conquering national news reporter, Emma Murphy, when she interned at the BBC nearly a decade ago. In a particularly lame piece of rebellion she knocked a glass containing pencils off her desk whilst sobbing her way out of the door. Somehow over the years that story had mutated into *'I kicked Emma Murphy's butt!'* She'd seen Emma doing an outside broadcast near the pier in the village the other day and had hidden from her in fear. Veronica knew deep down she was basically a bit of a coward.

'Fish and chips, times three!' Diego said looking at Ricky purposefully. He was pulling rank as second-in-command. 'And don't skimp on the sauce this time, or the cokes.'

'I don't want vinegar on my chips, and diet coke for me, thank you,' added Veronica.

Ricky pulled open the sliding door on the side of the van. 'You're a bunch of charmless cunts, do you know that?!' He didn't fail to notice that the sun was little more than a halo in the distance now, nearly completely out of sight. Ice puddles around his feet crunched. He looked towards a row of shops and houses, visible behind the small ornamental garden that separated the beach and the road. He could just make out the lights from the chip shop and estimated it was maybe one hundred metres away. 'Here, you cunts, pass me that hammer will you?' he said, pointing to the large lump hammer loose on the floor of the van. *You couldn't be too careful these days*, Ricky thought.

Ricky walked across the car park, watching where he placed his feet. It was getting dark fast. Even though the temperature was just below zero his hand was sweaty on the wooden handle. He was as big as a house but he'd never been any great shakes at fighting. He could take a punch alright, but he didn't fancy his chances of resisting having his neck torn out.

Ricky walked up the steps that led into the narrow ornamental garden. There was no sun behind him now and the light had gone beyond twilight into a dusky darkness. The well-trimmed bushes and trees in front of him were becoming impenetrable. Not for a second did he think it was a real vampire in the village, despite the reams of speculation he had read in the tabloid rags over the past week. In fact Ricky was ninety-nine percent sure *The Vampire Killer* was just some dude with a big screw loose.

Spooked, he half-ran half-skipped onto the narrow path and nearly slipped straight onto his backside. He was relieved to see the Christmas lights in people's windows and a very obviously open fish and chip shop across the road. It made him feel a little safer.

The chip shop was one of the best in the country, he had been repeatedly informed by the locals. The place was his preferred lunch and dinner outlet pretty much since the vampire story broke. He should have made a documentary like Morgan Spurlock, *Supersize Me Fish and Chips*. It was Boxing Day and the place was open.

A lucky one alright.

'You boys still here?' The chip shop owner said from behind the counter. Ricky thought his name might be Karl, but he wasn't good with names. The walls appeared adorned with a thousand and one business cards. How many businesses could a little village have anyway? It was weird.

'Last night mate. The bosses want us back and doing other stuff. This story is getting deader than a dodo!'

'You say that, but nobody's been caught yet. My guess is this is the genuine article. I mean ghosts exist, so why not vampires?' so-called Karl asked him. He started shovelling more fish into the chromed glass-fronted warming trays on the counter. Ricky saw two more local lads file in and queue quietly behind him.

'Ghosts? But...' Ricky trailed off. Perhaps this wasn't the time to be debating anything. He was too hungry for the fried food. 'Well it sure was the story that got the nation interested. But you know what they say: today's news is tomorrow's fish and chip wrapper!'

'Say what?' so-called Karl said.

'I said today's news is tomorrow's fish and chip wrapping. You know?'

'No, not heard that one.' Karl had a puzzled face, before it dissolved into a broad grin. 'Just fucking with ya!'

Ricky turned to go and the voice of the owner sounded again. 'What's with that hammer? You doing some home improvement or something?'

'Protection! Stop that fucker dead in his tracks if I have to.'

'Nah, don't reckon,' the chippy man said. With a little shake of his head, he turned to serve the two teenagers. Ricky walked out.

Fucking Royston Vasey!

Ricky took the three parcels of fish and chips, and three cans of various sugar and sugar-free cokes back across the road. It was night. There simply was no denying that the sun went down fast around here. On the other side of the garden he could see the news van brightly lit up, the engine running and all the internal lights on.

The wind was picking up off the estuary, the clouds were sparse, and the stars were already appearing. It was going to be a freezing night and he thanked god that the Travel Inn stocked plenty of extra blankets in their linen cupboards. Ricky walked tentatively down the steps and onto the beach, purposefully striding out the last fifty or so metres towards the van. *They better be grateful for this.* He was getting a little out of breath.

Three paces from the van he couldn't resist the urge to turn around and look behind him. It was a *'someone walking in your grave'* kind of feeling. There was no one in the gloom of the ornamental garden, and there was barely a chink of light that could be seen from the buildings beyond.

This really was a terrible place to park.

'Say, Diego...' Ricky said pulling the van's sliding door open.

Ricky's mind disconnected to some degree. His hands forgot what they were holding and the food, cans, and the hammer fumbled from his grasp. He began to back-pedal away from the van, slow at first, as if there was some kind of magnet repelling him. Ricky turned on his heels and went to run, to run faster than he had fifteen years and a hundred and fifty pounds ago. This wasn't a sarcastic punch-line, a throw-away situation: this was a getting your throat eviscerated and dying in the next thirty seconds type of situation. Ricky took another long stride and his foot went sideways on the ice and he fell hard onto the side of his body. A bone broke, perhaps his ribs. Ricky scrambled to right himself.

The van wasn't a van anymore, it had been something else. Perhaps an abattoir would have been a more apt description. Diego wasn't just dead, he was in pieces. An arm off, a head off... *how was that even possible?* The van looked like a red tornado had run through it. Everything looked either smashed or tipped over – cameras, monitors and wires, all broken and covered in blood and red flesh.

Ricky ran harder, his legs feeling like they were hardly moving. He felt like he was crawling towards the gardens. The naked thing with the bald head and devil ears had been looking away. It would have been the only thing that saved his life. Veronica had dead fish eyes. The thing had been eating her neck out.

He ran harder, slipping up the icy steps. He didn't want to look behind him, and didn't want to slow down, scared that the thing would be sprinting, gliding, flying or whatever else towards him. Ricky wanted to live; he didn't want to be a cynical angry person anymore. No he was going to love life and embrace it. He was going to hug his mother and tell her he loved her every day.

He chanced a half-look back. There was no one there, but he kept going towards the lights of the chip shop. They could lock the door, *call the police*. He ran into the road and never saw what hit him.

Chapter 22 – Reality Bites

Some part of Stixx was glad that two journalists were eaten by the local vampire, while another was pancaked by a two tonne ice gritter.

It was only a small part of him, granted, and no doubt only because he could feel the spotlight lifting away from him and Faye, the news crews having something fresh to chew on. For the first time in days there wasn't a news van camped outside the guesthouse. He was free from journos trying to talk to him, following him like lost puppies. Stixx liked being yesterday's news. Of course he did also feel bad for Veronica and Diego too, although he never met the one who got run over.

Unlucky bastard!

Stixx's mum had bought a selection of the national papers to read. They all had the story running on the front pages. *A vampire serial killer...* it was pure gold-dust to them. And maybe that was why he couldn't bring himself to totally empathise with the journos' fates. Nice as Veronica and Diego had seemed, he figured on balance that they wouldn't have hesitated to sell him and Faye out to the highest bidder if they had a new story.

He'd also heard he had been officially banned from ever seeing Faye again by Faye's mum, so in reality the vampire could have killed all the journalists and it wouldn't have registered very much higher on his caring scale.

Stixx and Faye were released from hospital that morning, none the worse for wear, apart from a cough the doctors said would last a few days, and a few shallow glass cuts. In the hospital car park Faye hadn't managed to speak to him, as her mum hurried her away as quickly as possible. Margie had told him, *'Don't worry, she'll come around in a few days,'* meaning that in a few days Amanda might eventually stop hating and blaming him for everything. Stixx wasn't convinced, and stayed unconvinced all the way back to the guesthouse, sinking into a brooding depressed silence, which he had stayed in ever since. A whole twenty-fours had passed.

He tried to go through the motions, the usual being sitting in his room sending texts to Faye that weren't getting answered, and listening to *The Cure*... none of which helped him combat the rising feeling of hopelessness. Stixx also suspected the reason Margie kept coming up the stairs to his attic bedroom every hour or so was to check he wasn't swinging from a light fitting. He stayed lying on his bed and staring up at the ceiling stars for some comfort.

'Can you meet me at the church? It's important!'

Stixx blinked down at the illuminated screen on his mobile phone. It was dark outside and he'd been asleep for hours. He scratched the sleep out of his eyes and texted back in a daze. *'How are you? Are you okay?'* There was no reply. He debated ringing her phone, but didn't want to ruin her chances of sneaking out of her house undetected.

Getting dressed quickly, he creaked his way out of the house. There was no sign of his mother in the lounge and the downstairs rooms were empty. He imagined she was tired and had finally gone to bed early. For a second he hesitated at the front door, something gnawing at his subconscious, something he had forgotten. Then it dawned on him he had nothing in his possession that even slightly resembled a weapon. He looked around the porch for inspiration, finding nothing better than an old umbrella. He decided to leave it.

It was cold outside, well below freezing. The weather reports said they were in for a cold snap, temperatures approaching minus ten. He would have started jogging, but imagined the additional heat wouldn't really be worth breaking his neck for. The ice had given everywhere a dirty-white veneer.

Stixx chose the quickest route from his house to the church, following the private road past the old lorry park and the line of small detached houses. There was barely a light anywhere, and if the distant street lights beyond the fields below him hadn't been illuminated, he may have suspected some kind of power cut. There was a deranged killer on the loose, and yet nobody wanted to spend a little extra on electricity to keep the boogieman at bay. It didn't make a whole lot of sense to him.

Stixx moved off his road and started the steep climb up the narrow path towards the church. Near the top there was a long row of terraced houses on his left, and walled gardens to his right. Stixx strained his hearing, trying to pick out even the smallest sound that might suggest he wasn't alone. His heartbeat ramped up, and he figured if a cat did jump out, that the likely result would be a heart attack. He wished he had brought the umbrella.

The church was in darkness and it crossed his mind that Faye had broken in again and was waiting inside on a cold pew. Stixx walked around to the main entrance but found it locked. He scanned through the sparse trees of the churchyard over towards the village primary school. *Freezing in a graveyard and there was no one anywhere around.*

Stixx moved around the building towards the window where Faye had crawled in a few days earlier. Then he saw some light, not from the church but from a small hatchback car with its engine ticking over. It sounded a little raspy. Stixx cautiously approached the side windows and the internal light flicked on. Faye was in the front passenger seat and there was a strange man wearing spectacles behind the wheel. He could guess who that was. Faye gestured for him to get in the back.

'This is Alan, my boyfriend,' Faye announced to the world before he was even seated. Stixx could see he had a particularly stupid looking goatee beard.

'Hi, Alan!' He hoped that didn't come out with as much venom and resentment as he was feeling inside at that moment. He gave Faye something of a stare as well, hoping she could read his mind.

'Hi, James,' Alan said, turning around to face him. There was a smarmy sound to his words.

Sarcastic.

Condescending.

Yes, he definitely did hate this guy.

An ex-teacher of Faye's? Surely that wasn't right.

Why couldn't he have been eating fish and chips on the beach last night? he wondered.

'Don't call him James,' Faye added, turning to face him. 'Everyone calls him Stixx... Alan turned up tonight. He's flown in especially to see if I'm okay, which I am, of course! I've told him what we've been doing and he's been really supportive. Alan's happy for us to keep digging as long as we're careful.' She smiled at Alan then, but it also struck Stixx that Faye wasn't exactly using her normal voice. It was like this was the posh-pitched version of Faye, with a voice sounding just like Mary Poppins.

'Well that is great! So is Alan part of the gang now?' he asked, giving Faye another of his best glares.

'No... no it's not like that, Stixx,' Alan said, turning awkwardly in the driver's seat to face him. 'I can see this is yours and Faye's endeavour. I'm not going to tread on any toes here. I think you two have stumbled onto something bubbling away under the surface that nobody seems to have quite latched onto yet. It all sounds very *Wickerman* if you ask me!' he said, and cracked a smile.

What the fuck is Wickerman?

'You think everything is Wickerman when you're in the countryside, don't you Alan?' Faye said, beaming at him. They were like some old couple sharing a private subliminal joke. 'Alan was from the city originally, so he's a little out of his element here. He loves cities!'

Stixx wanted to suggest that he should head back to the big smoke whilst performing some sexual act, but instead he kept playing nice. 'I'll look after her,' he said finally.

'Good to hear, Stixx! Good to hear!' Alan was ignoring him now, and holding Faye's hand in a definite non-friendship kind of way. Stixx didn't know how much more he could stomach of this.

'Listen, Alan,' Faye said. 'Do you mind awfully if I just speak to Stixx alone for a moment? It will only be for a minute.'

Puppy dog eyes.

Stixx wanted to be sick.

'Absolutely no problem,' Alan replied, flicking a slightly wary look towards Stixx.

Faye and Stixx got out of the car and into the freezing air again. He made sure they walked far enough into the churchyard to have at least a measure of privacy from the prying eyes of the jerk-off in the car.

'Fricking freezing out here, Stixx!' Faye cringed, pacing one foot to the other.

Stixx wanted somehow to articulate his true love, but his brain was beginning to freeze up as much as his feet. 'It's going to snow I've heard,' was all he managed.

'We could all go sledging?' she said, cracking a big smile.

By 'all' Stixx figured she meant Alan as well. *He really needed to get eaten.* 'Yeah... about the Flint thing. Bummer we lost the file in the fire. Do you remember the name of the victim?'

'Rachel Dowling. That's just it, Stixx. Alan has really helped us out. He's good at digging into records on the internet. Apparently Rachel Dowling's mother is still in the village, in one of those old people's homes on The Hill. He found her in a recent census.'

'So we can start afresh tomorrow, just you and me?'

'Damn skippy! Alan doesn't mind, he trusts me... even with a man-hunk like you on the loose.' She winked at him.

'Do you want to come back to the guesthouse?' He was really freezing now. His blood was forming ice flows.

'I can't. I'll text you tomorrow, okay? But don't come to my house yet whatever you do. I haven't quite persuaded my mum you're not the second coming of the anti-Christ.' She gave him a peck on the cheek and Stixx had no choice but to follow her back to the car.

The hatchback revved noisily and nearly stalled. Alan did some slightly effeminate wave, which Stixx didn't return, and it skittered away. Stixx was left standing in the darkness of the church. Part of him wouldn't have at all minded if the blood-thirsty monster had chosen that moment to step up and say hello. It could only be better than being broken-hearted and alone. Stixx set off to trudge back to the guesthouse. Fat snowflakes drifted down out of the sky. He held his hand up and caught one the palm of his hand.

It melted into nothing.

Chapter 23 – The Old Folks Aren't Alright

'James, are you okay?'

'Yes.'

'Are you sure you're okay? You've been so quiet the last few days. Is it because you've fallen out with Faye?'

'No Mum, I've not fallen out with Faye.'

'But you know you can't see her anymore because Faye's mum will call the police.'

Stixx threw the last morsel of Weetabix into his mouth. 'I'm not going to see Faye, and I'm not upset. My best friend is in hospital in a coma, or haven't you noticed?'

'It's going to all be okay, you know that, don't you? I love you, you know that too, don't you? I really wish you could stick around today so we could chat. I think that we should really do that.' She hugged him and Stixx got a heavy dose of his mum's perfume, *Brand Death to Small Marsupials*.

'I've got to go, Mum. I've got some friends to see, and I've not seen them all Christmas.' That was an out and out lie. He had no friends to speak of other than Red and now Faye. He hadn't even been in touch with Fat Les from his old workplace since being fired. The thought hadn't even entered his head.

'We need to have that talk!' Margie called after him as he left the house. Mothers always needed to talk, it was a universal rule.

Faye was waiting for him at the church, sat on the low wall looking curvedly gorgeous as usual in her red duffel coat. There was no sign of crap Alan and his crappy hatchback car, he was pleased to see. 'So, where's the ball and chain?'

'Alan wanted to come, but I asked him not to. I told him that this was our thing and if he loved me, he needs to stay out of it.'

'Did you really say all that?' Stixx went and sat next to her. She had perfume too. An Alan gift, he imagined.

'No, not really. Alan is busy – he's got to visit all his family today and wanted me to go as well. But he understood this was an important thing to me, too... the investigation, I mean.'

'And let's face it, three's a crowd!' Stixx gave her his best goofy grin to say he was joking, but inside it was exactly how he felt. There was a slight pang of guilt as well. It made him think of Red, and he knew that even if Red was well he might still be happier if he had Faye all to himself.

Faye just gave him a look, of the 'don't mess with me' variety.

Stixx decided to move it on. 'So, do we have a vague plan?'

'Don't we always?'

Ten minutes later and they were stood outside *The Hollies Retirement Home*. 'Quite a nice name for what's basically a death camp,' Stixx offered, but Faye didn't seem overly amused.

'So this is how we play this...' Faye started to tell him at length. The detailed intricacies of 'the plan' went on for another five minutes. Stixx tuned out a little, not because what Faye said was in anyway boring or uninteresting, it was more about Stixx's tingling sensation he got when she talked so intensely, like someone playing music up and down his neck. He loved her laughter lines, the light brown freckles on her nose... her nose full-stop. As well as every other single detail.

'Stixx, are you in any way, shape or form, listening to me?'

'Yes.'

'And to paraphrase the plan?'

'In a nutshell?' Stixx frowned.

'In any shell you like!'

'Well two things, or prongs, about sum it up, I guess... nobody in the old folk's home staff knows us. And B, the old folks are basically all mental, or they wouldn't be there. So we have a good chance of bluffing our way in!'

'And look at this,' Faye said, producing a small Christmas parcel from her pocket. It was wrapped in neat pink wrapping paper. 'I bought a glass ornament from the gift shop on the front this morning. Twenty quid!'

'Shame we're not on expenses,' Stixx said. He was feeling a little bit nervous. Role playing at school had never been his strong suit.

The Hollies was a grand Victorian detached house set on an elevated terraced garden. There were about a dozen such buildings along the cul-de-sac, some divided into flats, and others kept whole by rich people with big families. Stixx and Faye walked up the gravel driveway and the gently rising path to the front door. 'I think it smells funny already,' he said, wrinkling his nose.

'You are funny, not!' Faye pressed the ancient looking doorbell, and deep in the bowels of the house an electronic buzzer sounded out. It felt like an eternity before doors began to clank and keys turned in locks.

'It sounds like Fort Knox in there,' Stixx whispered, just before the door opened and Matron Anderson was standing at the door. Stixx knew it was Matron Anderson because the name badge said so.

'Can I help you two?' Matron sounded all business. Not like the *Carry On* films at all.

'We've come to visit our great aunt, June Dowling. We've been overseas for years and we're dying to see her again.' Faye sounded convincing to him at least.

'I'm not sure June is scheduled for guests today, I'm afraid.'

'We're literally just off the boat... err, and plane. We've only really just got back to this... err, our country,' Stixx managed. He was pretty sure his face had just turned magenta.

'What my brother means, is that we feel really bad not seeing her for so long. We've bought her a lovely little present and would love to be able to give it to her personally. We'll be very quick, I promise.' Faye had those puppy dog eyes out again. Stixx didn't want to be her brother.

'Well, I don't know. Perhaps you should just give the next of kin a quick call, just to be on the safe side. Mr Dowling, your father or is it uncle?'

'Don't do that!' Stixx blurted out.

'What?' The Matron was frowning now. Not a good look.

'My uncle was drinking last night. He's been drinking all Christmas. Basically he's sleeping it off today.' Stixx tried the stone cold bluff.

'Hmm...' There was a noise coming from Matron Anderson's lips, a little like an electric current. She was probably going to close the door in their faces, he figured.

155

'Please Mrs Anderson, it's Christmas, and she hardly ever gets a visitor.' Faye was the personification of *Bob Cratchit* from *A Christmas Carol.*

The Matron took a step back, and made some space. 'You'll have to be very quick, and in future you'll have to make a proper appointment. Come this way.' She beckoned them into the hallway. Stixx smiled at being right. There was, indeed, a bad smell.

'It is a real shame your uncle doesn't visit anymore. He used to come here a few times a week, and a year ago he just stopped coming over. I do hope his medical problems are on the mend.'

Stixx and Faye just ignored her. She didn't seem to mind and kept on chattering. They passed a lounge area off the hallway. Stixx looked in briefly and saw an ancient woman sat in an old fashioned armchair. She seemed to have dislodged her false teeth, which hung out of her mouth like a dirty white and red worm. Stixx averted his eyes.

'Miss Dowling is one of the youngest we have at *The Hollies*,' the Matron went on. Based on the woman with the escaping teeth, that probably wasn't saying much.

'She's only sixty-three years old. It's a tragedy how people's bodies can sometimes betray them.'

'What do you mean?' Faye asked, as they started up the wide carpeted stairs to the next floor. Looking at the floral design, Stixx thought the decoration was even more out-dated than Margie's.

'June Dowling is suffering from a form of early onset Alzheimer's disease. She has had it for a number of years as you should know. She has good days and bad ones. I think today is fairly good, but I can never be sure how long it will last.' The Matron gave them both another quizzical look. Stixx thought she was probably smart enough to work out that they weren't really relatives, and that they were trying to blag their way in here. Perhaps she sensed they had good motives, and thought a visit by a couple of friendly faces at Christmas wasn't going to hurt anyone.

'This is her room,' Matron Anderson said, and knocked on the white painted door. On the wall outside Stixx noted there was a black and white picture of the promenade. This one wasn't a hundred years old. Stixx put it twenty years at the most judging by the parked cars. There was no one in it he knew. The Matron didn't even knock before she opened the door and they all walked in.

June Dowling was sat at her dressing table, combing her hair in the mirror. She had a vacant, almost childlike face. Her long grey hair made her look a great deal older than her sixty-three years. There were framed pictures everywhere, on the walls and the marble mantelpiece, next to her bed on the bedside tables. It was her dead daughter he imagined, the one who committed suicide after Heathers Jr had his way with her. This was going to be the awkward part.

How far gone was she?

'Your niece and nephew are here to see you, June,' Matron said. 'Isn't that nice?!'

June turn around on her stool and smiled. She didn't speak, she just blinked, searching for some recognition that couldn't be there.

'Great to see you again, Great Aunt,' Faye said, reaching forward and touching her hand: making the connection. 'We've been abroad Auntie, but we're back now, and we thought we'd come and give you some Christmas cheer.'

Stixx noticed then that there wasn't a single Christmas decoration in the room. *Perhaps she didn't believe in it anymore?*

'Aunty, I've got you a present.' Faye gently handed over the gift. 'Sorry we weren't here for Christmas Day.'

June was silent, still looking a bit unsure. She was smiling a little though and held the present in the palm of her hand.

'Go on Auntie, you can open it, you know.'

June opened it and the grey box inside. She pulled out the glass swan like it was the most delicate thing in the world. Her eyes were full of wonder. Stixx thought it was nice, but also thought their chances of getting any useful information was somewhere between slim and none.

'I'll go and get us all some tea and biscuits,' Matron said quietly. They had won their alone time and had to make it count.

'June, you have a lovely daughter, do you know that?' Faye's words instantly had an effect. Sadness descended over June's face like a shroud. There were no words yet. The clock was ticking. She pressed on. 'What happened, June?'

'He… he broke her.' The voice was faint. Far away. 'He broke her!' She was louder now.

Almost too loud.

'Who broke her, June?' Faye asked, still holding her hand. They had maybe a few minutes.

Stixx felt bad for the old lady, but in the end they were trying to save some lives here. And anyway, who was to say she'd even remember any of this in a few hours' time?

'Heathers. That bastard Heathers! The police wouldn't save her. Nobody would save her. Nobody would stop them!' The old lady was talking fast now. Not really looking at them anymore. She was looking inward, remembering things that hadn't faded into the blackness of the brain disease.

'Do you mean Sergeant Flint?' Stixx asked, but she didn't seem to hear.

'I knew what they were doing in the woods. It was wrong. It was wrong…'

'Who was in the woods, June? Who was with the Colonel's son?' Faye was squeezing her hand, wanting to dig into the truth. Once Matron came back it would be over. There would be no covering up how upset June had become.

'Heathers was the worst. Heathers was the devil! What he did to her... the marks on her skin that never came out… the blood, then the scars.' There were tears now – big ones rolling down her cheeks. They definitely had gone way too far.

'We should go,' Stixx said to Faye, a little pleading entering into his voice. They both stood up and moved to the door. They had to get out now, before things got even worse.

What had they been thinking, coming here?

'There were three devils in the woods, doing their evil little dances. I saw them once when I couldn't find her. Do you know where she's gone? Where has she gone?' Her eyes were wet and bulging. She was looking straight at Stixx – straight through him.

'Who was with Heathers and Flint, June? You can tell us.'
Faye was speaking fast. Stixx thought he could hear the Matron
in the corridor.

'I don't know you! You're not my blood!' June was shouting
now, not holding back. 'Who are you? You're devils too, aren't
you?!'

Stixx opened the door and pushed Faye out into the
corridor. June's voice was booming out and other old people had
started shambling out of their bedrooms like ripe zombies,
attracted by the commotion, murmuring under their breaths.
Stixx slammed the door shut and they headed to the stairs. One
of the members of staff hurried past them, heading towards
June's room.

'Let's just get the hell out of here!' Stixx said to Faye, and
took the lead down the stairs. The Matron was at the bottom of
the stairs, a tray of tea and biscuits in her hands.

'Where are you two going? I've just gone to the trouble of
making all this.'

'Something just came up,' was the best he could come up
with. Matron heard the shouting then. June hadn't exactly calmed
down by the sound of it.

'Wait here!' The Matron sounded like she meant it.

Stixx waited until she was out of sight. 'We need to get out
of here right now.'

'Another fine mess and all that,' Faye frowned.

Stixx was relieved to be out in the freezing air, away from
the odours and claustrophobia of the nursing home. There was
the sound of a rapidly opening window above them and the
unmistakable voice again. 'I told you to wait. I've called the
police. I don't know what you think you were doing, but you're
in serious trouble.'

Neither of them looked up. They kept walking until out of
sight, and then broke into a jog to cover ground.

'They don't know who we are,' Stixx said breathlessly.

'She said there were three devils. What the hell was all that
about?'

'The Colonel?'

'That would make sense,' Faye said.

159

'We're not going to stop, are we? Not until we catch that thing?'

'We're just getting warmed up, Stixx! We're onto something, I just know it.'

They were unstoppable.

Chapter 24 – Beyond the Valley of the Friend Zone

'Hello, Stixx!'

It wasn't necessarily said in a completely threatening way, but it wasn't exactly pally either: somewhere in-between, with a lean towards the homicidal. Faye's mum stood blocking the threshold to her house before relenting and stepping aside when Faye appeared behind her.

'Mum's going to be very nice to you from now on, now I've explained that we weren't in that police station for any of those nasty nefarious purposes. I've also told her you don't suffer from any of those weird mental illnesses that some people have.'

'Neffa-what?' Stixx said under his breath.

Faye and her mum's house was a neatly decorated modern bungalow. Her mum must love her ornaments, Stixx thought. The vases told him that much, all perched on various vigourously polished display tables in their hallway. Faye's mum branched off towards the kitchen, and Faye gestured for him to turn into the lounge like an extremely cute traffic cop. Stixx half-expected Alan to be sitting there writing a thesis or something and was glad to see the room was empty. He did hope her mum made them sleep in separate bedrooms.

'So here we are,' Faye said, sitting next to him on the lush-green couch. 'I can't believe after all this time, this is the first time you've come home with me.'

'Well, I did walk you to the door a few times. I get brownie points for that, don't I?'

Faye's mum bustled into the room, two mugs of tea in her hands. She took her time putting them onto coasters on the coffee table in the centre of the room. Stixx felt she was looking at him and expecting him to wreck the place at any second. 'If you want any biscuits just give us a shout.'

'Thanks, Mum,' Faye said. Definitely the subtext in the tone was, *sod off!*

When she was out of the room, Stixx breathed a sigh of relief. 'You know, I don't think she likes me all that much.'

'You reckon?' Faye had the wrinkly nose thing going on again. It was like something out of *Bewitched*. There was an awkward pause and they both sipped their tea. 'Mum's just overly protective. She's not a mean person, but after what happened with my sister and my dad… well you know, it's to be expected.'

Stixx looked properly at the pictures on a corner table for the first time. There was a young girl with dark hair in them all, sometimes next to a young version of Faye. Fixed forever in time. Like Rachel Dowling, it was only photographs that remained of a young life.

'Your sister was pretty like you,' he said at last.

'For a bit of a dope, you can be fairly charming sometimes. You know what would be fun?'

When Stixx saw Faye dig out a bottle of red wine, vodka, and Malibu, out of a corner cupboard in the room with all the stealth of a seasoned cat burglar, he had a fair idea what she had in mind. It was three o'clock in the afternoon.

'We're going to my room to watch a film,' she said, and was disappearing along the corridor before her mum was even halfway out of the kitchen. Faye's mum gave him a look with daggers in it, but he couldn't think of anything to do other than shrug and follow where Faye had gone.

'So what do you think, cowboy?' Faye pulled two glasses off the floor and blew the dust off.

He was totally amazed to find Faye was even messier than he was. The bedroom was an exercise in organised chaos. The walls had artwork ranging from pictures with completely random paint strokes, to a huge one that swirled in yellows, blues and reds into a giant vortex or whirlpool. The paint was so thickly layered it stood up in great ridges on the canvas. A high bookcase against one wall seemed to mix books with cactuses, jewellery, and other random objects such as unopened luxury soaps in a display case.

There was a desk facing the window covered in sketch pads, loose paper and pencils. There were at least three different cups on the table, one of which appeared to be growing a new life form. 'Hey, what is this here?' he asked holding up a piece of paper. There was a pencil drawing of him wearing his best going out shirt, sat at a table in the local pub. He recognised it as when they'd first met. 'You must have spent hours on that!'

'Maybe five minutes tops!' She tidied them off the desk and pushed the drawing out of view. 'So what's your poison?'

They settled down onto two bean bags and started to watch a DVD of a *George Romero* zombie film called *Land of the Dead*. It wasn't exactly good, but Stixx didn't mind because mostly they just drank wine and talked over the top of it anyway. Faye said she liked zombie films because zombies were the only thing that scared her. It wasn't long before Stixx began to feel the warmth of distinct tipsiness begin to drift over him.

'So you know a bit about my fucked up family, but what about you, Stixx? What's your story exactly? It seems like in all the chasing around we've been doing lately you've not exactly given much away. Why so secretive?'

Stixx didn't really think of himself like that. What he did think was his story was pretty boring stuff. He also knew deep down he was a little intimidated by Faye. He wasn't as smart as her. He had left school at sixteen. He had no prospects to speak of, other than perhaps this vampire hunting. 'What's to tell?'

'Come on. Let the wine unwind that tongue a little.' She poked him in the ribs, hard enough for it to hurt. 'Spill!'

'Geez, you're a tough one. Okay, I don't know who my dad is. If you want to find some drama or whatever in my life, I guess that's it. My mum would never tell me. She always either clams up or changes the subject. Margie will talk about nearly anything on Earth, but I mention my dad ever and I might as well be talking to a brick wall. There are no photographs of him in my house I can find. My birth certificate says unknown. I have no fricking clue who the guy is!'

'That's awful. What's with that?'

'I don't know. You get used to it. He was probably just some deadbeat or whatever.' The wine was making him feel more emotional than usual. On the screen the zombies were getting smart and heading to the skyscraper where all the humans lived. They didn't seem that scary to Stixx. 'So, do you still see your dad?'

'Do you mean do I visit him? He's locked up for life in the mental health wing of a prison. And no, I don't ever want to see him again.'

'Will he ever be released, do you think?'

'If he is, then I'll kill him!' Faye looked away and went silent for a while, just watching the film. Stixx figured she must really mean it.

'My mum is a bit scatty,' Stixx said to change the subject. 'You know some people are a little flakey…'

'What like psoriasis?' He saw Faye had faint tears in her eyes.

'No, like she is a bit, you know… unpredictable. She has moved around a lot. You know before I was born she actually lived in the village for a few years. Then I was born and she hit the road. I think the first ten years after I was born she moved every year, always to totally random places like Cornwall and then the Scottish Highlands. I don't even remember half the places she went to because I was too young. I remember having my tenth birthday on the Isle of Man when we moved there. It was crazy!'

'Then she came back here?'

'She had a brainwave to get the guesthouse, and scraped the money together somehow. She still talks a lot about wanting to sell up and move on, maybe go abroad. But now I'm old enough to talk her down off the ledge.'

'So have there been other fellas in her life, crazy step-dads?' Faye opened the vodka. She was on a roll now.

'Nobody to speak of really. Sometimes she used to disappear, leave me with that Mrs Phillips for a few days. Nobody ever moved in properly. I saw her being dropped off back at the guesthouse sometimes, different guys, different cars. Not very often though. Mum can be a little secretive, I suppose. I've learned to live with it. Any step-dads for you?'

'I think after my dad, my mum's basically sworn off men altogether. She's basically a nun – a nun with a large vibrator!' She had the giggles. It was infectious.

When she stopped laughing, she started talking about Alan and basically wouldn't stop. If he didn't know better it could have been Brad Pitt she was talking about, such were the descriptions of hunk-ness hidden under the cardigans. Faye told him he'd been at the same sixth form college as she was, that there had always been *a chemistry* between them, even if they couldn't act upon it because it would have been wrong then. At one point she actually used the words, *'star crossed lovers.'* For a second Stixx thought he'd walked into an episode of *Hollyoakes* when he wasn't looking. He nodded his head, appeared interested, and drank a lot more vodka.

'So where is he then?' Stixx said at last. He'd half-expected the loser to walk unannounced into the bedroom at any moment – the cherry on top of the cake.

'Oh…' Faye said, pouring more vodka into her own glass, and offering him a top up. 'He had to go back to his teaching job in Ghana. He only came back to see I was alright. Alan was never supposed to be here at Christmas anyway. It was very lovely of him to come all that way, don't you think?'

'Oh yeah!' Stixx watched Denis Hopper get eaten by a zombie. If he squinted his eyes, he looked a little like Alan.

After the film finished, Faye disappeared to cook frozen pizza. Stixx took the opportunity to rummage through her room a little. There was no sign of a tell-all diary. He found condoms in a bedside drawer, hidden under some girlie magazines. There were old empty medication packets as well. He read the label on them – Ritalin. He'd heard the name before. It was a type of anti-psychotic medication.

Heavy stuff.

Stixx sat briefly on the bed.

Springy!

And then sat back down on his bean bag, a little guilty now for being so nosy.

A few minutes later Faye brought in a steaming Hawaiian and a meat-feast pizza. She put on a fresh DVD to watch. More zombies - Spanish ones this time. The film was called *Rec* and had a documentary crew being chased around an apartment building. It was making him feel a little dizzy, although that could just have been the vodka. 'How did you get those marks on your arms,' he asked randomly, instantly regretting the question.

'What?'

'The marks… on the inside of your forearms. I noticed them the other day.'

'Well, what do you think they are?' She was looking defensive.

'Sort of like knife wounds kind of thing?'

'I self-harmed for a while after my sister died. No biggie. Pretty standard stuff really, my psychiatrist said.'

'You had a psychiatrist?'

'Still do.' Faye washed the last of her pizza down with a gulp of the strong stuff.

'Oh!' was the best he could come up with.

'You know what scares me even more than zombies, Stixx?' He detected a slight slur on her words, just a faint one.

'Maybe werewolves?'

'I'm serious, man. This is from the heart okay. I'm scared that the genes from my bastard father that make him so mad and twisted,' Faye said, her fingers dancing in the air, '…that those genes are in me as well. Nobody can really say if I'm a bit mad because I'm meant to be, or a bit mad because of what I went through living with him. Nobody knows if I'll get better or worse. All I can do is keep popping those little white pills and hoping I'll turn out okay in the end. That I'll never hurt or kill someone I'm supposed to love.'

Stixx twisted around and hugged her. He didn't think about it, or analyse it, he just did it. Faye sobbed on his shoulder for a solid minute. He put his hand around her waist and held her tight.

'I bet I look a right old mess now,' Faye said, coming up for air. For a while they settled down and watched the film. He checked his watch – it was already past 8pm and dark outside.

As the credits came up on the film, Stixx leaned across Faye's body and went for a kiss. Her lips were soft, wet and pulling away.

'What was that?'

'You know what it was.' Stixx was the one on the defensive now.

'Stixx you know I don't see you like that, don't you?'

Somewhere deep inside his chest his heart was disassembling into small parts. Small ants were taking the chunks of meat towards a roaring funeral pyre.

'Well, how do you see me?'

'Come on, Stixx, we're friends. I like you heaps. We're on this crazy mission together!' She pushed him on the shoulder like he was her kid brother. He was older than her, he was sure he was. It was hard to think with all the vodka inside him and he had an impulse just to leave. Stixx shrugged away from her.

'I'm nobody's friend.' He stood up, tottered back a little and braced himself on Faye's desk. He wasn't drunk. *Tipsy maybe, just slightly tipsy.* 'And now I'm leaving!'

'Don't be an asshole, Stixx. You knew I had a boyfriend. He's probably going to propose soon.'

Stixx had decided not to listen to any more of the cruel words. He tried to ignore Amanda coming out of the lounge, who had her usual disapproving look about her. 'And you...' he started to say, '...you I don't like much either!'

He walked out into the freezing evening and stubbornly decided not to look back.

Chapter 25 – Faye

Faye threw some more water on her face, willing the headache to disperse, or at least ease off a notch or two. Red wine and vodka had been a *bad idea.*

She had gotten carried away more than usual. It hadn't helped that she had carried on drinking after a certain James *'The Strop'* Stixx had had his little hissy fit and stormed out of the house.

Faye looked down at her phone next to the washbasin – the little silver box of delight wasn't lighting up. She'd sent him three text messages and left a pithy voice mail. She'd even apologised, after all she knew she'd hurt his feelings. Popping two pills out of their little foil home, Faye dry swallowed the paracetamol.

'Mum, I'm going out,' she called out as she left the house. There was no reply – the silent treatment. Faye dimly recalled a fairly typical mother-daughter argument had also featured after Stixx departed. The gist of each of their contributions to that particular lively discussion had been somewhere along the lines of, *'...you're wasting your year before university hanging out with a total loser. He's a petty criminal who will drag you down. I wish we'd never moved to this village. Look how much you are drinking. It will affect your medication and your mind is a delicate thing. You don't want to end up being sectioned again... blah, blah, blah!'*

Faye's counter-argument had mainly revolved around her launching the vodka glass in her hand into a picture of her dead sister on the wall, and making four lettered suggestions on the theme that her mother was an annoying fucking android. At some point after midnight Faye passed out on her bed, face down and fully clothed.

Faye figured her mum could stick her guilt trip where the sun didn't shine, and walked out heading for the centre of the village. There was a weak winter sun in the sky, masked by a thin veil of wisping clouds. It was around a degree above freezing. The stone walls on the route had a two inch crown of snow and the road was covered by tyre tracks and compacted slush. Faye pulled her phone out her pocket and texted, *I'll meet you at the library. Stop being mad at me please x.'*

It was the 29th of December, and Faye knew this was one of the few days the village library would be open over the festive period. She wove her way down the road that led towards the promenade, took a side road, and finally found a small steep lane that took her to the steps of the library. There was a light on in the high windows. She kind of hoped Stixx would be there waiting, the usual idiot grin on his face. Faye went inside feeling disappointed.

The library was one of the smallest she had ever been in, no more than ten gun metal bookshelves in a space no bigger than a decent-sized living room. The first shelves were filled with books with *VERY LARGE PRINT*, catering no doubt for the village's older, near walking dead type of clientele. There was a small desk and chair at the far end of the room, but no sign of any customers or staff. She walked further into the room. At the far end there appeared to be some kind of dimly lit art display for local artists.

'Hello, Faye,' a quietly spoken voice said. Faye barely stifled a scream.

She turned, ready to fight, claw and scratch, to do whatever she had to do. The man standing in the corner didn't look like a threat. Spindly and wizened, he was a small man, perhaps approaching sixty years old. His crumpled suit didn't look like it had ever seen an iron. He was holding a small pile of children's books. *Ant and Bee.* They brought back childhood memories.

Her favourites.

'Timothy Berkley, chief librarian. I don't believe we've had the pleasure.' Timothy was offering his hand.

'I'm pretty new around here,' Faye said, still feeling unnerved, with no idea how he would know her name. 'I don't believe we've ever met before.'

'I've seen you in the papers, dear. You saw that *thing* in the field, didn't you? Lucky to be alive they said! I've been somewhat under the weather myself. Christmas flu. Barely over it, in fact.' Berkley sneezed, and produced a linen handkerchief from his pocket. Faye wished she hadn't shaken his hand, and rubbed it on her jeans in a way she hoped he wouldn't notice.

'So what's your poison? Perhaps a little *Dickens* for New Year, *A Christmas Carol*? Or perhaps some *Stephen King*? We have plenty of those if you don't mind the large print.' He tried to shepherd her towards the bookshelves on the other side of the library.

'That's not really what I came here for Mr Berkley, although I'm very, err, taken by your enthusiasm. It's very impressive!' Faye decided some flattery might help her cause. 'However what I'm looking for today is your newspaper archives. Your website says that you keep a complete record of the local paper here somewhere. I'd love to be able to see it... for research purposes.'

'It is a real shame...' he began to say. Faye's heart sunk. *If they drew a blank here...*

Berkley went on, '...that you young people have to work so hard. Essays and projects over Christmas, what a waste! University or sixth form? I can't place your age very well.' He stepped closer to her. Close enough that she could smell extra strong mints on his breath.

'Just sixth form history, I'm afraid.' It was an easier lie to sell than pretending to be at some university already. It would just be her luck that he would know whichever one she picked intimately.

'Well then, you are in luck. We have the records you seek, but not in here I'm afraid.'

'Then where?' Faye began to feel excited.

'Somewhere with no heating, unfortunately.' Berkley was pointing downwards with a bony finger. 'Down in the vault.'

He led her past his desk and into the back area where the art collection hung. From his pocket he produced a large bunch of keys and spent an age selecting the correct one. 'This is the only one I have. You can't be too careful, I find.'

Faye was beginning to think he was a bit of a creepy little fucker.

He opened the side door and flicked the light switch on the other side. There was a set of stairs heading down into a gloomy space below. Faye got a distinct sense of deja vu and wondered if she really should be doing this alone.

Perhaps she should go and find Stixx?

The mobile phone in her hand was still blank, her text messages unanswered.

'What are you waiting up there for? Come on!' Berkley said from halfway down the stairs.

Faye followed him down into the basement. He was right; it was as cold as a refrigerator down there. 'The heater busted nearly five years ago. The council are getting around to it soon apparently,' Berkley told her airily as Faye began to shiver.

Unlike the library floor above, there was nothing orderly, neat, or even particularly clean about *the vault*. From the sheer quantity of dust on every surface it was clear whatever cleaner the library had, their duties did not extend to this cramped space below stairs. The walls were lined in a mixture of obsolete and broken furniture and shelving, and boxes of slowly decomposing books that would probably never see the light of day again. At the end of the room was a small table, and what appeared to be some form of ancient chunky computer.

'Like I said, we don't get many requests for research here. In fact I'm really not sure if this little baby even runs anymore. Its innards may well be fried chicken by now,' he said, tapping the top of the grimy monitor the size of an old-fashioned portable television.

Berkley flipped a switch somewhere at the back, and after a brief electronic flash the machine started whirring and beeping. *Perhaps this was how Frankenstein's monster was created?* Faye pondered.

The screen threw up green coloured text and the librarian started pressing the return key. Faye noticed then that there wasn't actually a keyboard to speak of, just a few clunky buttons like a kid's play set, and a large flat space where she imagined the photo rolls fitted.

'There can't be many of these microfiche machines left in the county.' The guy seemed pretty proud to have one.

Berkley went to a filing cabinet hiding under a dust sheet. He produced another key off his magic key ring, and began to pile up boxes next to the machine. 'Now, I wouldn't want to exaggerate or to blow my own trumpet so to speak, but basically what we have here is the local weekly rag, *The Westmorland Gazette* reduced to microscopic size from approximately 1970 through to 1995. After that they switched to computer records. The end of an era, you could say. I should probably add that only in theory do we have these old records. The reality could be these boxes now home generations of rats or other vermin.'

Faye looked apprehensively at the three small boxes on the desk. She was too cold to particularly care if there were rodents, as long as they didn't bite her.

'Thanks.'

'I'll leave you alone, then. I promise not to lock the door. I wouldn't want to scare the local celebrity.' He was edging away from her, walking backwards: a creepier little man she had never met.

'Give me a shout when you're finished down here, or I'll have to send out a search party.'

After he left, Faye realised he hadn't even explained how the damn machine worked. *She was smart, she would figure it out.* Tentatively she opened the first box, ripping off the old cellotape. Inside were tightly packed A4-sized sheets of what looked like film negatives. She held one up to the dull desk light and saw the miniature boxes containing text and pictures, each box a page of *The Gazette*. She pushed the sheet into the machine and pressed the key. The screen lit up with a bright green rendition of the page. It was dated December 1994, and the headline read, *'PARISH COUNCI CONSIDERS A FREE BUS SERVICE.'*

This was going to be a long day.

It took Faye a further hour before she found anything that wasn't mundane, boring, or instantly forgettable. On page nine of the 17th August 1984 edition there was a short column regarding the inquest into the death of Rachel Dowling. It was so small that she nearly skimmed past and missed it.

'Today at the coroner's court it was ruled that Rachel Dowling took her own life by way of overdose. Her mother, June Dowling, was inconsolable and had to be assisted from the body of the court by police officer Sergeant

William Flint, who had earlier given evidence of discovering the body at Rachel's home address in the village of Greystones. Rachel was twenty-three years old...'

There was no mention of any causes or pending court cases. Faye's mind raced. *The Heather's sexual assault had obviously been buried. Flint covered it up and kept it to himself. He'd even taken her mother out of the way when she got too upset.*

Faye kept digging in the boxes, moving forward in time. She checked her watch, wondering how much longer she would have before the library closed. Pressing a button on her phone she noticed it didn't even have reception down in this dungeon.

Mention of the Colonel, Heathers Snr, did pop up from time to time. Usually it was only the briefest of mentions regarding his corporation buying or selling some land, or building, in Greystones. The company seemed to have owned pretty much everything in the village at one time or another. There was an entry for the purchase of the closed down Ridgeway Convalescent home on Hill Road; *'COLONEL PLANS APARTMENT COMPLEX FOR VILLAGE.'* For whatever reason it never happened, and nothing had ever been built. There was no more information she could see.

In 1994 it looked like the village had issues with gypsies. There was a picture of caravans and old battered vans in a field next to the woods. *'GYPSIES STAY ILLEGALLY IN VILLAGE,'* the headline sang out. The article stated that twenty Romany gypsies, including children, had set up a temporary home on one of the Colonel's grazing paddocks. Faye enlarged the photograph. Unmistakably, she could see in the background of the picture the same distinctive horse drawn gypsy caravan they had found in the photograph Flint kept in his safe.

There was another entry a few weeks later; *'GYPSY UPROAR! ARRESTS AS THE CAMP IS CLEARED.'* The article said a court injunction had been granted and the gypsies were forcibly removed. There was a picture of police in riot gear and batons drawn, marching into the camp. There was no sign of the horses or horse drawn caravan in this picture. It must have already been removed by then, Faye thought. There was a quote

173

from one of the travellers. *'Nobody cares about us. We can even disappear and nobody notices. The police do nothing.'*

There was a noise on the floor above, a series of heavy thuds like bookcases toppling over, a faint cry for help. The handle on the door at the top of the stairs rattled. She knew instinctively she was in massive trouble. Faye backed away from the machine and tried to melt into the shadows.

Chapter 26 – The Criminal

Stixx was hung-over and late. He also could add extremely tired to the growing list. Yesterday's clothes were in a heap on his bedroom floor and would do just fine.

Memories of the night before were already making him cringe. Would Faye ever acknowledge him in the street, never mind speak to him? Being so rude to her mother had probably sealed that deal.

Finding his mobile phone under the bed changed all that – she had texted him like nothing had happened. It was nearly lunchtime, but knowing Faye she would still be at the library. At the bottom of the stairs Margie popped out in front of him like some jack-in-the-box. 'Where are you going in such a rush? I've made breakfast... your favourite.'

'Not now, Mum!' Stixx had to physically duck under her arm. She clearly didn't want him to leave. 'I won't be long, okay?'

Outside Stixx hurried, half-walking, half-running his way to the library. The last message he'd received had been roughly an hour and a half earlier. He texted her back, *I'm coming. I'm also sorry about last night. See U soon x'* He would make it up to her somehow. From now on he would be Mr Mature.

Stixx headed up the steps to the library. It had been years since he'd last been inside, but heading through the outer door it still had the same distinctive smell of polished wood. The second inner door was partly ajar. There was a crumpled looking paperback wedged in the gap. It looked damaged and Stixx picked it up.

They should look after these things better.

He walked into the library reading the back cover, not really concentrating. The book was something to do with a romance between a Russian ballet dancer and a prince. It looked totally unreadable.

When Stixx looked up he realised the entire library had been trashed. There were shelves torn off the wall – hundreds of books on the floor. He looked around wildly, wondered if the person responsible was still in the room. There was a stain on the brown carpet, dark and probably red. He knew what it must be.

Where was Faye?

He shouted out her name, then shouted it again. He moved towards the back of the library, where there were torn and broken pictures and glass frames all over the floor. He picked up a wooden leg off a smashed chair and weighed it in his hand like a club. *It was better than nothing.*

There was an open doorway, and the stairs heading down into darkness. If Faye was looking for local records then they would have been down there, he knew that. He dialled '999' on his phone as he edged down. 'What is your emergency…' the operator cut off suddenly as the reception dropped out. There was a shape on the floor at the far end of the room, something crumpled and still. It could only be a body. Stixx edged nearer, tried to say 'Faye' but the words caught in his throat.

Stixx heard a wet sound and realised he was standing in a pool of blood. It was all over his trainers. It wasn't Faye, it was a man he didn't recognise. His throat wasn't there anymore, just a gaping empty hole. He could see white bone. Stixx ran back to the stairs, his legs feeling like rubber, dizzy with adrenalin.

Upstairs there were people in the room now. He couldn't process it.

'PUT DOWN THE CHAIR LEG!'

It was an order being shouted at him.

Stixx stared blankly at the two police officers, and saw more coming in behind them. They had their batons and taser guns out. He had red light dots dancing on his chest. 'There's a body down there,' Stixx managed to say, the words feeling thick, and ill-formed on his lips. He dropped the chair leg onto the floor with a *thud.*

That was their cue, they charged him. Stixx found himself bundled to the floor and roughly handcuffed behind his back. 'You're under arrest sunshine!' one of the officers screamed in his ear. 'Criminal Damage just for starters!' They pulled him to his feet and frog-marched him towards the outside doors. 'There is a body!' another officer shouted behind him. 'For God's sake, watch him.'

They thought he was dangerous.

'Faye is missing. My friend Faye Burns. You've got to check that she's okay!' Nobody was listening to him. Stixx was pushed towards a police van parked on the promenade. Already a small crowd was gathering. A journalist flashed a camera in Stixx's face. He was marched past Sergeant Flint who just casually shook his head. He saw dry mud on Flint's boots, soil streaks on his police jacket.

In a daze, in shock, Stixx found himself inside a reinforced clear plastic cage inside the van and was being driven out of the village. 'WHAT ABOUT FAYE?' He shouted it through the plastic. The officer on the other side just stared blankly at him, muttering something to her colleague he couldn't hear.

The van pulled sharply into the rear yard of the town police station. Already they had the custody area doors open, expectant faces waiting for them. Stixx felt like a proper criminal for the first time in his life. They were treating him like he was a murderer. Behind him he heard an excited babble of voices and before he was pushed inside the police station he glimpsed more journalists rushing to get into the courtyard area. It was all a horrible mistake.

Where was Hastie?

The custody sergeant appeared quite nice: a calm reasonable voice among all the tension and testosterone of the officers flanking his either side. Stixx hadn't held back, he demanded information about Faye.

'We're looking into it. I can assure you James, we are looking into it,' the custody sergeant answered. It was probably all a front. Stixx didn't trust any of them.

'But have you found her yet?' There was wildness in his voice, something approaching a total breakdown.

'We ask the questions,' the officer to one side said. Short, gruff and Scottish. Familiar from the hospital trips. 'Have you got any sharps?'

Later they stripped him naked in an empty cell and left him there with a blue paper suit and a blue PVC-coated mattress for company. Every fifteen minutes the slot on the metal door slid open and a pair of eyes looked in on him. There was nothing to

177

do but wait. Stixx didn't have a watch and was losing track of time. He had declined to have anyone told he was there.

Stixx imagined the longer he could delay his mother finding out, the better his eardrums would remain. Not that they would let her see him. It occurred to him that perhaps he'd never get to see anyone again. He could see himself behind Perspex glass with a telephone in his hand, talking to his ageing mother – the only person who would ever visit him in prison while he served out a life sentence. He thought of Faye being buried and not being allowed to go to her funeral, if they ever found her body. Stixx felt sick.

There was a red button on the wall. Stixx pressed it. Two minutes later the slot opened.

'What?'

'Just get me fucking Hastie!'

Another hour later Stixx was brought to an interview room and told to sit on a chair. There was a police tape recorder in a unit on the wall behind him.

What was it with police still using tapes for their interviews?

He would have asked the two police officers staring at him from chairs against the far wall, but they didn't look much for the small talk.

A familiar stooped figure walked into the room. The officers on the wall straightened their backs as if subconsciously saluting. Hastie had that sort of effect on people. 'No phone call, no brief… we are living dangerously, aren't we?!'

'Is Faye alright?'

Hastie didn't hold his stare any longer, looking away as if suddenly the small opaque window high on the wall was fascinating. 'We haven't found her yet.'

'Jesus! When can I leave?'

'Does it look like you're going anywhere?' Hastie had both hands on the desk in front of Stixx. Fingers like sausages.

'You can't seriously be thinking… thinking I could have killed that man? Eaten the guy's throat out? What sick fuck does that?!'

'A lot of people think you do, Stixx. The papers will be filled with it tomorrow.'

'Fuck the papers. I want to get out of this prison and go and find her. Can you please just let me go?' Stixx eyes got teary.

Hastie was staring at him, his eyes boring into him. 'Do you know much about gut instincts? You probably don't James, even if you live your entire useless life by them. So why should a person trust their gut instincts, James? It's science, that's why. It's your subconscious doing the extra hours for you, figuring all the shit out for you. And I bet you're sat there thinking now that good old Inspector Hastie is going to let you off the hook here, let you go free to burn down police stations and kill librarians whenever you get a fucking itch you think you need to scratch. But you know what my instincts are telling me now... they are telling me to lock you the fuck up. Get you remanded FOR MONTHS, James! And keep you the hell out of Greystones before we have even more bodies piling up in your fucking wake.'

Stixx twisted in his seat, trying to process what the hell Hastie was going on about. He wondered if he was going to stop jawing on at some point, and start beating on places where bruises didn't show. 'Look, I didn't kill the librarian, or Marco's parents or those two coppers or the two men that certainly weren't having a gay bonk up on The Hill.'

'Don't forget the three journalists, two of which stayed at your delightful three-star guesthouse.'

'I've got fricking alibis for most of that stuff, Hastie. And have you forgotten that big shit-stomping vampire type lunatic that put Red in a coma? It wasn't only me and Faye that saw that one!'

'I don't know how you are involved, Stixx, but somewhere along the line you are connected, even if you don't realise it... right the way up to your scrawny neck. I know it... I can smell it, Stixx.'

Stixx leaned forward on the interview desk and pushed a plastic cup of water out of the way. 'Can you taste it as well, Inspector?' Stixx said smiling. 'Well, I've got a tip for you. If I'm up to my neck in this, then that fucker Flint is buried under ten tonnes of the stuff. If Faye has disappeared then he has something to do with it. I'm telling you that now.'

But then Stixx trusted his own instincts and back-pedalled. He kept the details about Heathers Jr and Rachel Dowling and any mention of the three devils to himself, which basically left him saying that Flint had mud on him when he was arrested. Hastie looked less than impressed.

'It's actually very ironic. Sergeant Flint is the only reason why you're not being bussed off to Durham prison right now, on remand for murder.'

Stixx shifted in his seat again. 'What?'

'Well the sergeant was good enough to say he witnessed you walking along the promenade to the library about five minutes before the boys in blue arrived en masse. Even a slickster like you, Stixx, couldn't have wrecked the place, messily killed the librarian and the disappeared Miss Burns in that timeframe... not to mention clean yourself of all that blood. What that leaves us with is two viable possibilities – either Faye did it herself... which is possible but unlikely. Or your friend from Planet Transylvania has made another appearance. I am prepared to provisionally go with the latter.'

Stixx experienced a plummeting feeling. The floor was opening up. 'Where the hell is Faye?' *And what the hell is Flint up to, giving him alibis like that?*

'I won't kid you, Stixx. There was other blood at the library. And I'm telling you this, even though you have no real right to know. We think Faye Burns may have been taken.'

Chapter 27 – Missing

He had spent the night staring, awake for over twenty-four hours. Stixx had lost count how many hours he'd examined the ceiling of the tiny police cell with forensic detail, while Hastie and his investigators no doubt chewed the fat, choosing the criminal charge.

Any charge that would stick.

Then in the early hours of the morning, with the sun peeping over the roof of the police station, he'd been cut loose with a promise that they'd want him to return for follow-up interviews. Arrangements were made and he was driven back to Greystones by a heavy-set Jamaican-looking officer, who said his name was Greer. But instead of walking through his front door for a grilling by his mother, Stixx had walked straight into the village. Straight to the library, for whatever that was worth.

It was cordoned off, of course. Yellow police tape was stretched across both the upper and lower entrances to the library lane, guarded by police sentries. Stixx could see the familiar white-suited Scenes of Crime officers making in and out with clear plastic evidence bags, full of books, it looked like. He imagined they must have paid for Christmas with all the overtime they have racked up in the past week or two. Stixx noticed a media van parking behind him, with the journos inside already eyeing him up. He didn't want the hassle, so quickly turned and walked away. One of the last things Hastie had said to him as he had gathered his belongings from the custody sergeant's desk had been, *'Get ready for your trial by media now, sunshine!'*

Stixx found himself on the beach, tracing the pebbled jagged path around the curving estuary. There was nobody around other than dog walkers and the occasional fisherman, trying their luck with the local radioactive flounder. As Crocodile Dundee had once said, *'You can eat that stuff, but it tastes like shit.'*

Stixx kept on walking, trying to gather his thoughts in a head that felt full of candyfloss and dead air. He was numb. *Maybe he was in shock?* Faye was out there somewhere, trapped and injured, Maybe even close to death. He rounded the next bend and saw the first evidence that people cared, that people were looking for the girl he loved more than anyone or anything.

There was a line of police estate cars on a farm track off the beach, with open cage doors at the back. Policemen had excited looking dogs on leads, setting out on the numerous paths that led from the beach up through the woods and onto The Hill. Stixx reminded himself there was still a policeman out there somewhere too, missing, no doubt presumed dead by now.

Stixx imagined this was the same all around the village, people looking for the missing girl they barely knew anything about. Stixx thought her picture would be in the national papers, another victim of the vampire killer. The whole country reading it and expecting her to turn up dead and mutilated: *just another victim.*

He spat on the ground. It wasn't true and it wasn't going to end like that. He edged closer to the policemen. There were others, people from the village, no doubt offering to help with the searches. More eyes on him, not friendly eyes, eyes that said we know what you did. No one was saying hello or offering any of the flasks of coffee that seemed to be getting handed around to everyone else. He was a pariah, but he didn't mind that. He was used to that.

Stixx didn't linger, and pressed on around the bay. He didn't really have a real plan or a destination in mind. The path broke down into a combination of wave-smoothed limestone and ankle snapping rocks shelving downwards towards the water's edge. Way back in the village life boat station he heard the faint boom of the bore tide warning, signalling the approach of the fast-flowing inrush of water from the sea: a miniature tidal wave.

He remembered nearly drowning on more than one occasion with Red, trying to body surf with pieces of timber that barely kept them afloat. The fleeting memory triggered more emotions. Too often these days he was forgetting his best friend, lying in a coma. All those adventures and crazy turns they had done. His feelings for Faye were drowning Red out, tuning him out of his head. He felt so alone.

Stixx found himself up on the cliff path, walking faster now. The water had come in quickly to cover the salt marsh glass and flat quicksands on this part of the coast. Far Greystones, a tiny hamlet of no more than a handful of houses a few miles from his village, had come into sight. He remembered he'd passed by here once with Faye, on the first day after he'd met her. Stixx remembered taking her on a tour of her new surroundings, a tour that had ended up at his little cannabis enterprise and barely escaping Flint and Heathers Jr.

Stixx saw a faint outline of a path around the next tree, heading steeply upwards towards The Hill. Stixx left the cliff top and followed it – a random decision. Out of breath, he knew why nobody used it. The path was treacherous with mud and tree roots, and generally steep as hell. The exertion was a welcome distraction from all the depressing thoughts constantly circling around his mind.

Finally there was a clearing, a small field in fact, halfway up the climb. It was elevated enough that it afforded him something of a view of the estuary and beach, and the horseshoe curve of the coast. Inland he could see the woods and fields that marked the Colonel's estate. Hidden there, Stixx could make out one corner of the great house, the mansion where the recluse lived with his son and probably a whole array of minions and butlers. Stixx stood and stared for a long five minutes, searching for some inspiration that finally escaped him.

Hours later at the guesthouse he pushed his way past three journalists, not answering their questions, barely even hearing them. During the long walk back he had been excited by the thought that Faye had been found, that she would be safe again, perhaps in a hospital bed. In his mind he had imagined he could visit and bring her books and grapes – that they could just live quietly and forget about all this vampire rubbish. Stixx didn't even care if she did marry Alan. Instead he would happily settle for being her best friend.

But a journalist shouted, *'Do you know where Faye Burns is?'* to him as he pushed his front door open. The illusion shattered and he knew she was still lost, still out there.

Still dying.

His mum had hugged him and cried, like a vice with a water leak she had squeezed him and refused to let him go. 'This has to stop, Stixx!' she said over and over.

'I know, Mum. I know.' But he didn't mean it, not even slightly.

Later he ate her food, and dozed fitfully on the couch as *Sky News* played in the background. The police had issued a statement. Apparently he was, 'helping them with their inquiries.' It was as if he was guilty already. If anyone needed a scapegoat he would be it. One talking head journalist on the TV called the village, '...a place of death and mystery now gripping the nation.' Outside the guesthouse Stixx could count five news vans – a new record. Later his mother roused him from the couch and pushed him up the stairs to sleep in a proper bed.

Five hours disappeared in a heartbeat before bad dreams began to surface, along with a full bladder. The worst of the exhaustion had passed and he lay on his bed spooked by the shadows in his room. Every time he closed his eyes he seemed to see Red being bitten by the thing in the fields, or worse now, Faye being drained, bleeding and alone, waiting to die. Finally he couldn't stand the anxiety and the fear any longer. Stixx dressed silently and slipped out of the house.

At somewhere near midnight he found himself back-garden hopping to avoid the waiting media. The excitement of feeling like some kind of fugitive for a moment pushed the last tendrils of sleep out of his body.

Stixx found himself wandering past more places he had been to with Faye – the church and the vicarage were both in darkness. No doubt the resident vicar, McClintock, having long retired to his slumbers. There was no one around. No wind in the trees, just the crunch of his boots on the icy road.

Aimlessly he carried on through the streets, using the cut-throughs and hidden paths where possible rather than the main roads where he would be easily spotted. At the back of his mind he knew what he was doing, he wanted the thing from the field to seek him out, to find him. And then it would talk to him. It would tell him where to find Faye, even if he had to break every bone in its body. Stixx felt like he didn't even need a weapon in his hands. There was an energy running through his body now, like an electric current. Something that couldn't be stopped.

At some point he found himself about to take an unlit path down to the beach when he heard the engine of an approaching vehicle. If it was the media he would run and lose them. Momentarily blinded by the headlights, he could make out the distinct shape of a police car. It pulled alongside him and the passenger window whirred downwards.

'James Stixx out on the prowl again, I see.'

Stixx strained his eyes to see the two officers in the patrol car. It was dark in the car's interior.

'What do you want?' Stixx answered. It didn't come out sounding friendly.

Both car doors opened simultaneously and the officers approached him. Stixx didn't recognise either one of them. 'Have we met before?'

'We've been around,' the ginger haired female cop said. Her pale skin shone white in the moonlight. 'We met your friend Marco the night his dad was killed. We heard he gave you something of a beat down that night, as well.'

'What can I say? Marco has a mean left hook when he feels like it.' Stixx took a pace backwards. Ginger's partner, a tall Asian looking person was edging closer. He had seen him before, another officer from the town. He thought they might be preparing to jump him, to haul him back to the cell.

'We're just going to search you, okay?' he said. 'Nothing for you to get excited about.'

Stixx held his arms out. He had nothing to hide. He knew he had to go with the flow. They could find nothing other than his door keys. If he had been carrying anything resembling a weapon he had no doubt he would have been arrested on the spot. He knew he was a marked man now.

A target for nearly everyone.

'So why are you out so late Stixx, in these dangerous times we are living in?' the ginger-haired officer asked. She had a calming voice and seemed genuinely friendly.

'Not your concern.' He noticed her flinch a little when he said it. Stixx knew he was being an asshole, but being the nice guy wasn't going to get Faye back alive.

'Steady there, Mr Stixx,' the male officer was trying to calm him down with his gloved hand rummaging in his pocket. Finally they both stood back. Ginger went off and talked in hushed tones on her radio, far enough away so he couldn't eavesdrop. She didn't take her eyes off her partner for a second. They obviously thought he was dangerous.

'Can I go now?' Stixx asked finally.

'Of course you can, James,' the Asian officer said. 'Nobody said you couldn't.'

Stixx walked across the road and straight down the path to the beach. They couldn't follow him down there. He felt a little mad, a little violated, and couldn't seem to throw the feeling off. It sat in his stomach like bad indigestion.

A half hour later he was outside the house, not pressing on the doorbell. His fist was hammering on the door. Nobody was answering though. Nobody was home it looked like. He hammered on anyway. It felt kind of good. There were murmurs of voices somewhere behind him, from the other neighbours. He turned and saw a few people in their windows watching, some with phones in their hands. The sun was coming up. It was dawn already.

'FUCK YOU!' he shouted at the house. He knew Flint was inside there somewhere, hiding with all his secrets and lies. Stixx walked away.

For now.

Chapter 28 – New Year's Resolution

New Year's Eve arrived in a blur. Stixx had barely eaten. Food seemed tasteless and a waste of time.

He wasn't an idiot; he knew the chances of Faye still being alive were next to non-existent. There was no solace in that thought, no reprieve from the certainty that he was now very much on his own.

Nobody had seen the killer vampire for two days. There were no new leads he knew about, although to read the newspapers anyone would think it was Stixx who held all the vital clues. The truth was he had nothing. And any second he expected the police to come along and serve him up like some kind of sacrificial lamb. He felt he was as every bit as doomed as Faye.

Over the last few days his mother had continued to watch his every move, his every expression. This was a marked contrast to the lead up to Christmas where she had always been out running one errand or another, even if she had chosen not to reopen the guesthouse after giving the journos the heave-ho. Even the regular guest Mr Schmidt had packed his bags and left early. Stixx doubted they would be seeing him again in a hurry.

So Margie had sat with him, eaten with him, and basically followed him around the house all the time he wasn't sleeping. It was driving him crazy. Not just fun crazy either – crazy, tear your eyes out with a spoon crazy.

In Stixx's nineteen years he felt, generally, he had shown a decent amount of honesty when talking to his mother. In the last few days that had disappeared, along with everything else. He promised not to go out at night. Swore on people's lives he wouldn't go out again after dark. *And yes he knew he could be killed, that he could just disappear, and people still loved him.* He had watched his mum's tears rolling down her cheeks like buses on a regular service route. There would always be another one along in a minute or two.

It was the numbness that made the lying easy. As soon as the sun went down he planned to be out the door again.

Searching.

He just didn't care about lying or deceiving anyone he had to. There was a purpose in him, a singlular purpose to find Faye. There was no plan as such, no real hope of success. But the drive and desire burned in him, and it wasn't going to be stopped by a few tears. He would find her or die trying.

But by New Year's Eve his mum had finally worn him down. Perhaps it had been her threat to call a doctor and have him sectioned. Or maybe it was when he looked in the mirror he barely recognised the haunted face staring back at him, the black rims around his eye sockets, and worse, his dead eyes themselves: eyes without hope.

Zombie eyes.

Stixx knew Faye wouldn't want this, wouldn't want him to wear down until there was nothing left. He knew that soon he wouldn't function properly; wouldn't be able to help her or anyone.

'Give yourself a break, James,' Margie had pleaded that day. 'I know what you're going through. I know how much you care about Faye, and how much you want to help save her. But just stop for one night. Think about something else, even if it's just temporary. Even if tomorrow it all has to start again." Margie paused. 'I've asked someone to meet you.'

'What! A fricking doctor?' He felt the anger boiling up, ready to spill over.

'No, it's Faye's boyfriend Alan. He's very worried about what's happened, obviously. He says he feels partly responsible. Alan wants to have a drink with you down the pub. Just go and give each other some support. It will be good for you, James.'

'I can't believe you did that, Mum! With Alan? For God's sake, the guy is a cretin!'

'I made you better than that. Just do that one thing for me, okay? Be nice, see in the New Year. Go and enjoy yourself for a few hours. It would mean the world to me.'

Stixx relented. Anyway, he figured that perhaps Alan had heard some information that the media didn't know. It wasn't like the police were telling him a thing, even if he was ringing up practically every hour. He wasn't family, but Alan near as damn well was.

Alan could have some answers.

Stixx walked into *The Noble Man* at around 7.30pm. It was still over half-empty as most of the village's more youthful members preferred to go to town first and get the last train back into the village at around 9.30pm. Still there were plenty of 'regulars' to stare at him when he came through the door. He wondered how often his name had come up in pub banters over the past few days. If he was a betting man he would have said a lot.

Alan was propping up the bar, and by propping up Stixx meant he was sat on a high bar stool looking like a well-dressed moron. 'Hello, Alan!'

'Stixx, good to see you.' Alan gave him a hug. There was a slight slur on his words, like a lisp. He had a large glass of red wine in front of him on the bar. 'What can I get you?'

Stixx went with the local *Thwaites* lager. He would save the German beers for later. 'How long have you been back?' Stixx dived into the small talk, blocking out all the people staring at his back.

'I came back this morning. It feels like all I've done this Christmas is bounce around on planes. I don't know what to do, Stixx.' There were genuine tears in his eyes, real feelings. It made Stixx feel a little fake.

'What have they told you?' By *they* Stixx meant the police.

Alan went on to outline nothing Stixx didn't already know. There were no leads. There were no suspects beyond him.

'The librarian has brain damage. He can barely string a single sentence together. The police think he may need a carer to look after him the rest of his life.'

'So he's basically a semi-vegetable?' Stixx's comment didn't seem to overly please Alan. There was a frown on his goatee face. Even inebriated he was still a pompous asshole as far as Stixx was concerned.

Half a wine bottle later and Alan had his finger waving uncomfortably close to Stixx's face. It was in his air space and was likely to be shot down sometime soon.

'You know I had my doubts about you. Everyone has you pegged as a suspect in the papers, and probably around the village too. But not the police, not the people that count, otherwise you wouldn't be sat here now. You'd be in prison already, being bum-raped and trying to get on library duty, or whatever people do inside… I don't know.'

Stixx could see Alan was going to struggle to even make it to midnight at this rate. 'You're not what one would call a good drinker, are you, Alan?'

Alan wasn't listening. '…but I know Faye trusted you. And I trust Faye. In fact I loved Faye… which, of course, makes this all very sad. Anyway, I know you and Faye were onto something. I don't know exactly what it was, because Faye couldn't or wouldn't articulate it to me. And frankly I don't want to know that much. I might travel a bit Stixx, but I'm not built for danger.' With that, Alan slipped off his bar stool and staggered off in the general direction of the toilets.

Stixx saw that people were filing into the pub now, and filling up the spare seats. The last train from town had obviously arrived. Stixx recognised a few faces from the past. Some had gone to the same village junior school as he. Some had even gone to the same secondary school. At best they were barely acquaintances he never kept in touch with. None came over to say hello.

There was another face hiding in the crowd, a face that made his skin bristle.

Sebastian.

Sebastian of the funny toilet graffiti and who he last saw falling unceremoniously into the store Christmas tree after he had pushed him. *What the hell was he doing here?*

'Another round?' Alan was back on the barstool next to him, slurring enough that he might not get served by the barmaid.

'No, my shout!' Stixx opened his thin leather wallet. There was enough Christmas money to last him another day or two. It dawned on him he would need to get a new job. There was the prickling reality that he would have to go back to his mundane dead-end job existence, left to be haunted by the girl who lit up his life for two short minutes. God, he hated New Year!

He moved on to German pints. The pub was so noisy it drowned out most of Alan's drunken warbling. At one point he talked about buying a house for him and Faye to live in: 'A nest for the future.' It made Stixx feel miserable and inferior.

He found his eyes wandering around the room, people watching. Stixx estimated that over a hundred people were crammed into the small pub like sardines. He caught sight of Sebastian again, seated near the bay window. There was one of the local village girls with him. Perhaps a girlfriend? Sebastian caught him looking, and raised his drink in his direction. It was wine as well.

He'd probably love Alan.

'So, do you have any ideas?' Stixx was nearly shouting to make himself heard. A pub band started to play in the corner. The increased noise felt like it was invading his every pore. He felt sweat rising on his forehead.

'What?'

'Do you have any ideas how we can find her?'

'You've got to let the authorities do their job, Stixx. It's what they are trained to do. I'm just a teacher, man!'

'You're an asshole!'

'What?'

'YOU'RE AN ASSHOLE!'

Stixx rocked off his barstool and pushed his way through the crowds to the door. 'Hey, watch it psycho!' He'd knocked someone's drink so it slopped over his hand and shirt.

Outside, the wind off the estuary bit into him. Fresh ice had formed on low railings on the edge of the beer garden. It would be another bitter night. Stixx crossed the road and wandered slowly over the rise that led to the pier. He could see silhouetted figures on there, fixing up the fireworks display they had at midnight every New Year. He checked his watch: 11.52. Time had flown. It was a cloudy night, nothing to see over the bay but inky blackness.

'Hey, Stixx!' Alan was skittering down the path towards him. 'Why did you just take off like that?'

'There's going to be fireworks. It's a village tradition.'

People from the pub were trailing past them, waiting for the show. Sebastian was one of them.

Fucking Sebastian!

'Faye would have loved this.' Alan might have been crying again. Stixx wasn't sure in the poor light.

'I hear you've got yourself in a bit of bother.' The voice instantly grated on him. Sebastian was standing up close to him, breathing alcohol fumes on him.

Did nobody have any concept of personal space?

'...did you hear me, Stixx? I said...'

'I'm not fucking deaf, Seb. What do you want?'

'Just to see in the New Year with my woman. What else is there?' Seb was spreading his hands. He had a champagne bottle in one hand. His other arm was around the local girl. She looked barely fifteen. 'You should enjoy it Stixx, from what I hear they are going to put you away pretty shortly. That temper of yours got you in trouble in the end, didn't it?'

Sebastian was on the ground before Stixx even realised how much his knuckles hurt. He looked down at the offending fist. It had a mind of its own sometimes. The fifteen year old was crying. There was a shout, 'Someone call an ambulance!' A crowd formed around Seb, his champagne bottle smashed and spilling over the road. The fucker looked just fine to him.

Play acting a bit.

People were staring at him like he was some kind of monster that had just confirmed everything they said about him behind his back. Stixx looked at Alan, but he had moved away too, the same wary expression on his face as everyone else. The fireworks began to explode in the air overhead. Stixx turned and hurried away.

Chapter 29 – A Radical Solution

Stixx sat on the low wall of what the locals called *The Boat Yard*, although it hadn't contained a single boat since a 1980 storm had turned a number of expensive yachts into matchsticks.

It was now no more than a rubble-filled concrete space looking out over the estuary, but close enough to Greystones that Stixx could still see the last of the midnight fireworks erupting over the bay. Watching the bright exploding lights, he tried, and failed, to collect his thoughts. The clouds seemed to be clearing and there was just enough moonlight to see his breath condensing in front of his face.

Stixx half-expected to see a line of locals with pitchforks and burning torches coming to get him. Nothing would surprise him anymore. What he did know was he had to keep moving. It was so cold that he could feel his veins furring up with frost – his red blood cells being weighed down with ice. He stood up and stamped his feet. He had to get going again.

An idea popped into his head. Not a particularly rational idea. Not an idea Faye would have sanctioned. But Stixx wondered what he really had to lose. Stixx knew he was around five millimetres short of the police pinning a murder rap on him. There had been so many deaths in the village he was losing count. He'd seen enough TV series to imagine that the hunchback bastard Hastie was under some pressure to get a result.

Any result.

Would a jury ever believe that he was innocent, that he wasn't somehow tangled up with all those bodies somehow? A flash of anger ran through him then: the thought that Faye would never have a chance to defend herself. That the two days she had been missing would soon stretch to a week, a month.

Forever.

Picking up the pace, he cut up off the beach, looking for the most direct route he could think of to get him to where he wanted to go. It was pitch black on the forest trails, the leafy canopy above blocking out the night sky. On occasion he slipped on the icy-smooth limestone that appeared everywhere. There was a boiling anger inside him. If the vampire came for him now out of the blackness, he would tear it apart. There would be nothing left but bloody entrails and pointy teeth.

Short of breath, Stixx dropped down the steep path on the far side of O'Halloran Hill, trying not to break his neck. This was the first New Year's Eve he remembered ever spending outside for any length of time. He estimated it must be at least minus eight degrees centigrade, maybe even colder. Ten minutes later and he was next to the boundary fence. He didn't stop, didn't even think about stopping. He knew if he did, it would be over. There were no more neat clues. The only card he had to play was one of blunt force trauma. He realised if he was going to go down, it might as well be in flaming wreckage from a very great height.

Colonel Heather's mansion was enormous. There wasn't another house or building anywhere near the village that was as big or as grand. Stixx wasn't sure of how old the building was, or even what type of architecture it was. The white-painted walls reminded him a little of The White House. He supposed that the Colonel had for years been the unofficial ruler of the village, pulling the strings that nobody else even knew were there.

Walking around the perimeter he tripped a security light and was bathed in white light bright enough to make his eyes burn. He ignored it and tried a set of French doors, both sides of which were securely fastened. Stixx wondered about alarms. This wasn't some dumb church, and he knew he wasn't just going to find a handy window open. He was going to have to gamble. *There were no other options left.*

Alongside one of the great lawns Stixx found a rock big enough to suit his purpose. Then he half-threw half-pushed it through one of the French door glass panels. He held his breath and waited.

No alarm.

Not an audible one at any rate. Stixx threaded his hand through the broken window and turned the latch to open the door.

The manor house was vast. He knew what he had in mind wouldn't exactly be easy. Stixx tiptoed along the long hallway, aided in part by a table lamp that cast a dim light at the far end. Stixx's first impression of the Colonel's grand residence was that it was a classic aristo-type set up. There were numerous huge portraits filling up walls of vast height. He presumed they may be older generations of the Heathers' family line.

Standing at the base of a particularly grand staircase, Stixx knew that somewhere in the manor there would also likely be the semi-psychotic Heathers Jr: the wild card. What he really needed was a map, and more importantly some luck for a change. Stixx padded up the lushly carpeted stairs with hardly a creak. There was really nothing Miss Havisham about the Colonel's house, the whole place was spotless and immaculate. Somewhere in the bowels of this place could be an army of staff, Stixx thought.

At the top of the stairs Stixx stood under a painting of what looked like a giant wolf hound.

So many choices.

In the end he decided to follow the corridor with the most light. He had no idea where it was leading, and it crossed his mind that perhaps now would be a sensible point to retrace his steps and get the hell out of there. He didn't though. He didn't have anywhere else to go. Stixx started to try the doors.

The first one he opened took around a minute of painstaking, silent, slow-motion teasing. By the tenth door he was pretty much wrenching them open without much of a care. Each room appeared as bare as the next, with little more than a cold fireplace and a wooden floor on show. Stixx moved up to the floor above, losing track of how long he'd been inside the great house. The clock was ticking. A faint smell in the cool air caught his attention. It was familiar, but he couldn't place it. There was more light in this corridor, *strange blue light.*

Stixx looked closer at one of the table lamps. It wasn't a normal lamp or a normal bulb. It was a UV lamp, which Stixx knew according to the movies made vampires' faces melt off. He guessed there must be a few people in the village doing strange stuff like buying UV lamps now. He also knew he must be near to where somebody had their bedroom. Around the corner he saw a whole corridor filled with the blue glow, UV lamps spread at short intervals.

He was close.

The garlic and possibly the crosses on the door gave it away. Clearly somebody with a large fear of vampires was going to be inside this room. Stixx only hoped they didn't own a crossbow or other deadly weapons. It would be somewhat annoying to have come so far out on a limb only to be killed stone dead. Stixx put his hand on the doorknob and twisted. Well oiled, it didn't give any resistance. A blazing fire in a vast fireplace was giving out a ferocious heat. Stixx flicked a quick glance around the room; four-poster bed.

Empty.

An arm chair was facing the fire. A wrinkled hand.

'It took you long enough,' the voice said, deep and guttural. Stixx had a strong urge just to run. *Was this the killer?* He took a short step forward, if only to see a little more.

'Don't run,' the voice said. 'That would be quite pointless.'

The man in the armchair was ragged looking and in an advanced stage of old age. The light from the raging wood fire made the liver spots on his face practically sparkle. What little hair was left on his head looked silver more than white. The old man looked ninety years old at least, and practically shrivelled up inside his dark blue silk pyjamas. He'd surely found the Colonel.

'I've been watching since you came in through the West Wing. I even turned the alarm off so you wouldn't turn tail and run. It was very kind of me really.' There was a throaty laugh, and then a brief coughing fit. He looked too old and infirm to be dangerous. Stixx stood his ground and looked at the small CCTV monitor set up on a table next to his chair. The screen was divided into a further dozen smaller frames, each showing high resolution footage from all over the manor. 'There are simply dozens of cameras in this house. My son, Jr, is such a paranoid fellow.' That laugh again, demonstrating with a flick of his craggy finger just how many different screens he had access to.

'Are you going to call the police now?' Stixx wondered if he already had done.

'What would be the fun in that?' For an old guy he could move his head very quickly. One eye looked milky and off-colour. Cataracts.

'Where is Faye?' The question sounded stupid when said aloud. There was a slight stammer to his voice. His stomach full of butterflies.

The old man ignored the question, and drank from a tumbler of what looked like whisky. 'You're James Stixx, aren't you? I've seen you in the papers a lot lately: always in the eye of the storm. It looks a little like the world out there thinks you're a killer.'

'I don't care what those stupid journos think. Can you just answer the question and I'll go on my way.'

'Why such a rush, James? You break into an old man's home, you can at least show enough courtesy to allow him time enough to collect his thoughts. I imagine you have quite a few burning questions to ask. Please sit down.' The Colonel motioned towards the other empty armchair. 'My son usually sits there, although not so much lately. Too many irons in the fire, so to speak.'

Stixx sat down but waved the offered whisky tumbler away. The last thing he needed was to be drugged by a crazy old bastard. The heat from the fire was ferocious.

'I've heard a lot about you too, Mr Heathers. You pretty much own everything that is worth anything in this village, don't you?'

Heathers leaned towards him. When he smiled there weren't any teeth. Somewhere in the room would be a glass with a set of false teeth in it.

'Money gets you so far... in fact it gets you a long way. But it doesn't buy you everything,' Heathers hissed.

'I didn't come here to hear stuff out of fortune cookies. I want to know where my friend is.'

'All in good time, James. Aren't you the slightest bit curious why I let you in here? Why there are special lamps all over the corridor outside, crosses and garlic? Does your mind not possess such normal curiosity?'

'I'm guessing that just because you are rich, it doesn't stop you being as stupid as everyone else around here. You think there is a real vampire running around sucking out people's blood. And you know what, I saw that thing and I think maybe

197

you are right. But I'm also pretty sure crosses, lights, and vegetables, aren't going to stop that thing tearing you into little pieces.'

'Touché. Maybe you're right. But please indulge an old man's fear. Even at my age mortality is not something to be taken lightly. Can you imagine anything worse than having some foul creature pinning you down helpless whilst your neck is slowly eviscerated, feeling every drop being drained from you? That would give any man pause to create a few measures of protection. Although, granted, come the morning the lights, crosses and garlic, do appear somewhat foolish.' The old man chuckled to himself and took another sip of whisky.

'Okay you want a question, I've got one for you. That fuck-stain Flint, what the hell is going on between him and you and your crazy son? Me and Faye know he covered up some God-damned nasty rape, assault or whatever you want to call it, against Rachel Dowling. That girl killed herself and, from what I could see, it pretty much sent her mother over the edge. You tell me Colonel, if Flint has anything to do with Faye disappearing, because I think I already know he did.'

'Sergeant Flint is a troubled man, I won't deny it. He was once a good friend of my son, until Jr became too worldly for him after university. I don't think Flint ever forgave him for casting him aside as he did: all that bitterness and loneliness bubbling away over the years. He imagined all his Christmases had come at once when that slut Dowling made up some false allegations and was idiotic enough to end her own imperfect little life. Flint thought it wise to blackmail us, thinking even if the slut was dead he had enough information in his files to hand over to the media and slur our family name. It became so boring in the end we even considered handing over the deeds to that empty convalescent home on The Hill. We dangled it in front of him like something of a juicy carrot. Flint probably imagined he was going to get rich converting it into apartments, that he was going to make millions. But we knew the site was bad, riddled with subsidence and toxic soil. The surveys as good as condemned the whole area. The old home is good for landfill only, as good as worthless, alas. Still, in the end Jr didn't want to even give him that worthless dump. That idiotic little man is of no consequence to us whatsoever.'

'No one fucks with the Colonel, hey?' Stixx shifted in his seat and thought about leaving. 'So Flint is pissed off his blackmail deal of the century has gone south. What does he do? He starts to think how he's going to get back at the great Colonel and his son. And while he's thinking about it, me and Faye come along and uncover some of this blackmail shit. Now, I think he had something to do with Faye's disappearance. What happened in that library was during the day. Flint says he saw me going to the library and he's definitely lying about that. I think he's trying to make it look like the vampire did it, and he's gone and done it himself. In fact, when I've finished here I'm smashing my way straight into his stupid house to beat the truth out of him.'

The Colonel leaned closer still. It looked like there were a million wrinkles under his eyes dancing in the firelight. 'Do you ever see what's under the surface Stixx, or just what's in front of your very nose? This whole village has something of a history, James. Looking at you, I don't imagine you remember much past the last week. Officially the village was discovered in 1797 by Robert MacAoidh, who later also made the railway viaduct the villagers so love. But before that, way before all that, it is believed there was a Celtic tribe known as Ir Sentanti who lived a Neolithic lifestyle. And know what one of those is? Superstition, ritual and sacrifice is what it is, Stixx. Do you have any idea how many bleached bones have been found buried in those woods over the years? How many children's skeletons... how many baby skeletons there have been hidden in shallow pits over the years? Imagine the happy families sat on O'Halloran Hill with picnics, eating their sandwiches on a beautiful summer's day, all the time sat atop a children's graveyard. But you wouldn't hear any of that. We like to keep things like that quiet, so quiet that sensitive little ears like yours never have to hear about it.'

'Nice story. I think I was asleep there for a minute. I don't really give a shit, honestly. If it's true you know everything, just tell me where the fuck Faye is?'

'But my dear boy, I truly have no idea.' The Colonel was looking past Stixx's chair, and Stixx turned slightly to look into the shadowy corner of the room. There was a figure there. Stixx thought perhaps he had been there all along. 'I rather feel you have worn out your welcome now, James Stixx,' the Colonel said, his tone a rancid sneer.

Stixx was on his feet, stepping back close enough to the fire to feel the back of his legs start to dry out and scorch.

'Hello there, Stixx!'

He thought at least it was good the person was speaking and not trying to eat him. But it wasn't the vampire, it was the tall, ginger-haired brute Jr, and he was holding a somewhat lethal looking double barrel shotgun in his hands.

'What you want to do now is move away from my dad,' he growled.

'...so you can shoot me?' Stixx was thinking perhaps *human shield*.

'Step away, James!'

'You pull that fucking trigger, Jr, and I'll come back and haunt you.' Stixx moved away from the Colonel. He considered making a run for the door, but at the back of his mind he knew Jr would have a pretty easy time pulling the trigger before he got even two steps. Jr motioned for him to start walking.

'Are you going to let him kill me, Colonel?' Stixx tried to find the voice of reason in the room.

'Now James, my son has been known to take a very dim view on burglars. And you have broken in, haven't you? My son here is his own man and can do as he pleases.' The Colonel turned away from him, the fire dancing on his face again. Jr nudged him with the barrel of the gun, and he was pushed out into the UV-lit corridor.

'You people make me sick,' Jr said from behind him. Stixx wondered how long he would take to die when the moment came.

Chapter 30 – Red Devil

'You're one of the three devils, aren't you, Jr?! Doing sick things to that Dowling girl in the woods! Bet you got a kick out of killing all those animals too.'

At some point outside the manor, on the sharp gravel driveway, Stixx and Heathers Jr had stopped walking and started fighting.

Jr punched Stixx in the gut and sent him down again. 'I can see your mother never taught you how to speak with your betters. Perhaps it's not too late for a lesson.'

Jr was at least six foot two and Stixx guessed the ginger-haired psychopath must be at least as old as Flint, maybe his late forties. Unlike Stixx's slender frame, Jr was built like a rugby forward. He hit Stixx on the side of the head with the butt of the shotgun and sent him sprawling onto the gravel. Dazed, Stixx felt his throbbing ear and had blood on his fingers.

'That's just a warm up. They are never going to find your body. Just another mystery that can't be explained, in a Christmas full of them.'

Stixx scrambled back to his feet, one arm lifted high ready to fend off the next attack. 'You, your dad and Flint, you were the three devils, weren't you?! Some sick cult in the woods. Doing bad things and getting away with it just 'cos you had money.'

The next blow caught Stixx lower down, on his thigh. He was on his knees again, helpless and bleeding. The pain was making his vision blur.

'You're talking about very old news, Stixx. Talking out of your arse in fact, with everything back to front. I've met very many smart people in my life Stixx, and I can assure you that you aren't one of them. In fact I would suggest you are about as intuitive as a cardboard box!' Jr hit him again, a sharp jab on his shoulder with the butt of the gun, sending Stixx over onto his back. His hands burned from where he'd tried to break his fall on the gravel.

Random thoughts bounced into Stixx's head.

It was a bluff, he wouldn't kill him here... Not on the driveway of his own house...The gun probably wasn't even loaded...

Stixx propelled himself off the ground and made contact with Jr just below his knees. It wasn't so much a rugby tackle as a desperate torpedo of a move. Jr went over like a bowling pin. Stixx scrabbled on top of him and sent fists down into his face. His knuckles screamed at first, and then went numb to the pain. There was a reason fighters wore gloves.

Stixx had never tried the mixed martial art, *ground and pound* technique before. What seemed to work for Randy Couture seemed to work for Stixx for all of three seconds before Jr bucked him forwards, sending him hurling face first into the gravel again. Jr had him by the hair now, ready to dish out more pain. Then there was a flash of blinding light and the distinctive crunch of approaching tyres. Stixx felt Jr's hold on his hair loosen a little and managed to roll away from him. Flashing blue and red lights told him it was a police car.

Stixx saw boots in front of his nose and looked up to see Flint's unpleasant scowl looking down at him. 'You're making friends in high places I see, James. Can you not stay out of the shit for more than a single day?'

Stixx felt fairly elated to still be basically in one piece. 'That fucker has a shotgun!'

'The Colonel rang to say you'd burgled his house. You wouldn't be the first intruder here to get filled with buckshot. Looks to me like you got off lightly.'

Jr was on his feet next to Stixx and kicked him hard enough in the ribs to wind him. Stixx's eyes watered and he curled up holding his middle.

'Who says I'm finished with you? I've got all night!' Jr announced.

'I think the lad has had enough,' Flint said firmly, and pushed Jr backwards with an open hand. 'You were never very good at knowing when to stop, were you?'

'You want to do this now, do you?' Jr said, and spat at Flint's feet.

'Get in the car,' Flint said in a low voice to Stixx. He wasn't stupid enough to disagree and crawled into the passenger seat of the patrol car. Through the glass he watched Sergeant Flint face off with Heathers Jr. There was a blur of movement and Jr was back on the ground. Flint had the shotgun in his hands, open, and throwing the two cartridges into the field beyond. It had been loaded after all.

So much for instinct.

Flint climbed into the driver's seat of the patrol car and drove them away at speed. 'You might be a fucking idiot, Stixx,' Flint said. 'But that fucker is a whole different league.'

The trees flashed by and Stixx wondered with all the ice on the road how likely it would be that he would now die in a tragically ironic motoring accident. *What would the papers write then?* 'Can you slow down a little, Flint? One near death experience is enough.'

'It's only two a.m, Stixx. The night is young.' Flint gave him a funny look. The look didn't speak of law and order, police officers and pillars of the community. The look reminded him of a programme he had once watched on television about lunatic asylums. Flint looked like one of the inmates.

'You can drop me out anywhere, Flint. I've really had enough.' Stixx's ear was aching and with his fingers he felt crusted blood forming.

Flint didn't reply. He didn't stop. The village was racing past as they descended on the road that headed down to the promenade. Flint veered off left, taking the turn that led towards O'Halloran Hill Lane with enough momentum that the back wheels of the police car skittered out and fishtailed. Flint was laughing now, but not a natural laugh. 'You never lose it, Stixx. I did a police pursuit course twenty years ago. *Twenty years.* The skill is still there buried in my skull, waiting for days like this.'

Stixx could smell alcohol on his breath. He was drunk, and he noticed that he wasn't even wearing a tie. The police radio wasn't switched on. There was no way he was on duty officially. 'I guess you will get to drive fast when they ship you back to the town with all the other community coppers?'

Flint punched him on the arm, hard enough to bruise. He was laughing again. 'Well, you burning down my police station pretty much sealed the deal on that one, didn't it? They want me to retire now. Thirty years of service and they want to push me out with a lump sum and a pension. But I'm not here to talk about my problems, Stixx. It seems the time has come to set you straight on some more pressing issues, before you go and burn the entire village down.' Flint was accelerating the police car. The speedo read over sixty miles an hour.

'Can we not do this in the morning?'

Flint had that inmate look on his face again. The patrol car hit the base of the steep climb up O'Halloran Hill hard enough that the suspension bucked and the tyres briefly scraped on the wheel arches. Stixx knew where they were going and felt his heart rate increase another notch. He didn't forget about Faye though. He wouldn't run until he was sure she wasn't there.

Flint parked the patrol car close to the old garages of *The Ridgeway* convalescent home. 'Did the Colonel tell you this should have all been mine?'

'He said you tried to blackmail them with what happened to Rachel Dowling, that this whole place is pretty much worthless anyway. They fucked you over, didn't they Flint?!'

Flint looked at him from the shadows as they stood next to the home. 'Those two are on borrowed time. Now come on, let me show you around.' Flint gave him a push forward. He had a set of keys in his hand. 'You and Burns have been doing a lot of digging around haven't you? While Hastie and the rest chase a vampire, you break into my house, my police station... you chase me instead!'

'What happened in the library, Flint? What the fuck did you do with Faye?' Stixx was no more than a foot away from Flint's face. He was ready to fight again, for what it was going to be worth.

The sergeant turned away and pushed a key into the lock of a side door. 'I'm not the enemy here, Stixx. It's about time someone lifted those shutters off your eyes and got some truth in there. Just because I have a Hammer Horror poster or two in my house and have locked horns with the Heathers, does not mean I go around kidnapping and killing people. Now come on, because we have plenty of other things to talk about.'

Stixx thought of Faye and walked ahead into the blackness beyond the door and found himself in some freezing hallway where he couldn't even see even a foot in front of his eyes. 'Get some lights on for Christ's sake!'

A face loomed up towards him, making Stixx nearly topple over in fright. It was Flint playing a joke, lighting up his face with a torch. 'Afraid of a little darkness, are we?'

Flint shone the torchlight ahead and set off walking. 'This place was a palace back in the day; a palace for the infirm and the sick to rest and get some relief from their tired little lives. Do you know, at one time they even had a ward here for people with leprosy? Well segregated from the rest of the residents, of course. I mean who suffers from leprosy anymore? This place is immense. It could house two or three thousand people. It would literally be filled with people.' Flint was babbling at him. It was clear he was obsessed with the place.

'Yeah, that's fascinating, but are you going to get to something resembling a point Flint? Is Faye here somewhere?' They were in an enormous room with what looked like a very high ceiling. Flint flashed his torch around. It looked like some kind of circular ballroom.

'You really are quite taken with Faye Burns aren't you, Stixx? I would have thought she was quite out of your league. The papers described her as a smart, academic young woman, with a very bright future. And then there's you, who can't even hold down a job stacking shelves in the local supermarket. What did you think was going to happen after you stopped chasing the vampire around, Stixx? Did you see her marrying you and settling down in this shitty village? Well I suppose there is a vacancy going down at the local library now.' Flint was laughing again, in that slightly unhinged way.

'Fuck off, Flint, I'm leaving!' Stixx walked out of the light, and started to retrace his steps out of the ballroom.

'Now don't be like that.' Flint's voice came from behind him. Stixx went to reply, but his foot slipped on the shiny polished floor. There was some liquid on it. Flint's torchlight illuminated the wet patch just as Stixx was torching it. It was dark and sticky, and undoubtedly fresh blood. Stixx started jogging, getting some distance between him and Flint.

'What the hell are you doing, Flint?' Stixx shouted back. He ran blindly, knocking a wall table over. There were too many corridors by the look of it to be sure of the original route. He saw light on the stairway ahead, coming through a window on the landing above. Stixx made the decision it was better to have light than stumble around in the darkness, and ran up the stairway.

'Where the hell are you running off to? I was only joking around. Don't be so sensitive about these things!' Flint was shouting after him. Stixx could hear the rage in Flint's voice plainly enough. He meant him harm.

Stixx ran down a corridor, using another window at the end as some form of guide. He knew two policemen had been killed in this building, and kicked himself for letting himself be brought here as well.

'Slow down, Stixx. You're going to suffer for making an old man run.' Flint's voice was at the top of the stairs. He was tracking him. It probably wasn't hard with his footsteps echoing loudly on the old wooden floorboards. Stixx took a corridor that branched off, then another one. He hoped he wasn't just going around in a circle.

Tiring, Stixx turned another corner and saw a doorway. Inside, he could just make out an old wooden stage raised at one end of the room. It looked like a small theatre of some kind. Perhaps the former guests like to put on Gilbert and Sullivan productions to pass the time. Stixx strained his eyes to make out what was in the room. He passed a stack of metal chairs, but that wasn't enough to conceal him. He jumped onto the stage, panicking because there seemed nowhere to hide. The stage sounded hollow when he landed on it, so Stixx looked for a way inside, brushing his hand around the wooden surface, while all the time his eyes looked towards the door, expecting Flint to come bursting in at any second. Finally he found something: a handle.

A trapdoor!

He pulled it up and pushed the thought of a thousand spiders out of his mind. Trying to control his breathing, he jumped down into the black space.

For what felt like five minutes he heard nothing, then the door creaked and there were footsteps on the wooden floor. There were tiny chinks of light coming through the floor of the stage above Stixx's head. He felt exposed, like at any moment an eye was going spy him through one of the gaps: that soon he would have company in the darkness. The dust was heavy in the air. Not for the first time he gripped his nose in his hands to stifle a sneeze.

Above him the wood creaked. The footfalls were softer, harder to follow than he imagined Flint's would be. Stixx couldn't see, but in his gut he had a terrible feeling it wasn't Flint in the room, that it was someone or something else. His mind began to race. He hated himself for not running. *What madness thought it was a good idea to hide under a stage?* He was going to die here.

The feet above moved again. There was another creak on the stage and it sounded as if the person or thing was now stood directly on the trapdoor. Stixx wondered if these were the last seconds of his life, that somewhere there was a clock ticking down for him.

A final countdown.

His heart felt it was ready to explode and finish the job anyway.

A cracking sound. Stixx thought it was the trapdoor being lifted, but then he heard the light footfalls moving away. He realised that whoever it was had jumped off the stage and was moving towards the door again. Stixx was sure it had left him. He closed his eyes and listened even harder. There was nothing to hear. It would be a waiting game.

How long it was he waited, he wasn't sure. It was still dark outside, there was no change in the light as yet. Then he heard voices. Raised, shouting voices. They weren't close enough that he could make out the words, but there was definitely more than one person. There was a female voice in there, he was sure of that. It somehow fortified Stixx, made him feel safer. It must be the police, or at least enough people that he could be safe.

He stood up, and feeling braver by the second pushed up the trapdoor. There was no one else in the room, but the door to the room was ajar, not as he'd left it. The voices came again, raised but still garbled. He guessed they came from the floor below. Stixx tiptoed across the room. If the vampire was in the building, he knew the sounds should distract it from him as well.

Stixx was sure he heard the word 'Flint' shouted from below and hoped it was other police officers, finally come to arrest their crazed colleague. He went to the stairs and descended. It had gone quiet again. There were no external doors he could see. Stixx had no choice; he picked a corridor and started to sprint. The swing door ahead looked familiar, but it was only when he ran through it he realised why. He had enough time to compute that he was back in the vast ballroom when there was a gunshot from one side of the room.

A hand grabbed roughly at his shoulder and bright light shone in his eyes for a second. The hand pulled him to the hard floor. 'Help...' It was Flint's voice. There was enough light to see a hole in his eye socket. Blood was spreading from the gory socket like an overflowing tap. Blood was everywhere and Flint had stopped moving. Stixx thought he could see the silhouette of another person at the far side of the ballroom. Stixx sprang back to his feet and ran.

'Oh fuck!' the words sprang out of his mouth. He'd found the door where he had come in. It was open. There was freedom and there was also Heathers Jr lying prone next to the door. The thing with dirty-red skin was sucking on his neck with a hungry gargling sound. There were chunks of flesh discarded on the floor next to him. Jr still trembled and spasmed, as if somewhere in his defiled body there was a spark of life remaining.

Stixx moved again, as fast as he ever had. The vampire watched him nonchalantly as Stixx careered through the open door to greet the outside world with flailing arms. Down The Hill, and through the trees, Stixx could see the tell-tale flashing blue strobes of emergency vehicles coming his way.

He didn't stop running.

Chapter 31 – The Hounds of Hell

Stixx kept on running, something which amongst all of his D and C grades at school, he'd always been commended on. His games teacher had written, *'He has a good engine'* one year, and Stixx always remembered that one.

Twice he nearly fell on the icy sludge on the footpath, craning his neck backwards to see if *the thing* that had been chewing on Jr's throat was after a second course. It wasn't in pursuit as far as he could tell. More light was coming through the trees. Dawn was breaking, another card in his favour if the thing was for real.

Stixx had chosen not to wait for the police to arrive. It had not so much been a conscious decision, more an instinct. He'd lost count of the number of crimes he had committed or had been accused of committing in the last week. There was the real fear that being found at yet another murder would have meant something sticking this time. Too many people in the village had him pegged as a murderer already. Stixx wasn't going to be the fall guy, or an accomplice, or anything else for that matter. Faye was still out there someplace and he didn't have another day to waste answering a thousand police questions.

Stixx dodged down a back alley behind a row of terraced houses and came out at the end of the private road the guesthouse was situated. Around the corner he stopped, thinking there might be a few fresh journos, but in no way expecting to see armed police officers climbing out of a riot van outside his house.

Stixx gawked a moment too long. The words 'STOP RIGHT THERE!' were being shouted among choruses of 'DON'T MOVE!' and 'ARMED POLICE!' Stixx knew he had them at a disadvantage. They were at least eighty metres away and wearing a tonne of kit, he figured they wouldn't be able to run for shit. He turned and darted back the way he'd come.

Stixx knew enough to be sure they were now madly scrambling other officers and patrol cars to cut him off. He had to be very smart to make an even halfway decent getaway. Sirens started screaming up the road that led towards the church. There was no choice but to cross the road or risk being surrounded. Running into the road he looked right and by inches was missed by the leading police car. Tyres screeched and burned the tarmac, and with a manoeuvre somewhere approaching a hand-brake turn the police car was back facing him. The officer was looking homicidal.

Stixx kept running, jumping a wall and scrambling over a loose rockery and a lawn. From all the sirens, police were clearly going to do whatever was necessary to catch him, which he hoped didn't include shooting him in the back.

As he straddled a fence at the far end, something shot past his head, followed by a loud electrical fizz and frantic clicking sound. A police officer was in the same garden and had tried to hit him with a taser. Stixx flung himself over the end fence, rolled and ran again along another line of terraced flats. He knew the fences were going to slow the copper down.

If they had a helicopter it would be over, but the local force couldn't afford one. The nearest whirly bird was with the next constabulary along, Lancashire. It hadn't been over the village since the first murders. He knew he had some time to play with, but probably not much.

Stixx had a destination in mind, but needed to change direction and be unpredictable. From all the noise he could tell the superior police numbers weren't far off boxing him in. The taser shooter wasn't getting over the fences very fast though – too many Happy Meals by the look of his waistband. He'd had his Hail Mary shot, and missed.

There were more sirens ahead.

Just how many police were there?

 The village must have been swarming with them.

At the top of a high stone wall between gardens, Stixx briefly had time to assess his surroundings. Looking back to the road where he had come from originally, he could see at least four more police cars parked haphazardly. He could see eight police officers closing in through gardens in that direction. Looking towards the way he was heading, there were sirens but Stixx couldn't see fluorescent vests.

There was a chance.

He took a deep breath and sprinted through the next yard. An old woman was hanging out her washing. She made a slightly surprised high pitched sound and stood frozen to the spot with a pair of large granny knickers in her hand.

Stixx battled his way over to the Educational Institute, the village's cultural hub. They had chess on a Thursday evening and some of the most abysmal amateur dramatics in the northern counties. The concrete backyard also had a manhole cover that lead into a drainage tunnel. Or it did have five years earlier when he and Red, as cheeky, bored thirteen year olds, had pulled it open and spent an evening scaring themselves stupid because they'd just watched *Stephen King's IT*.

Panting for air, Stixx searched for the circular metal cover. It was still there, which was a start, but Stixx could see it was badly corroded. He pushed his fingers under the sill of the sunken handle and pulled.

Nothing happened.

In the distance he could hear barking. Stixx knew they had police dogs on the hunt. He bent his knees and tried to lift again. The heavy cover came up slowly, and it took every fibre of his limited musculature to scrape it over the concrete to one side. The hole below looked as black and uninviting as he remembered.

The metal ladder in the manhole was so rusted that the surface rubbed off as powder in his hands. Stixx made a half-hearted attempt to move the cover back in place above him, but it was hopeless. He had to keep moving. Stixx nearly slipped at the base of the ladder as underfoot it felt like the slime had turned to slush and ice. It was so dark he couldn't even see one foot in front of his eyes. Looking for a reference point, he tried to remember the way. Mainly all he remembered was Red screaming like a girl a lot and making him jump.

He picked a direction and set off, trying to go fast enough to make progress without suffering a critical injury. He was in a Victorian storm drain that followed the line of the road the police were parked on above. Stixx was banking on the fact that hardly anyone knew the tunnel was there. But a second after those chickens were counted, he heard voices behind him.

Boxed in.

There was daylight ahead, although he knew from experience it would be useless to follow the drain too far. There was a steel grill at the end, and there would be no way to get that open. Instead he found the ladder he vaguely remembered and using his back he levered up the manhole cover above him. Stixx fought his way upwards and blinked back into the daylight again. He was in a parking area at the far end of the promenade. If there had been a car tyre parked on top of the cover the game would have been over.

This time he did push the manhole cover back into place, hoping it would confuse them, or slow them down at least. Stixx sprinted down onto the beach and then took the steps up the concrete causeway two at a time. He vaulted the wall into the grounds of the derelict outward bound centre he had gone to with Faye and Red, that first night. It looked different in daylight, far less scary and foreboding. Stixx bypassed the main buildings and headed straight into the tree line. The slope was severe and his legs burned before he got to the top. There was a crazy idea in his mind, and only a small window of opportunity to pull it off. The barking dogs seemed closer.

It had been perhaps three years since he had last climbed the trees in the old centre and Stixx didn't find it any easier than the tree he'd climbed before the fight with Marco last week. The skills just weren't there anymore for the nimble stuff.

He and Red used to climb trees all the time back in the day. In the outward bound centre they had called it 'the circuit.' Stixx went up their old starting tree: a big ancient willow that had plenty of handholds. The trees on the slope were densely packed together and in the main overlapped. He and Red had taken note of this and had happened on something of a brainwave. Like those old days, Stixx moved from the willow to the next tree, across a thick branch he hoped hadn't turned rotten. He was at least twenty feet off the ground and getting nervous.

Stixx kept moving and listening out, finding the old handholds and routes through the trees, sometimes with difficulty. Across the grounds he couldn't see any police yet. In the end, he'd covered perhaps a hundred metres, finding at the end the huge old oak tree still had pieces of wood nailed into its trunk providing a makeshift ladder.

Gingerly, Stixx made his way down. From the distance there was another fierce bark. Stixx was banking on the fact that any trail those dogs were following was now going to get very cold. He at least had a stop-gap to buy some more time. Dogs couldn't track if the scent wasn't at ground level.

He moved out of the far end of the grounds and up a track he knew would lead eventually to O'Halloran Hill. There were hardly any houses on the route and he hoped none of the elderly residents would report where he went. This time he stayed out of their gardens and tried to keep a low profile. At the end of the track there was a stile, a short field and then the woods of The Hill stretching on as far as he could see.

The world's biggest hideout.

Stixx ran to the tree line and then had to walk as he was close to being completely knackered.

He moved off the main paths immediately and cut his own way through the trees. The last thing he wanted was to meet any walkers out for their post-breakfast New Year's Day stroll. A half hour later he made himself comfortable, lying against the fallen remains of a stone wall, flanked on all sides by a barrier of thorn bushes. There were no barking dogs, just the odd chirp of a bird and the natural rustle of tree branches on the wind. As an afterthought he checked his pocket for his phone. He must have left it at home or in the pub but consoled himself with the thought they wouldn't be able to track him that way either. Finally he closed his eyes and tried to doze. It was going to be a long New Year's Day.

When he woke it was still daylight and he was shivering uncontrollably with the cold. Stixx knew the only thing keeping him alive was the thick-lined coat his mother had given him for his eighteenth birthday. It was looking pretty dirty and frayed around the edges, but was still just about waterproof. Stixx stood up on stiff limbs and stamped his feet trying to gemerate some warmth. He was hungry and thirsty, and only had a remedy for one of those things. He moved on through the woods.

On the far easterly side of The Hill there were basically no paths, just a tangle of more thorny bushes, ancient trees and unforgiving gradients. He and Red once chased a pheasant this far into the woods with a catapult that was neither deadly nor accurate. On the odd occasion they had a direct hit, the bird just ruffled its feathers as if to shrug at them. Stixx wasn't there for the birds though. There was a small spring, no more than a trickle from the earth, over on this side of The Hill, and Stixx found the moving water under a thin film of fresh ice. He had no idea how clean it was, but it had to be better than eating ice off the dirty ground.

Again, he compulsively checked his pockets methodically for something resembling an edible substance. There was nothing to find but fluff and an old penny. He put the penny in his mouth and then spat it out. His stomach rumbled in protest. This was getting unpleasant. There was nothing else to do but sit and wait. He lay down on the uneven ground and stared up at the tree canopy and the off-white wisps of cloud high above him. There was no insulation and he was in for a hellish cold night.

Faye had been gone over four days now. He wasn't stupid; he knew she had probably been dead that long as well. In the back of his mind was the thought that scared him most: that everyone in the world now thought he killed her too. Whatever Hastie had told him, to go back now would guarantee that he would be charged. A tear rolled out from the corner of his eye. The first one.

Eventually, after what felt like an eternity of waiting, it became dark. At least now he would be able to see the police coming with their torches, although in truth he hadn't seen a soul all day. There still had been no helicopter, no thermal imaging to root him out. His luck seemed to be holding. Stixx set off to move around O'Halloran, a fresh plan buzzing in his head. He had hours of darkness to play with.

He continued to stay as far away from as many of the main paths as possible. The next part of his plan would involve some risk, but it was risk he had to go with if he wasn't going to freeze and starve to death in the woods. Popping his head over the wall, he looked at the road. It was the road that linked Greystones with the coastal hamlet of Far Greystones: just a back road, not often used at night. It looked empty. There was a layby nearby, but no cars were using it. Stixx climbed over the wall, listened, and then ran across the road to a barbed wire fence.

Carefully he scaled the fence, still managing to snag his jeans on the wire barbs and scratch a line on his leg underneath. Halfway down the field to the distant edge of the Colonel's land he heard a noise, and saw headlights of a vehicle coming over the rise from the village. Stixx dropped to the ground and flattened himself out. There was no cover to hide behind. He was a person clearly lying face down in a bare field. He kept looking at the road.

It was a police vehicle, one of the bread van types that wasn't quite a car, and not quite a van either.

A regular patrol.

It was firing out a powerful spotlight from its roof, scanning the tree line beyond the field, the very direction he had been heading in. The light traced across the field, now no more than five feet away from where he lay. *He must have been seen, there was no way he hadn't been.* He got ready to sprint, although he didn't fancy his chances so much, this time. The police vehicle seemed to slow but didn't stop as its light moved on to the next field. Stixx waited until it was out of sight and ran for the trees, his heart beating out of his chest.

Minutes later Stixx was standing in the shadow of the Colonel's old greenhouse. He hadn't been back there since he and Faye had run when Flint and Jr showed up. As they were both now dead he thought he had at least a fighting chance that the place was still a secret. Inside was the familiar smell of old soil and decay. The trapdoor was intact. He would make it harder to see, with dirt and leaves. Walking down the wooden steps into the cellar area below, Stixx flicked a switch and was amazed to see actual electric light. He felt a little like falling to his knees and praising the lord.

The marijuana plants and most of his hydroponic equipment was long gone, no doubt dumped in a skip somewhere by Flint, who was not exactly renowned in the community for relishing complex investigations. The rest of the room, like the trapdoor, was intact. There was still a table, a wooden chair, and if Stixx wasn't mistaken, there were still his hiding holes. He never imagined he would ever be properly on the run from the law, but whether it was for fun or from latent childishness, he had hidden food, matches, and cigarettes, in a metal box under a loose floorboard. There was an old transistor radio as well.

Later Stixx sat at his table smoking and eating a Mars Bar. The radio was crackling, but it was still working. The BBC newscaster was talking about him.

'...police widen their search for the suspected vampire killer, James Stixx, who was last seen earlier today daringly evading capture following a dramatic chase by police through the Cumbrian village of Greystones. They warn that nobody should approach him and that any sighting of the nineteen year old should be reported immediately to police. It has been confirmed that Sergeant William Flint was found dead by a gunshot wound at what was previously The Ridgeway Convalescent Home on Hill Road in Greystones, along with another named person, Myles Heathers Jr. Heathers, who was the son of a prominent local businessman was also discovered murdered at the same location this morning, following a report to police of gunshots being fired. In a statement issued this morning, Inspector Neil Hastie, confirmed that these latest deaths were indeed believed linked to what is now a death toll of ten people in this village over the Christmas period, all now seemingly victims of the so-called vampire killer. James Stixx is now the second suspect to be named in the investigation, following the earlier questioning of Down's Syndrome sufferer, Marco Marx. Inspector Hastie also confirmed that Marx no longer forms part of this investigation. He also reiterated that there had been no new breakthroughs in the related case of missing Greystones resident, Faye Burns. The eighteen year old, a friend of the wanted Stixx, disappeared during an incident at the Greystones village library on the 29th December, which left the librarian with serious head injuries...'

The radio droned on into the night. Stixx had long since fallen into a deep sleep.

Chapter 32 – The New Lost Boys

Stixx paced around the cellar. It was as cold as a grave and felt small and dirty. The radio was reduced to a low hiss of noise, the batteries having all but given up the ghost. Hungry again, he rummaged through the treasure box he'd dug up earlier. There were three boiled sweets and a tube of Polo Mints. The first mint was covered in grime where the silver foil had rubbed off in the box.

Terrific!

He realised he was probably going to starve to death.

Stixx lost track of time. Pushing up the trapdoor, more freezing air met his face. It was night, but a night with at least some stars visible between the thin cloud banks. There was also a watery moon: a light bulb dialled down on low. Stixx stood hunched in the old broken greenhouse looking out at the tree line on the edge of the clearing. There was nothing to see but the blackest foliage, tendrils of branch, leaf and dirt, that gave nothing away. Squinting, Stixx tried to see beyond the trees, looking for small gaps that might show even a partial view of the road between the village and Far Greystones.

There were no gaps.

There was something else – a rustling, a snap of twigs from near the clearing. Stixx turned towards it, expecting perhaps voices or another dog bark to tell him the police were closing in.

There was nothing.

The sound came again. Angry, hard footfalls. Stixx moved back inside, trying not to give away any movement behind what was left of the glass panes of the ancient greenhouse. He got a foot on the first of the cellar steps when he heard it; a growling hiss. There was the blur of a figure moving in the darkness, dancing on the edge of his peripheral vision.

Stixx skittered backwards, bringing the trapdoor down too noisily. It would have been heard. There was no lock. There was nothing to do now but turn off the light and hold tight to the coarse rope handle on his side of the door. There was no way to be really safe and secure. Glass was breaking in the greenhouse,

217

not just one pane, but all of them it sounded like. It could only be one thing really. It could only be the vampire, come to finish what it started in the field. It had seen him at *The Ridgeway*. He had been a fool to think it wouldn't find him here.

Heavy feet on the floorboards over his head, then nothing. A silence that invited him to think everything was safe, to think that the thing had left to tear somebody else's throat out, not his.

Then it began.

At first it was scratching, scratching that sounded so deep into the wood that at any second he expected the vampire to gouge his way through the wooden boards and rip its way into the cellar. A thudding pounding came next, so hard that the wood began to splinter and break into matchstick pieces. Stixx tried to flick the lights back on but now they wouldn't work. He was alone in the dark, sitting helpless on the stairs of the cellar. The wood was being ripped away above him.

A face appeared – a red face looking down at him. It was lit up somehow, illuminated as if on fire. The ears looked more pointed, the hairless head again more lizard than human. This was the real vampire. Stixx had the truth but would never get to share it. The red face was still but the arms like talons worked on tearing the hole wider.

Stixx opened his eyes and it was gone. There was nothing above him but an open sky and a moon that loomed too large, like an interested spectator. Then the vampire dropped down in front of him, like a spider off a web.

Stixx woke up and knocked the radio off the table. The lights were still on. There was no hole in the ceiling, no monster trying to kill him. He was sweaty and cold all at the same time. He looked in the tin on the floor. There were no sweets left, he'd eaten everything.

It dawned on him then that his time was running out, that being a fugitive was harder than he imagined. The thought cut off when he realised somebody really was in the greenhouse above.

You've got to be kidding!

With the dream still gnawing at him, his rebellious streak kicked in and he threw the trapdoor up. Daylight streamed in and he stood paralysed and blinded.

'Who the hell?' he barked.

Through a haze of white light, Stixx could see two figures in front of him. It crossed his mind that it was the ghosts of Flint and Jr coming for him.

'Jesus man, you look like Saddam Hussein after they dragged him out of that pit! Have you never heard of human hygiene?'

'Fuck me, is that you Red?' Stixx's vision was slowly clearing. Red and the crazed Down's Syndrome dope fiend, Marco Marx, were standing there right in front of him.

'Stop looking so worried. We're not fucking ghosties!' Red shouted, and hugged him hard enough that it hurt. Marco joined in too.

'I thought you were dead!' Stixx said. He was crying but he couldn't stop himself. Marco was smiling like a lunatic.

Later the three of them were sitting on the grass, leaning against the outer walls of the greenhouse. For the past five minutes Stixx had been eating greedily from a lunchbox containing a squashed up Christmas dinner.

'My mum was so happy I'd miraculously recovered they had Christmas Day all over again yesterday at the hospital, with a home cooked Christmas turkey and all the trimmings!'

Red told him that he was still supposed to be in hospital, probably for another week, but he'd run away in the early hours of the morning when the nurse's station was empty. 'Getting a cannula out of your arm is a right bitch, I'll tell you that for nothing!'

Marco Marx had not said a great deal of anything. Stixx figured the little guy must have been a little shellshocked still over losing his dad. 'I can't wait to see him,' he said after a while.

'Who, Marco?' Stixx had asked.

'The vampire of course. I'm going to kick his nuts!' That was more like the old Marco.

Stixx spent a great deal of the next few hours explaining in detail just what Faye and he had been up to while Red had been lying comatose in a hospital bed. Stixx couldn't believe how well his best friend was looking considering. Clearly he was a little thin and shaky on his legs. He still had some hospital issue plasters on his hands, and on his neck and the back of his head was still a matted with a nest of ugly scabs from where it had nearly been bashed in.

'...and now you're on the run and living like a dirty Santa,' Red said at last.

'Yeah, that's just about right.'

'Fucking hell, mate. You're fairly fucked, aren't you?!'

'Thanks for pointing out the painstakingly obvious there.'

'You should have a bath,' Marco said, throwing his hat into the arena.

'You know my theory,' Red said, shaking his head at Marco. 'Two possibilities that I can see – it's either real or it isn't real. But, vampires aside, that Flint must have seen it as some kind of opportunity to turn the screws on the Colonel and Jr. They'd not given him *The Ridgeway* like they might have promised, even with it being supposedly worthless because of the soil or what-not. They were basically laughing at him. So he thinks, fuck it, there's a lot of people dying in this village so he gets Jr to the home and somehow gets the vampire there as well. The vamp is supposed to do its job and eat Jr. You've been a thorn in his side all along, so you're there to be some sort of fall guy, I'm guessing. But it all goes tits up and Flint ends up taking one in the head from Jr first.'

'I told you Red, I think I saw somebody else there in that hall. It doesn't make a heck of a lot of sense that it was the Colonel. I mean the guy can hardly walk unaided. He never leaves his manor house anymore. No, there's something we're missing. I think Faye figured something out that we haven't. That was why she was taken.'

'Yeah well,' Red said, 'I'm pretty much out of inspiration. And I'm pretty gutted to have missed all the action.'

'But you're back now!' Stixx said genuinely.

'Ah come on, admit it. Faye is your number one best bud now.'

'No way.' Stixx was squirming a little.

'It's okay, you know. That birds and bees shit is just natural. You were bound to meet a girl eventually. It doesn't change anything. It just means you get some other things going on in your life.'

'You know, if I didn't know you'd been in a coma for the last few days, I'd think you'd been sat in your hospital bed OD-ing on Oprah!' Stixx laughed. Red cracked up as well, and Marco joined in.

The wind was getting up and rustling the trees around the clearing.

'So, where do we go next do you think?' Stixx asked Red after a few minutes. 'I can tell you now that both the convalescent home and the library are both well off-limits. The police forensics are still all over those places, with cordons and police guards. Besides what would we find that they haven't already bagged and tagged?'

'So what else can we do?' Marco asked them.

'Play fight!' Red started wrestling with Marco on the ground. The cold truth seemed to be they were all out of plans.

It was a waiting game.

When it got too cold they moved into the cramped cellar under the greenhouse. Or, 'Stixx's hobbit hole,' as Red referred to it. Stixx found a dog-eared pack of cards and they tried to teach Marco how to play *Texas Hold-Em*, with only partial success.

'Well, we can keep bringing you food, but how long do you think you can stay here like this?' Red was serious, which was something of a rarity for him.

Stixx would have said, 'As long as it takes,' but it was a dumb answer. Instead he was honest. 'I'll try one more time to find Faye. After that I'll let them catch me and face whatever is coming. I just want one more shot, that's all.'

'You shouldn't bend over in the showers.'

'What, Marco?'

'That what my dad used to say. When you're in jail if you bend over in the showers they bum you up the bum!'

'Thanks, Marco. I'll look out for that one.'

They were all laughing again, and Stixx dealt another hand.

The hours ticked on with small talk and rubbish card games. Stixx was told via Marco that nobody had seen the Colonel since his son had died, which wasn't exactly unusual. Most people in the village now thought Stixx was responsible for what happened, or at least someway involved. The media were speculating it was all an elaborate hoax, and Stixx was some kind of criminal mastermind trying to get the world to believe in vampires by creating fake vampire killings. Some journalists had actually written now that he, Faye, and Red, faked the attack in the field, that they were all some kind of amateur illusionists trying to fool everyone. He was being portrayed as a loner, a classic psychotic, delusional serial killer; *Bonnie and Clyde*, yet with Bonnie now missing and presumed dead. It was a red-hot New Year's news story by the sound of it.

It made him sick.

Red sat up straight from where he had been picking at a loose floorboard. 'I think I've got it!'

'Got what, Red?' Marco asked, while Stixx just wrinkled his nose at his friend.

'The thing. The connection. It's obvious when you think about it.'

'Spit it out.' Stixx was all ears.

'When you saw the vampire at *The Ridgeway*, you said you thought it was red, like a red devil or whatever. You know, before it bashed my head in that field, I kind of remember the same thing. There were patches of red on that thing's skin, and it sounds like there was even more last night. So it's dirty right, but not just with any old common garden dirt...'

'...the old Far Greystones cave used to be full of red clay. We used to get covered in the stuff!' Stixx finished Red's sentence for him. Stixx remembered now the sheer number of hours they'd spent down there when he'd first moved to the village. 'But the cave isn't really there anymore, Red. It collapsed eight years ago. There's just a pile of rocks where the entrance used to be.'

'I know what you mean. It's a long shot. But have we really got any other shot out there to go after?'

Another hour and it was dusk enough outside for them to risk leaving the greenhouse. Between them they had one small torch and nothing even resembling a weapon, as per usual. They skirted the edge of the Colonel's property, before picking the right moment to move back onto O'Halloran Hill again. They hadn't seen a single policeman or police vehicle since they set off. It felt like the calm before the storm.

The air was damp and colder than ever. There was still ice underfoot, slush that had re-frozen into treacherous slicks. Stixx felt the mud from the trails crunch around his trainers like concrete treacle.

'We are basically The Lost Boys, aren't we? The new Lost Boys,' Red said.

'I guess that makes me Corey Haim,' Stixx told him.

'No, you're the other one, the more weasel type one. You're Feldman and I'm Haim. Potentially you could be Jason Patrick, but I don't think chicks dig you that much.'

'Did you just call me a weasel? 'Cos the last time I watched The Lost Boys, I don't remember Corey Haim being a short-assed imp!'

'Yeah well, technically you may have a point. But in essence, my essence of character is much more Haim than Feldman.'

'So who am I then?' Marco asked expectantly.

'Other Frog brother!' Stixx and Red said in stereo.

They were doing so well. They got within a quarter of a mile of the old cave entrance and then they heard the first voice. The three of them froze and listened, trying to pinpoint the sounds. 'They must be on the other path,' Stixx said finally. He figured it to be some kind of search party.

The cave where they had often visited as kids, to blow up aerosol cans on bonfires and stupidly burn trails of firelighters deep down the wider passageways of the cave, wasn't hidden. It wasn't like the water spring lost in the middle of the woods. The old cave was on one of the main paths, not far from the cliff paths around the coast. It was even close to a caravan park for tourists.

Stixx remembered years ago the cavers with bright coloured hard hats going down the caves with all their professional gear, looking somewhat down their noses at his and Red's rampant attempts at pyromania. Sometimes parties of kids were brought over from the outward bound centre when it was still open. The truth was, since the rockslide closed off the entrance the caves were forgotten about. Eight years was a long time.

'We should go back,' Marco said nervously. He knew the woods as well as any of them, and was probably right.

'No,' Stixx whispered. 'We can beat them there.'

'And then what?' Red shrugged at him.

'Gut feeling!' Well it was, Stixx thought. They started to jog, covering the ground.

There was a shout from their right and a flash of a torch beam streaking through the branches: a lone police officer who must have broken away from his colleagues on the path was charging right at them, kamikaze style.

'STOP WHERE YOU ARE! DO NOT MOVE!' The policeman was deliberately shouting loud enough to alert the other officers.

Stixx, Red and Marco didn't stop, they just ran harder. The officer looked lean and fit, and they were in a heap of trouble. It was a hundred metres to the old cave, for all the good it was going to do them. Marco suddenly stopped running.

'What are you doing, Marco?' Red shouted. The little Down's kid wasn't listening, he was running back the way he came straight at the copper. Like a cannon ball hitting a ship, Marco's head hit the officer's stomach. They tumbled onto the muddy forest floor.

'Come on!' Red shouted to Stixx. A sound like thunder echoed overhead. A massive beam of light cut through the canopy of the trees like a blinding sun.

'Now they get the helicopter!' Stixx shouted above the rising din.

Around the corner was what was left of the cave entrance. Stixx shone his torch on the rocks, all covered in moss, lichen, and dirt. His heart sunk. It was just as he remembered it. There was nothing to see here. More shouts came from down the path, officers moving past where Marco had been fighting. The helicopter beam was strafing to where they stood looking at the rock fall.

It was over.

'Here, get here!' Red was shouting.

There was a hole in the rocks, barely more than a badger hole. Stixx pushed more rocks away. *It was a way into the cave. It must be,* thought Stixx.

'Mate, you can't do this!' Red kept shouting. Stixx was already on his knees.

'I've got to do this. I've got to do it for Faye.'

'I love you but you're a fucking moron! I'll do what I can to slow them down.'

Red erupted in the ten thousand watt glare of the search light. Blindly Stixx pushed himself through the gap and allowed himself to be swallowed in the suffocating blackness.

Chapter 33 – Underground

Stixx kept knocking the small torch on and off as he dragged himself through the tunnel. At times it got so narrow that he could feel his ribs painfully compressing. It was pure agony. He had to take shallow rapid breaths just to try and make more space for his body. When Stixx fought against the rock it clacked and rumbled around him, as if reminding him that at any second the whole unstable mass could decide to come thudding down on his head.

Choking on the rock dust in the air, Stixx could tell the opening was getting smaller. The tunnel had reached a triangular junction between two great slabs of limestone. From there the tunnel rose in a steep incline, almost like a tilted chimney. He couldn't see far enough to be sure there was even an opening at the top. Not for the first time, he wondered if this had all been a terrible mistake, that he should just start inching his way back before he got stuck and died a horrible death. In the dulling torchlight he could see his hands had the dark stain of the red clay on them. Stixx pushed on up the chimney.

At some point he stopped moving. The incline was deceptively steep and as the walls narrowed the friction was starting to snag. There was a feeling that he couldn't move up or down. A panic was rising, nearly causing him to drop the torch. Arms were jammed helplessly by his sides, his breath struggled into his lungs and sweat poured out, despite the icy cold.

Stixx tried to wriggle forward, managing only to move only a few centimetres despite a huge physical effort. The panic was coming in waves now. He tried to push his back against the slab above him.

Nothing happened.

Stixx tried to calm himself and slow his breathing. It took a long time. There was one more thing to try. He breathed out – breathed out all the air he could.

Like an empty husk.

Then he moved, he wasn't a human in his mind anymore. He was snake slithering through the tall grass. *Slow and steady wins the race.* He was moving, the rock tighter and tighter on his abdomen: squeezing and crushing. The pain increased. The rock dust was choking him. Stixx kept moving, getting more light-headed. The world was blinking in and out. Stixx reached, one hand finding itself free and in the air. Stixx forced himself on, vaguely noting the feeling of falling before cracking his head and blacking out.

Stixx blinked back to consciousness on the hard, wet cave floor, touching a trickling wound at the back of his head. His whole body felt like it had been compressed and squeezed out through a tube of toothpaste. Stixx's ribs felt warped and out of space. The breath burned in his lungs. He was dizzy and disorientated, but elated to be alive.

He sat up and felt around the damp gritty cave floor for the torch. The dull beam of light was still on and focused on the wall. He estimated that he was at least twenty metres underground, in an area of the cave not affected by the cave-in eight years ago. He stood up, only having to stoop slightly to avoid catching the top of his head on the ragged cave ceiling. It was hard for him to remember where the cave tunnels went next. There was something else just around the next corner. Stixx could see it shining in the torchlight – a bare foot, discoloured and mottled dark purple like a bruised plum. Stixx slowly walked closer, each step he took revealing more of the body. It was a female, so thickly coated with the clay-dirt that he couldn't make out the colour of her clothes. Her hair was matted and dark, her face hidden because she was lying on her chest. There was no movement, no sign that the person was alive.

Was it Faye?

Stixx edged as close as he dared.

Stixx reached out and touched the girl's neck, recoiling when he felt her as cold as the rocks in the cave. Stixx took a deep breath and reached out again, pulling her by the shoulder so she rolled towards him. It wasn't Faye. He shone the torch into the girl's dead face, half-recognising her but being slow to remember from where. Then it came to him, it was creep Sebastian's young girlfriend, the local girl he'd seen at New Year. Her throat was just a blackened hole of congealed blood and jagged flesh. Stixx stepped back wildly shining the torch around. There was nothing but bare seeping rock and the cave's inky blackness. Stixx was sure he wasn't alone, that there was some presence down here with him.

Around the corner the cave narrowed again, but not to claustrophobic proportions. Shadows danced on the walls from the increasingly feeble torchlight. At one point he had no choice but to climb down a ten metre wall of rock with the torch in his teeth. Twice his feet kicked out of the slippery footholds and he nearly fell. Already his head was beginning to pound with a headache, no doubt related to his bloodied head injury. Stixx wasn't foolish enough to think that another crack on his head wasn't going to cause serious damage.

Getting his bearings, Stixx had two choices. The cave was branching into two opposite directions, neither of which looked in any way inviting. Stixx pushed his body into the gap on the right, being forced to walk sideways while the pressure of the rock made his ribs shoot with pain. 'Fuck me!' he said under his breath. He banged his forehead on a high rock outcrop and hot blood ran down the side of his face. The wound didn't seem deep.

On the far side there were blocks of stone that appeared like steps. The cave opened up into a cavernous area, Stixx didn't remember ever seeing before with Red.

There was a sound.

Not an innocent sound. Not an explicable sound: the sound of a monster. Stixx remembered it from the field, a deep baritone of forced angry air coming out of the thing's mouth.

A war cry.

It echoed around him, making it impossible to know how far away it was or in what direction it came from. It stopped just as abruptly. Stixx moved down onto the cavern floor and kept himself moving.

The torch lost more brightness and Stixx wondered how much time it would last – maybe no more than ten minutes. Fumbling around in the dark was a frightening thought. There would be nothing to do but wait for his throat to be torn out or at best suffer a slow death from dehydration. He moved on, randomly choosing another branch of the tunnel that somehow felt right. Every three paces he snapped his head around to look behind. He knew that thing was in there with him. He heard subtle sounds around him: the faint echo of small tumbling stones, the occasional footfall. Stixx was sure he was being stalked.

He groaned to see the cave narrow yet again into another tight gap. Moving awkwardly he ducked under a low outcrop of rock and into the gloom. A trickle of ice water ran down Stixx's back, shocking him with the cold. Just when he was sure the way was going to be a dead end, it opened up around a corner and Stixx could stand up again. He tapped the torch with his hand, trying to get more life out of it. For a second it blinked out, leaving him lost in total darkness. Two desperate taps later and the torch blinked back to life. He found himself hyperventilating.

The noise came again. The raging sound. Stixx's mind was racing. He was closer this time, he was sure of it.

'I'M DOWN HERE!' he shouted. Better that the vampire came to him now, he reasoned, than when he was weak and in the dark.

There was no attack. Stixx moved on, the torch beam visibly receding before his eyes. 'Hello!' He shouted this time for Faye. 'HELLO!'

There was no chance.

The wet cave floor had become slippery and Stixx was finding it hard to maintain his footing. He was deep under The Hill, of that much he was sure, deeper than anyone would be able to find him for a very long time. The police would take days to get through the cave-in at the entrance. They would have to do it safely. Nobody was going to risk their necks going in the way Stixx had.

He glanced behind, for at least the hundredth time. Stixx stared, trying to take in what he was seeing. On a ceiling ledge above him there wasn't just wet rock and shadows; there was a shiny doomed head and a hint of eyes that caught the light. The vampire was still, cocking its head slowly to one side as if it was also drinking in his details. The torchlight around the creature narrowed, closing up like a flower. Then there was nothing but blackness and the sound of scurrying.

Stixx paced backwards, immediately butting into the rock wall. He braced himself, unsure of what to do next. He decided to run, trying to remember the direction the tunnel went. There was more movement on the rocks above him, footfalls somewhere in the blackness. He fell, head-over-heels, landing battered on the unpleasantly hard floor. Something had hold of his leg and Stixx felt sheering pain as needle teeth tore through his skin. He kicked out with his free foot, making contact with what may have been a shoulder. The teeth didn't stop. He kicked again and again. 'Get away, you fucker!'

Free at last, he crawled and stood with some difficulty. His eyes weren't adjusting to the darkness. There just wasn't any light for them to adjust to. A hand grabbed at the clothing on his back. Somehow it had got behind him. Stixx spun away disorientated, lashing out his hands and feet, grazing his knuckles on the rough cave wall. The claw-hands had him again, pinning him against the rock, nails digging into his skin. 'GET THE FUCK…'

Rotting meat breath was near his nose and Stixx dropped his weight instinctively, realising that the vampire was going for his neck. He dug his feet in and pushed forward as if in a rugby ruck, driving the vampire across to the other side of the cave tunnel. There was a satisfying *clunk* as its body hit the rock. 'It fucking hurts, doesn't it?!'

Nails slashed across his cheek, drawing more blood. Stixx hit back with his fist, making contact high on the creature's head. It had no effect. They were locked together, Stixx feeling the teeth tear at his clothing, getting closer to his face. He punched its head over and over, forgetting the pain in his fist, any damage to his hands now irrelevant.

The vampire was overbalancing, holding onto him and trying to drag him to the ground. Stixx brought his knee up making a solid connection to thing's chin. He followed the blow with kicks, wild soccer kicks to what felt like its face, arms and torso. The vampire had stopped moving. Stixx kept kicking it until he was exhausted, then staggered away, leaning on the walls for support. He felt like his body was one giant abrasion now, pain screaming out from every extremity. Blindly, he moved down the tunnel, realising the torch was still around his neck, swinging from its cord.

He flicked the switch, amazed to see a small amber pool of light. It was back to life, although probably not for long. He started to jog, hunching down so as not to smack his head. Stixx saw a shoe on the ground, a female training shoe. He wasn't sure if it was Faye's, but he wanted it to be. There was a sound behind him, back down the tunnel. The thing wasn't dead. Stixx broke into a full-blown sprint.

He was in a small cavern, a cavern with death in it. Stixx smelled the rot before he saw it. One of the bodies was in what looked like a police uniform, a bloated face turned black: a yellow florescent protective vest darkly stained around the neck no doubt by blood and other fluids of decomposition. It could only be the policeman who had disappeared from The Ridgeway. Stixx wasn't looking at him though.

It was Faye next to the policeman, lying motionless, almost touching the other body. Her skin was also dark, mottled with dirt over her body. Stixx was now only dimly aware of the clattering of stones in the tunnel he had come from. The world was fading away, tuning out.

'Faye?' he said, the word getting lost in his throat. 'Faye?'

He reached down and touched her face. She felt cool, but there was a flicker on her eyelids. 'Faye, can you hear me?'

Faye's lips were dry and flaky. Her lips moved, but there was no sound.

There was life.

Stixx picked her up in his arms, pointing the fading torch back towards the tunnel he had come from. There was no sign of the vampire yet. There were other tunnels heading off into multiple directions. 'We're going to get out of here, okay.'

The tunnel he picked was going down. *This is bad.* Stixx's arms were already starting to burn with Faye's weight. She was stirring a little, her head rocking from side to side. There were puncture marks on her neck it looked like, blackened and infected. The vampire had been there, with its stinking meat-mouth. For the first time since he entered the cave Stixx felt more angry than scared.

There was a sound, and,for a moment Stixx didn't know where it was coming from. Then he looked down and saw it was Faye's lips moving. It was barely a whisper. 'Up there,' she said. Stixx thought she was trying to lift her hand, trying to point.

Stixx shone the torch into the deep shadows along that side of the tunnel: irregular, broken rocks. But there, at waist height was an opening. Stixx got onto his knees with Faye still in his arms and crawled through the space, the torchlight starting to fade out, the batteries finally exhausted. There was a guttural scream, perhaps no more than ten or fifteen metres away.

'Where is it?' he muttered.

'Gotta keep going,' Faye whispered, she was finding her voice again. 'Leave me…'

Stixx could feel her fading away before his eyes. He saw she was attached to a loop drilled into the cave wall by a thin steel chain on her wrists. Stixx began to pull on it with everything he had, the metal biting painfully into the palms of his hands. Finally it gave way, sending them both sprawling into a heap.

They had to move now. Fast.

The climb was steep. Stixx saw it then, no more than a chink of white in the infernal blackness. He dragged Faye with him, trying to keep his balance. She seemed to be drifting in and out of consciousness.

'I can crawl.' Her voice was faint but defiant.

Stixx didn't know what she meant, but then it became obvious.

At the top of the rise the light was glinting out from the base of the cave wall. It was a crawl space no more than a foot high and a body width wide. 'It's okay Stixx, don't be scared. I watched him do it.'

Faye was taking the lead, her body snaking through the gap, her legs still tied. Stixx threw the now useless torch away and followed. The light was blinding, clearly daylight, there was no other explanation. The tunnel height was reducing, making it harder for him push Faye ahead of him. The pain was back in his ribs. Stixx felt like he was moving in treacle.

A hand gripped his foot. Stixx strained his head back to see the vampire's face, bloodied and staring back at him with dead fish eyes. Stixx kicked hard, making a half-decent contact with its looming face. Stixx broke the grip and squeezed himself forward, moving on pure adrenalin.

'Hurry up, Stixx!' Faye was already out, lost in the light somewhere.

Stixx crawled as if his life depended on it. Ahead he couldn't see anything but the burning white letterbox shape. The vampire was making horrible screaming sounds, pulling itself towards him like a snarling animal. Stixx could see its black teeth, gnarly long curling fingernails. It was bleeding though.

It wasn't indestructible.

Blinded, Stixx's vision turned white for a moment. He'd been underground all night and when his eyes refocused he saw he was halfway up a cliff face somewhere on O'Halloran Hill. Stixx didn't recognise it, had never been there before. Faye was stood on a small ledge to his right, looking pale and frail.

'Come on, Stixx, get here will you!'

Stixx took a step out onto the ledge, which was barely a foot-width wide. Together they started to traverse the cliff face. Flailing arms and the bald head shot out of the hole next to them. The vampire was angry, spitting, jabbering non-words from its mouth.

It happened fast. The creature tried to jump from the cave opening to where Stixx stood on the ledge, taking hold of him, teeth snapping for his neck. Stixx felt himself pulled forward off the cliff ledge, the ground coming up in a rush, as they plummeted the fifteen feet to the leafy forest floor. Stixx landed on top of the naked vampire, being vaguely aware of a cracking sound of splintering bone, before the reality of not being able to breathe hit home. Winded, he rolled off the vampire's chest. There was no air going into his lungs, the world was on the way out. Faye's voice was out there somewhere.

Everything was black.

Chapter 34 – Home Is Where The Heart Is

'Come on Stixx, wakey wakey!' Faye was kneeling next to the prone body of Stixx at the base of the small cliff face.

The icy wet mulch of leaves on her knees felt like bliss, as did the fresh air and the sky. She couldn't believe that after days of being trapped in the blackness of the cave she had come out alive.

And free.

Her head pounded with a migraine from the lack of food and her limbs felt like they were moving in slow-motion. She felt as weak as a kitten.

'Stixx, I know you're not dead. Wake up, will you!' She shook the shoulders of the lanky lump, not hard, just lightly. There weren't many exposed areas of his face or hands that didn't have either dried or fresh smeared blood. The back of his scalp had various raw looking cuts but they didn't look life threatening. Faye could only imagine what sort of state she looked. Her neck bites were definitely red raw with infection, and it made her literally dizzy to think about it.

Stixx opened his eyes and made a noise... a bit of a groan. His eyes focused on her. 'Soft landing!' he said and tried to sit up. 'Christ, is the world spinning?'

'No, just in your head.' Faye was smiling like a fool.

They were both okay, against the odds they were going to walk away from this, or at least hobble away. She helped Stixx to his feet and with some struggle he finally helped rid her of the shackles on her wrists and ankles, breaking the locks open with a large rock. There were grooves cut into the skin that she guessed would scar, hopefully faintly.

She'd spent days working at getting free, losing skin for little progress, and felt sore all over. She was sure she was running a high temperature from the infection on her neck.

'You know, I think I recognise the guy. I've seen him somewhere,' Stixx said, kicking the body on the ground with his foot. In the harsh light of day the vampire was looking a bit less like a bloodthirsty creature of nightmares, and a little more like a naked man with a tiny penis, covered in clay and dirt. He looked surprisingly small, curled into something of a foetal position. His bald head was off-set awkwardly to one side. There was little doubt that his neck had been broken by the fall. An ugly line of healed stitches ran across the back of his head.

'I recognise him too,' Faye said triumphantly. 'I saw him in a picture in June Dowling's bedroom at the old folk's home. The matron said she used to get visited by her son, but he got sick and stopped coming. Now I think we know why.'

'He decided he was a vampire and wanted to live in a cave. That's some kind of crazy shit!' Stixx said, kicking the body again. No doubt he was wondering if he was going to sit up any second and try for a second bite. The vampire man, however, was looking distinctly and permanently dead.

'Well he didn't do it all on his own.' Faye told him then how it had been Flint who had come into the library, grabbed her, knocked her half-unconscious and drugged her. That he'd taken her into the woods and left her chained up for that thing to take her into the caves. Faye told him how she'd woken up in the darkness, bolted to the wall and disorientated, with the vampire-man licking blood from the vein on her neck like some bloody cat. She had been forced to lick the damp stone on the walls for water just to survive.

There was so much to say, and Faye splurged it out in an endless stream of consciousness. Her lips were sore and her throat felt like sandpaper. She wasn't really sure how much Stixx was taking in. The poor guy looked tired and possibly in shock. In the end she just stopped talking. There was more, but there would be time to tell him everything later.

'So where the hell are we, exactly?' she asked him at last.

Stixx was vaguely pointing. 'We must still be on The Hill, but I haven't seen this place before. If we had I reckon me and Red would have loved messing around on this cliff.'

They started walking slowly, as slow was all Faye could manage. Stixx told her that he thought he'd broken a few ribs. She just felt weary, like there was no energy in her muscles, and every step was an effort. She'd found two bars of chocolate on the corpse of the police officer. She had been lucky the guy had been a snacker. After a while she hadn't even noticed the stench from his body anymore. The chocolate and the rock water had somehow kept her going, although there was little doubt in her mind she wouldn't have lasted much longer.

'Look at this,' Stixx said, pointing at a barbed wire fence. The cliff was in one of those protected areas of O'Halloran Hill. There were no paths, no public rights of way. 'I guess it explains why Red and me never came here.. Red is a bit of a dick, but he's also a bit of a hippy conservationist on the quiet.' Stixx filled her in about Red and Marco's miraculous return. That he hadn't seen her mum, but was sure she was okay as well.

Faye couldn't stop smiling. 'We've got to tell them. Tell them we're okay up here.'

Over the wire there was enough of a clearing to see down to the coast. They could just see the tops of a few static caravans from the holiday park near Far Greystones. 'I know where we are now, come on.' Stixx led them down the field and through the steep bank of trees, eventually coming out on a narrow tarmac track. Beyond the row of static caravans there was a pebble beach and the estuary.

'Any second now we're likely to get arrested, you do know that don't you?' he told her.

'We'll be okay you know. There's a body in the woods that must be a forensic goldmine connecting to all the dead bodies. I can tell them what that psychopath Flint was up to. Don't worry about it, okay.' She felt herself have another dizzy spell. Putting one foot in front of the other was becoming an effort on the uneven ground.

Stixx took her past the first row of caravans and they followed the track as it doubled back on itself to head back towards Far Greystones. The caravans were all dark and empty. Nobody holidayed in the winter. 'It's still here,' he said pointing ahead. Faye could see he was pointing to a red phone box.

'I didn't think these things existed anymore.'

'They do here.'

They spent a whole minute debating who to ring, while digging in their pockets for anything resembling legal currency. In the end they decided against ringing '999' and instead spent their fifty pence piece on ringing Margie. 'Because she'll know what to do,' had been Stixx's winning argument.

Faye watched tears well up in Stixx's eyes when he spoke with his mum. Obviously she must have thought he was dead. Her heart sunk thinking of her own mum thinking the exact same thing. 'We'll ring my mum when we get to your house, okay,' Faye told him after Stixx had finished on the phone. 'It's the first thing we do!'

'Agreed!'

They moved to the tree line, to be at least hidden a little if a police patrol did choose to drive past. Sitting on the grass, trying to keep a worn out looking Stixx awake, Faye kept talking. 'So, it wasn't a real vampire. That's pretty obvious now. He was just a bog-standard nutter with something wrong with his head.'

Stixx blinked at her. 'Yeah, well you know even in the field, when we had that fight with him, I wasn't totally convinced. I mean, yeah, he was really strong, and I did tell Hastie that it could be for real at the hospital. But it was just the dark playing tricks on us really, the power of suggestion or something. That guy lying back there in the woods doesn't even look a heck of a lot like Dracula. More like an escaped mental patient or something.'

Stixx was right. She'd seen plenty of mental patients in her time.

'Sorry,' Stixx said, and put his hand on top of hers. Even after all that had happened, he knew enough to see he'd reminded her of her own father.

There was the rumble of an approaching car, and Faye and Stixx edged back into the shadows of the trees. 'It's okay. IT'S MUM!' Stixx shouted ecstatically. She was alone in the car. No police escort. No media.

Margie practically flew out of the little hatchback. 'Geez, Mum, I have got injuries here!' Stixx squeaked, while getting a vintage hug that never seemed to end.

'I can't believe you're okay, that you're both okay,' Margie cried, beckoning Faye to join in for a group hug.

In the car and driving through Far Greystones, Stixx asked the question that was making him nervous. 'Have you told anyone that you were coming? The police...?'

'I haven't told anyone. I know you've got yourself in a jam and a half. We'll get home and figure it out. We'll get Faye's mum, and then probably we'll have to look at getting you both to the hospital. You both look like you've been to hell and back.'

'I just want to call my mum,' Faye told her wearily, slurring her words slightly.

'Mum's not big on mobile phones. We'll use the landline as soon as we get to the guesthouse,' Stixx told her.

'You know among all the bad luck, you've had some good luck as well. The Colonel's mansion was burnt to the ground last night, by the look of it with the Colonel still inside. From what the media are saying they think it may be foul play of some kind. Anyway, the media have kindly decamped from the guesthouse and the police are pretty distracted over on that side of the village with the fire crews.'

Faye was keeping her head down on the back seat with Stixx. She dabbed her fingers on the puffy, infected skin on her neck again. It felt bad. Basically she'd need nuking with antibiotics once she got to hospital. A week in bed wouldn't hurt either, together with a lot of giant fry ups.

'It's clear!' Margie announced when they arrived at the guesthouse. 'We'll go in the bottom way. It'll be quicker.' She unlocked the door to the passageway leading to the cellar rooms of the guesthouse. It seemed a safer option than walking up the steps to the front door with the whole world watching.

'Watch your step,' Stixx said, as they walked down the dusty corridor, past what looked like old rusting oil tanks and Stixx's pushbike. Margie unlocked another heavy wooden door and Faye found she was at the base of the cellar steps, next to the room they'd played table tennis in on Christmas Day.

'I had a fire going in the private lounge when you called,' Margie said opening the other door. 'It's the warmest room in the house right now.'

Faye followed them into a private lounge room. It was one of the only places in the guesthouse that Faye had never seen.

Margie was right, it was gloriously warm. The cold from the cave felt like it had seeped into her bones over the last few days.

It was a sizable lounge, with the open fire against the far wall. There was an upright piano in one corner, and what looked like a raised platform in another corner, smothered in bright and obviously home-made cushions. There was a wicker settee, a chair, and a round glass-topped coffee table in the centre of the room. There were also old relics like an old black and white television and a turn-table record player. If the room could be summarised in a single word it would be *lush*, a very seventies kind of lush.

'I'm going to call your mum. Then probably we'll have to go straight to the hospital,' Margie said. 'You just relax for now, okay. Put some music on or something. Stixx loves my *Toyah Willcox* LPs.' Margie disappeared out of the door, and Faye heard her steps heading up the stairs.

'How are you holding up?' she said to Stixx, wincing.

Stixx squinted up his eyes, like he did sometimes when he was in pain. 'My head feels a little like somebody has forced wire wool in the back of it, and then poured in some petrol…'

'Good job you don't keep anything essential up there,' Faye joked.

'What about you? You were pretty skinny before, and now look at you. You've lost weight my girl!'

'Why thank you! A girl takes a compliment where she can find it.' Faye was getting a little bit of a fuzzy warm feeling when she thought about Stixx. She looked at him lying slumped on the settee, covered in crap and with those Thom Yorke geek looks. He was no rocket scientist, but he was the bravest idiot she'd ever known. He'd never given up. 'Stixx, it was pretty special what you did, you know. I'm not going to forget what you did in a hurry.'

'Think of it as my Christmas present,' he said with a tired smile.

Footsteps were jogging back down the stairs. 'I've called your mum, she's coming straight here right now. And I brought you nourishment… soup,' Margie said, handing over a cup of soup to both Faye and Stixx. 'It's tomato, not from a packet either. It's a start. You don't want to overload your stomachs, especially you Faye!'

They sat and waited. The soup was delicious, Faye thought, not too hot, not too heavy. Faye could feel her body sighing, overwhelmingly ready to receive some much needed nutrients. She drained her cup and saw Stixx had already finished his. Faye settled back down into the comfortable cushions, feeling a wave of tiredness washing over her. Stixx already appeared to have dozed off.

'It won't be long. She'll be driving like a bat out of hell,' Margie told her.

Faye smiled at her. She was such a lovely person. Faye couldn't think of what to say, so instead let her eyes explore the room a little more. There were pictures above the fireplace.

Lots of them.

Mostly they were black and white photographs of the village. Somewhere at the back of Faye's mind was an itch. She saw pictures of the estuary, more of O'Halloran Hill, a few pretty close ups of old knotty oak trees and fishing boats. There were pictures of the guesthouse and Stixx when he was younger on a chopper bicycle that looked far too big for him. It made her smile.

'It won't be long now, honey,' Margie was saying softly.

Faye scanned the pictures again, feeling a little confused, feeling she was missing something important. She just wanted to close her eyes and go to sleep. Then she saw it, a small rectangular picture frame. In the picture was the horse-drawn gypsy caravan. The man was smiling, happy to be photographed. It was identical to the photograph she had seen in Flint's safe at the police station. He was the gypsy the papers had said had disappeared. Stixx's mum had been the photographer. She thought of the other pictures, the darker ones, the ones with the animals.

'Have you figured it out yet?' Margie whispered in her ear. Faye shivered and looked up to see Stixx's mum looking down at her.

'You were one of the three devils. It was you and Flint and Jr all along, wasn't it? We thought it was the Colonel, but that never made that much sense.' Faye looked over at Stixx. He was still asleep, slumped over in his seat. Her own eyes were so heavy. 'You're connected to everything, aren't you? You knew what Flint was doing, didn't you?' Faye wasn't stupid; she figured there must have been a sedative in the soup, at worst a poison.

'It's all history now... you're looking very tired, Faye. Perhaps you should shut your eyes and rest a while.'

'Just tell me about the three devils.' Faye needed to keep her mind sharp.

'You want to know about the killing, don't you? The immature thing we all did when we didn't know any better. It was Jr who was the psychopath. Flint was just curious. He killed animals as well, of course. Even I once killed a rabbit. It really didn't do anything for me though. I don't even know why we were all together... just an extension of school, I guess. The truth was Flint always had a little bit of a crush on me. He became enraged when I started my little dalliance with the traveller. Flint hated that I found a gypsy more interesting than him. The truth is I'd have found a rock more interesting than him really!'

Margie was pacing in front of her. 'One day, Jr and Flint were talking to him at his caravan when I went to meet him. Then Flint held him down right in front of me, and Jr slit his throat like he was just one of those animals, like it was nothing. Jr told his father of course, and there were lots of tears and recriminations. We were only your age Faye, we had our lives ahead of us! The Colonel made sure it was covered up and nobody found out. Just a disappearing gypsy nobody cared about, except me, I suppose. Jr was sent away to university. I left this bloody village and travelled for years. Flint was the only one who stayed in Greystones, joining the police, of all things. *How very ironic.* I don't remember us ever calling ourselves the three devils, although probably that's what we were!'

'All that death, all it was ever really about was money, wasn't it?' Faye hissed at her, and staggered to her feet. The room felt as if it was tilting and she struggled to keep her balance.

'Money, isn't it always about money?' Margie said following her around the room, just out of arms' reach. 'I had none, I needed it. It was my idea to blackmail the Colonel. I wrote to

Flint thinking he would probably still on some level be in love with me. It was pretty mercenary really, but I was desperate. I had debts that weren't going to go away. I had to meet him and sleep with him. There was of course that cost, but I was willing to pay it. I said we should blackmail the Colonel, get some money out of the old bastard before he went and died.'

'And let me guess, this guesthouse didn't pay for itself,' Faye said, trying to fight off another wave of tiredness.

'Yes, I got this palace,' Margie said, waving her arms about. 'They gave Flint nothing, just teased him that one day he'd get The Ridgeway convalescent home. It drove Flint even more crazy than he was already, he went right over the edge. It was all just an amusing game to the Colonel, I think. Probably he was planning some horrible revenge himself but he never got the chance to pull it off.'

'So, somewhere along the line, June Dowling's son gets involved. She's already lost her daughter to suicide, and her son gets... what? Some kind of problem with his brain?'

Margie sneered at Faye. 'You think you're pretty smart keeping me talking don't you. How long before you pass out, honey?'

Faye's balance finally gave out and she sat down suddenly on the floor next to the fire. 'Indulge me, would you?'

'Okay, so Flint wanted his retirement fund, even if it was just some toxic waste ground. He said he had a plan to scare the money out of the Colonel, said June Dowling's son was going to help, that he was crazy enough to pretend to be a vampire. The Colonel, for all his money and influence, was apparently scared to death of the things, and also believed in all that occult nonsense. Flint was going to use the vampire as some kind of psychological warfare, let the crazy vampire make a few appearances, to prey on the old guy's mind. *Wear him down you see.* It was a typically idiotic Flint idea, and it took about five minutes to go completely off the rails. June Dowling's son had a tumour in his brain. He went from play acting a vampire to running a bloody rampage around the whole village. Flint couldn't control him, couldn't even track where he was hiding with any accuracy. Of course he couldn't say or do anything or it would have been

242

his neck on the line. He had just to sit tight and hope a police sniper took the vampire down as soon as possible.'

'And then me and Stixx started our own... investigation.' Faye could barely keep her eyes open for more than a few seconds. Her eyelids felt like dead weights.

'Yes, and then you two started digging and finding out far too much. I love my son,' she said pointing to the slightly snoring Stixx. 'But without you he would have stayed oblivious to all this. He became obsessed with you, and you were obsessed with finding out all there was to find out, which would mean, of course, getting me into a great deal of trouble eventually. It wasn't my idea to kidnap you in the library. It certainly wasn't my idea to leave you in the woods in the hope the vampire took you. But don't imagine if had it been me, I'd have been so kind.' Margie revealed the knife she was holding up the sleeve of her blouse. It looked like a very sharp carving knife. 'As usual, I guess I'll have to sort things out myself.'

'You don't have to do this.' Faye was trying to get to her feet, but they were having none of it.

'I'm really surprised that you're still awake,' Margie said calmly, her knuckles going white as she gripped the knife handle.

'Well, half a lifetime of taking anti-psychotics will do that for you! This thing you're about to do, they'll find out. And if they don't find out, Stixx will know. There's no way you'll get away with another murder!'

'You'll just disappear. I'll tell Stixx you got up and left. Your mum doesn't know you're here, nobody does. The story will be you left and became another little village mystery, of which there are far too many now. I'll just dispose of your remains when the time is right.' The knife blade was being raised towards Faye's neck.

'The shooting at the Ridgeway, that was you too, wasn't it?' Faye was stalling for time. She already knew the answer. Margie was looking increasingly unhinged.

'Of course. I arranged to meet the old gang. I shot Flint, and would have shot Jr as well, but the vampire got there first. Just a lucky coincidence I suppose. I had no idea Flint would be bringing Stixx with him. That was never part of the plan.

Surprises can be a bitch, don't you think? This is all about Stixx really. I was trying to protect him from all the trouble and accusations you've brought down on his simple head. I wanted him to have a clean slate again.'

'You waited too long.' Faye lunged forward and kicked Margie as hard as she could in the knee. She missed though and only landed a glancing blow to her thigh. Faye made for the door, but Stixx's mum brought the knife down in a stabbing motion, and Faye felt it strike bone in her shoulder blade. Instinctively Faye grabbed Margie's hair and tried to swing her off-balance causing them both to fall to the floor. Margie swung the knife again and sliced across Faye's forearm. Blood was flowing freely and Faye gritted her teeth against the pain.

The knife blade was coming down again but Faye caught the bloodied hand and made Margie stab the floorboards instead. There was a door jamb against the door. It looked slightly ornamental, with a polished oak finish. Faye grabbed it and without a second thought plunged it into the chest of the woman trying to kill her. She saw it wedged deeply, like a stake through the heart.

Faye left Margie lying flat on her back gasping for breath. Moving away, she crawled her way slowly up the cellar steps leaving a bloody trail in her wake.

Epilogue

Stixx and Faye stood on the grassy bank in the woods, and watched. Stixx had said he wanted to be there, and after all that had happened Hastie was kind enough to let them.

Probably they looked like a pair of Frankenstein monsters, faces black and blue with slowly healing wounds and bruises. Faye's right arm was in a sling, but the doctors didn't think there would be permanent damage if she had the right physiotherapy. At worst, there would always be just a little numbness around her shoulder muscle on that side.

Stixx had a large white medical dressing on the back of his head. He was still getting regular headaches, but again the doctors said they should eventually ease.

He wondered how much the whole experience had changed them. There was definitely a bond there now, something tangible and lasting. They weren't just two silly kids anymore. He looked at Faye, noticing the faraway look in her eyes he'd seen a lot since the fight at the guesthouse. The doctors said a certain amount of post-traumatic stress was to be expected, that there were pills you could take. Faye hadn't seemed very interested in any of that.

They were standing in a cordoned off area of the Colonel's estate, in a clearing surrounded by bare winter trees, that ironically wasn't far from the old greenhouse hideaway. Below them, the diesel engine of an industrial digger worked hard at breaking through the frozen ground. There was a crane, with various workmen in orange tabards working hard to get the thing out of the ground. Someone was shouting, 'lift again!' and the crane chains clanked tight.

Policemen were standing at the perimeter of the distant cordon, stopping errant journalists getting through to take pictures. Hastie had given murderously clear instructions to keep the area sealed. Words to the effect of, 'If I see any pictures on the front cover of The Sun tomorrow, I'll be having someone's bollocks for earrings.'

They knew that Hastie had, in the end, turned out to be a decent cop, and that he fought off extreme pressure from his bosses to pull the trigger on Stixx for murder. Hastie had told them he had trusted his gut feeling that something else was going on, even if at the time he struggled to put his finger on what that something actually was. He'd even suggested that Stixx should apply to join the police, but a tell-tale twinkle in those mean eyes had suggested that part was probably a joke.

The crane winched up another few feet. Someone in the pit shouted, 'There's somebody in there. I can see bones.' Forensic officers in white suits swarmed forward then, hopping down into the pit with the workmen.

'You know, that vampire guy must have wanted you to be his queen.'

'What?' Faye said, blinking back to reality. 'What are you on about?'

'I mean that must be why he didn't kill you, just sipped on your blood or whatever. He must have thought he could change you into a vampire.'

'It's a shame it never happened, because I would love to be immortal.'

'But is being immortal and living in a cave really that cool?'

'We could have decorated. Perhaps I could have done some cave painting to brighten the place up.'

'Or even moved a few virgins in there for company.' Stixx grinned. He was feeling a little empty inside, and the humour was very welcome.

Faye was looking serious again. The cute frown lines were back. 'Are you sure you really want to stay? We don't need to be here. Let's go and watch another zombie film, or perhaps something without people getting eaten this time?'

'No, I'm good.' Stixx was watching the men in the ditch, wondering what they were seeing now. He couldn't really see inside the gypsy caravan from this angle. The yellow paint had flaked or rubbed off, exposing the rotting wood. The roof was partially collapsed, but he could see the wheels were still intact. It was being carefully lifted out of the hole, to be placed on supports on the ground. The people in white coats were erecting a large white-sheeted tent around it all. It was yet another murder investigation.

Maybe, the final one.

Hastie had given him a letter the day before, written by his mother who was now on remand in the hospital wing of Durham Woman's Prison. Faye's makeshift stake had missed her heart, but not by more than a centimetre or so. She would recover in time, like they all would. Hastie said she had confessed on tape to killing Jr and Flint, and also stabbing the Colonel in his sleep, before burning the whole manor house to the ground.

But the letter hadn't been about any of that. It had been about the past and the gypsy man who was now surely a rotting corpse in the caravan below them. Stixx had never known who his father was, and now it was blindingly obvious why not. Margie had written to say she had been pregnant when Jr had slit the man's throat. And after the Colonel's minions buried the evidence on his land, she had run away, scared she might have been targeted next in the ensuing cover-up. She only knew the gypsy as Kieran, saying that he had never told her more than that. Margie thought Stixx would have liked him, he was a gentle man. She said she was sorry for everything. Hastie said he expected it to be a life prison sentence, at least twenty years.

'There's one thing I need to ask you,' Faye said, still looking the picture of seriousness.

'Ask away,' Stixx said, slowly drawing his eyes away from the caravan.

'I did kind of drive a stake into your mother's chest. I wondered if you're going to hold it against me. Are you ever going to forgive me?'

'Yeah, it's alright. No worries,' Stixx said flatly. He generally felt emotionless thinking about Margie Stixx these days.

'No worries? Are you crazy? I drove a piece of oak into her ribs, Stixx. That's your mother!'

'Don't worry about it. I get to stake your mother and then we're even.'

'You leave my mother alone. She's had a very stressful Christmas.'

'Am I invited over for tea yet?'

'Mum says when hell freezes over, maybe you can!'

'So that's progress, right?'

Faye took hold of his hand as they set off walking away from the pit. The hand felt warm and soft and safe to Stixx. They were going to be okay.

The End

BIOGRAPHY

Remy Porter is a British ex-pat living in South Australia with his wife and daughter.